GRANDFATHER GUARDIAN

ANTHONY W. EICHENLAUB

To grandparents who do their best, even if they sometimes fall short.

CHAPTER ONE

"Some invitations are impossible to refuse," Ajay Andersen explained as the rusted sedan drove itself past soybean fields recently darkened by the spring thaw. It was true. Whether the invitation employed a weaponized amalgamation of targeted manners or subtle tour-de-force innuendo or the machine gun rattle of repeated offerings, there were simply some times when one's presence was absolutely required. He sighed. "This is one of those times."

Kylie's teenage scowl was partially hidden by the curls of dark hair that fell in front of her face. "What if I don't want to meet her?"

Ajay pinched the bridge of his nose. Retirement hadn't gone as expected. His estranged daughter had died after returning with her children, leaving Ajay to care for the youngest grandchild—a teenager now on her way into high school. He loved the kid the way a parent loves a child, and like a parent and child, that love was a source of eternal unending conflict. It made him feel his age in his joints, which, judging by his knobby knuckles and aching hip, was substantial.

"We're going, and we need to be on our best behavior," he said.

"You're the boss."

Ajay bristled. Even when he had been a superstar hacker for the NSA, he had prided himself on sticking his thumb in the eye of authority. Being the guy in charge did *not* make him comfortable. "I didn't say that."

"Got it. Reject authority."

Yes. "That's not what I said, either."

She raised an eyebrow.

"Never trust authority, kid," he said. "That's all I said."

"Uh huh," she said as if it were something interesting.

Teenagers were the worst. He watched her closely for a few miles. They passed dense stands of tall pine—windbreaks on the vast plains of northern Minnesota. Her jaw was tense, her shoulders hunched the way she got when she was nervous. "It's only dinner," he finally said.

"Dinner and hacking," she shot back.

Hacking had always been his talent. He'd found ways in and ways out that no other programmer had ever imagined. In his days at the NSA, he had ruined countless lives and nudged whole governments to the edge of collapse. There was little to be truly proud of from those days, but he found himself feeling proud anyway.

He had been *good*.

"There's not a problem a sufficient amount of hacking can't fix," he mumbled.

"That's the exact opposite of what you told me last week, Papa."

Recently, he had taken the hobby of attempting to make the world a better place through judicious and well-researched hacking. It had, predictably, gotten him in some trouble.

"What makes you think I'm there to spy on her?" Ajay asked.

"Olexie infiltrated her staff. Your countercapitalist people have been getting pretty worked up about how close he is," Kylie said. "I read all your notes."

Now it was Ajay's turn to grind his teeth. Olexie *had* been trying to help. The old Russian was the one who pulled Ajay into the movement in the first place. "Don't use your ability while you're there."

"But—"

"No." The authority reverberated in his voice, and he hated it. "These people. Your grandmother. If they know what you can do, they'll want to exploit it. Best to keep it a secret."

"I'll be sneaky about it," she protested.

"You don't know how to properly defend yourself yet." Kylie had a computer in her brain, which was as much a vulnerability as it was an asset. With the right tech, her senses, her abilities, even her identity could be altered. Her father had done the same to her sister Isabelle. "There are things they can do."

"Maybe a summer survival camp would teach me how to defend myself."

Ajay scowled. She'd asked about the camp before. He didn't know where she got the idea, but it was dangerous. Ajay didn't know what it would do to her, and he hated the idea of not seeing her for so long. Survival camp? It sounded dangerous. "We're safer at home," he finally said.

As good as he had been at hacking, Kylie was better. They had taken the self-driving car all the way from Bemidji to an estate on the lakes north of Duluth. Now, they sat in silence. The beautiful young lady—his ward—fidgeted nervously, tapping her painted nails against the clutch purse that matched her crimson suit. She'd done her hair—a rarity for her—and her lips were colored to match the outfit. Her child's beauty was betrayed by the worried look in her eyes.

"It'll be fine," Ajay lied in an effort to avoid the growing conflict.

It didn't work. "I don't want to go."

At her feet, Ajay's bloodhound Garrison shifted to look up to her. Ajay had allowed her to bring the dog for support on this trip, and she visibly calmed when she ran a hand along his smooth fur. Maybe Ajay had made one good choice after all.

"Some invitations are—"

"I know, Papa," she snapped. "I'm going to go. I'm just not happy about it."

Ajay glanced out the window as the car turned onto a driveway that meandered through a tunnel of bare aspens. The brick driveway passed a wall made from large river boulders. The mansion itself was a comically enormous take on a Romanesque design, its facade dotted with enormous semi-circular arched windows overlooking Lake Superior over the top of the gray expanse of trees. The car stopped in the area specifically positioned to show off both the enormity of the mansion and the splendor of its view.

"I didn't know she lived in a palace," whispered Kylie.

"We're early," said Ajay. "We can wait a bit if you aren't ready to go in."

"No," said Kylie, setting her jaw. She clipped Garrison's leash to his collar. "I'm ready when you are."

Ajay drew the cheaters up from their chain around his neck and placed them on the bridge of his nose. He clicked the head of his cane and brought up the digital interface in the glasses. He no longer wore the fidget interface, which would have fit on his left hand and displayed a holographic image. Not only were those devices falling out of fashion, but his old eyes were starting to have trouble with the tricky task of focusing on the smaller semitransparent images. His cheaters could laser that text directly onto this retina, which worked better under most light conditions. Plus, his cane could hold more computing power than the typical handheld device.

"You did well with this thing," he said, tapping the knobby top of the cane.

A hint of a smile flashed across Kylie's lips. One of the diminishing number of things that calmed her was arts and crafts. She'd helped build his new cane from the computer insert to the retractable taser tip to the detachable drone hanging from a mount on the handle.

His bones ached when he unfolded himself from the car. It took him a moment to stretch his hip until it regained its full range of movement.

Beyond the mansion, the sky was dark, even though it wasn't yet late in the afternoon. The spring's first real rain approached. "We should build an umbrella into this thing next," he said.

"You look good, Papa," Kylie said, perhaps sensing his apprehension. This wasn't something he wanted to ever do, and over the past couple years Kylie had grown passably good at reading him, even though she often had trouble with other people. She straightened the collar of his old blue suit coat and snugged the ragged brown tie that his ex-wife had once told him complemented the light brown of his skin and the dark brown of his eyes. He felt like he swam in the outfit, as if he'd shrunk over the many years since he'd last worn it. Maybe he had. On his wrist, he wore a multicolored bracelet Kylie had made for him. She flashed a quirky grin. "Pretty good, anyway."

He waved her off like she was an insect and focused on the text flowing past on his cheaters. The car had a memory unit that recorded all of its movements, and it wouldn't do to leave it intact.

Hacking was one of those things that had changed immensely over the years while also staying pretty much the same. There were some universal truths that Ajay could always depend upon.

First was that people were always the weakest point of any system.

No people here. Automated cars were common, even north into the Iron Range where many still drove their old gasoline trucks out of sheer stubbornness. A fair number of people didn't bother owning their own vehicles anymore. They just summoned an auto and took it where they needed, not even caring that the vehicles recorded their every movement.

Not that it mattered for most of them. Every device people carried with them also recorded their movement, and it was almost trivial for someone like Ajay to find the records. He and Kylie weren't ready to be found, which was part of why engraved invitations sent directly to their little Bemidji home were so hard to refuse.

Kylie and Garrison walked up the brick sidewalk toward the large double doors.

The second universal truth was that someone always misconfigured something, especially when it came to networks. There was always a way in because some doofus left the door wide open. The car's guest wireless login had access to a file that contained all the passwords ever entered through the system's universal interface.

Breaking in after finding that was trivial.

He started to walk as he cracked the last layers of encryption.

People still used encryption. They still almost trusted it, even though it had been dead for over a decade. Quantum computing had cracked it wide open, and after riding a career on cracking encryption, Ajay had turned in his resignation by making the whole thing public. The world knew that encryption would never hold.

They just didn't care.

"We'll have our dinner," Ajay said, catching up to Kylie. "Then we can leave. No need to linger."

"It's okay, Papa," Kylie said. "I'm not nervous anymore."

Ajay narrowed his eyes at the thirteen-year-old. Her parents had experimented on Kylie's older sister, Isabelle, and Kylie had the same modifications that allowed her to alter her own brain in seriously disturbing ways. Many of the children that Jackson Garver experimented on later didn't survive. It also gave her the ability to directly communicate with wireless devices, but that didn't worry Ajay quite so much. She was getting pretty good at doing that without accidentally lobotomizing herself.

Oh, the many stresses of parenting.

"It's not that." Kylie pointed at her temple. "I'm not doing the thing. I'm just excited to finally meet her."

"Good," he said. "You're doing well, dear."

She scowled. "Does everything have to be a lesson?"

"Can you name the layers of an OSI network?"

"Physical, data link, network, transport, session, presentation, and application."

Dang. "Which layer is the most vulnerable?"

Her scowl darkened.

Ajay said, "The deeper you go, the longer the tech has been around. Physical, data link, and network layers have been unchanged for decades. They're proven technology."

She rolled her eyes. "And applications are new every year. More potential for errors."

Ajay sighed. The auto's encryption popped with a flash of blue text in his left eye. He delved into the vehicle's records and searched for its most recent journey so that he could purge the logs without leaving a trail.

Nothing.

The third universal rule of hacking, which Ajay had found frustratingly true throughout his career, was that there was always someone better.

Always. Even if she didn't quite know everything yet.

Kylie glanced over at him in response to his grunt of frustration. "I got the car already."

Ajay poked around in the text interface. "You left a deletion record."

"No, I didn't." They were at the door, and Garrison lay down as if he thought they would be there a while.

Ajay spent another moment looking around the auto's system as it pulled away from the mansion. Then, he removed his cheaters and let them dangle from their chain. "You're right," he said, allowing a proud smile to slip across his lips. "You did very well." With that, he rapped three times on the door. "Are you ready?"

"I'm nervous again," she whispered.

He gripped her hand in his and gave it a squeeze. She was so young, and he needed to constantly remind himself that she really was just a kid, even though she sometimes acted much older.

The door opened, and a dark-haired young woman in a black suit greeted them. She looked down her thin nose at the two visitors and rested the slender fingers of one hand on the doorframe. "You must be Mr. Andersen and Kylie?"

"Present," said Ajay. His throat tightened, and he felt a little bit of the nerves Kylie had admitted. He drew the thick cream-colored invitation from his suit pocket and held it out. "Sorry we're early, we didn't know how long the drive would take." He had known exactly how long the drive would take, but Ajay hated walking into a room full of people.

The woman raised an eyebrow at Garrison, who managed to make rising from his spot look like a tremendous effort. Sometimes Ajay understood how the old hound felt.

"He's a service dog," Kylie lied.

The woman stepped aside and held the door for them. "My name is Melinda. Please let me know if you need anything while you are here."

"Are you the butler?" Ajay asked.

"The staff will do their best to attend to your needs," said Melinda.

The foyer was an explosion of dark mahogany and shining bronze. Three high arched doorways led out from their central room into the gloomy dark hallways. The floor was covered in an elaborate rug, which muffled the clack of Ajay's cane as he followed Melinda into a side room. One wall of the small room was dominated by a steel vault.

Melinda gestured at the vault, which looked like a solid brick of steel with an elaborate door mechanism. A box the size of a guitar was mounted to the front, beside which a console glowed. "You may place any weapons in here for safe keeping."

Ajay cleared his throat, which did nothing to relieve the tightness in it. He gripped the head of his cane with two hands.

"We didn't bring any weapons," Ajay said.

"I didn't know we were supposed to," said Kylie.

Melinda eyed Ajay's cane but must have decided it wasn't enough of a threat to worry about. She scanned it and registered an exemption on the weapons safe control panel.

"Again," said Ajay, "we apologize for being early." As he stepped through the storage room door, a red light flashed on the control panel and an alert bell pinged.

Melinda held out a hand. "Not to be alarmed," she said, "but if you don't hand over your weapon, a powerful microwave pulse will make the evening significantly less pleasant for everyone."

Ajay furrowed his brow. His palms went slick and his heart pounded. He didn't want to leave his cane just because of some stupid scan. "I don't—"

Images flashed across Melinda's glasses. "A knife?"

"Oh." Ajay removed the multitool from his pocket and handed it to her. "I'll want that back."

"Of course." She placed it on the entry platform for the safe and cycled the machine. It boxed and stored his extremely dangerous three-inch blade and its accompanying array of gadgets.

A voice from the doorway connecting the west wing to the foyer said, "I'm so glad that you decided to come, Mr. Andersen."

He turned. The woman he saw wore a golden dressing gown. Her skin was clear as ivory, offsetting the dazzling blue of her dangling earrings. She wore gloves to match her gown, but as she strolled across the wide room, Ajay noted that she was not wearing shoes.

The tightness in Ajay's throat finally won, and he found no words with which to greet the woman. He had accepted the invitation because he had no choice. She had found him. Found Kylie. What she did with that information was entirely up to her, and the only way to influence that decision was this one night. This one party. It was his only chance.

When she finally reached them, the woman held out a hand and said, "It's nice to finally meet you, Ajay Andersen."

"Likewise, Jocelyn Garver." He took the hand and, not knowing the social protocols, kissed the back of her hand gently. That was something rich people did, wasn't it? It seemed to earn a dismissal.

Jocelyn turned to Kylie. "And you, Kylie." She drew a long, slow breath. "I've heard so very much about you and your sister."

Kylie placed a hand on Garrison's head, as if for support. She licked her lips. "I wish I could say the same," she said. "Dad never really said anything about you." She swallowed hard. "Grandma."

CHAPTER TWO

When Jocelyn disappeared, Melinda gave them the polite equivalent of a gentle shove out the door. She placed a hand on Ajay's shoulder, and he couldn't help but imagine her immaculate fingernails clawing into his neck. "Mingle," she said.

Ajay peered out at the courtyard. "With who?"

Melinda's glasses flashed. "The other guests are arriving now."

The courtyard was a paradise on the cusp of a spring bloom. Lime green buds peeked from the gray branches of the crabapple trees, preparing to burst forth at the nearest hint of warmth. It wasn't cold exactly, Ajay found. Not in the courtyard, where they were protected from the wind on three sides by the huge building. The sky still furrowed its massive brow in a hint of an impending storm, but it wouldn't rain for hours. It was pleasant.

Kylie led Garrison away through the meandering

paths, leading him on his leash as if they were searching for hidden passages or buried corpses. Ajay wondered if there was a non-zero chance of finding either.

"Dinner will be soon," said Melinda before she left. "Ms. Garver requests that her guests take some time to peruse the garden."

It seemed like a rude way to run a dinner party, but Ajay had to admit he was not well versed on the nuances of dining with the rich and famous. In fact, he wasn't much for social gatherings at all. If it hadn't been for the arrival of his granddaughters, he might still be safe and snug in a little house in Red Wing, Minnesota. Alone.

This was better, even if it took him out of his comfort zone. Even if it put him in danger sometimes. He strolled through the garden, passing hostas with hints of growth in their centers, roses with the barest nubs of green, and a wall of tall lilacs that were clearly meant to block the view to a utility shed a nine-iron's distance from the house. When he stepped from the path, he saw a monstrous black metal rig towering above the neighboring apple trees, looming over a narrow path between the garden and the driveway.

"Huh," he said to himself. When he returned to the path, he found the view of the construction equipment blocked. He wondered how superficial the rest of this place would be.

He returned to the center of the garden and

settled his aching bones on a bench, cane clutched in both hands. Maybe this wouldn't be so bad. Jocelyn could get to know Kylie. They would have a quiet dinner, and then they could leave. He would place a tracking program on the network if he found the chance, but it wasn't really that kind of job. Olexie had messaged him with a vague idea that there was something dodgy about the woman's estate, but it wasn't enough to warrant a full infiltration. Feelers. That's all he wanted.

Plus, this was Kylie's grandmother. She deserved something resembling the benefit of the doubt, didn't she?

After a short time, a round-faced boy of twelve or thirteen arrived with a tray of ridiculously tiny sandwiches.

"The other guests will be here soon," said the boy.

Ajay took a sandwich and peered at it suspiciously. "Aren't you a little young to have a job, son?"

"I'm twenty-two, sir."

Ajay moved his suspicious gaze from the sandwich to the boy. The boy had a mop of curly hair framing his big eyes. Yes, okay. Fine. Twenty-two. He believed it. Twenty-two got younger every year, though. Pretty soon thirty-year-olds would be in diapers and forty-year-old men would play foursquare in the parking lot.

"What's your name?"

"Zach," he said. "Zach Smith."

"Thank you, Zach," Ajay said, dismissing the boy with a wave.

Zach didn't leave.

"What is it?" Ajay asked.

"It's just," the boy stammered. He pointed at Ajay's sandwich. "It's just you probably don't want to eat that."

Ajay's suspicious gaze returned to the sandwich. "Deadly poison?"

Zach gave a quick shake of his head. "They're just not very good, sir."

A gentle breeze swirled through the courtyard—not enough to feel cool, but enough to carry a sharp voice that Ajay thought he recognized. He tucked his sandwich behind the glossy leaves of an alpine currant shrub. "Thanks for the tip," he said to Zach as he hurried away.

"I'm certain I don't know this one," said a woman's voice up ahead. This woman spoke with a nasal timbre, as if her nose were so high in the air she had no choice but to speak through it.

Ajay rounded an aggressive stand of viburnum to find an elderly couple arm in arm, walking along the path. The woman was as slender and stylish as the cigarette she pinched between two fingers. She wore a dress of shiny material so light it fluttered in the wind, which would have been truly ravishing on a younger woman. By contrast, the man's thick frame was draped in an immaculately tailored suit made of the softest blue Ajay had ever seen.

The man cleared his throat. "Percival Trow-bridge." He jabbed a hand out for a shake. "And this is my beautiful wife Loretta."

He knew them. Not personally, of course. Ajay would never have met such people in passing. He only knew them by name. Percival and Loretta Trow-bridge were on Olexie's list of the richest people in the nation, but they were recluses.

Ajay shook the hand dutifully, noticing the gruff strength in the old man's grip. *Old*, of course, being a relative term. On closer inspection, Ajay decided the man was probably younger than him and certainly in better shape. The blue of his suit set off the hazel of his eyes against the gray of the cloudy sky.

"Ajay Andersen," Ajay said, finally, when he figured out what they were waiting for.

"Of the Andersen Art Center Andersens?" Loretta asked.

Absolutely not. "Something like that."

"Charmed." Loretta glanced away. "I'll let you two get to know each other. I think I see Robert now, and I'd like to speak with him before we settle on more serious topics." She wandered away through the garden.

"Serious topics?" Ajay asked Percival when she was gone.

Percival only smiled ruefully. "An invitation to one of Jocelyn Garver's new palaces simply must be about business."

"Of course." What? Ajay opted to deflect from

the fact that he had no idea how Jocelyn Garver made her money. "Have you been to this kind of thing before?"

Percival nodded toward the garden—a gesture that might have been an invitation but came across as more of a command. The two started a slow walk. "Loretta is pleased to be here. These social things are all a bit much for me, but I'm told this is quite an honor."

"I've never been very good at that sort of thing."

Zach passed with a tray of wine glasses, and Ajay flagged him down. He selected a glass of the white wine without bubbles, figuring it was probably the safest option. Percival took a glass of aggressively red wine.

"Are you here with anyone?" Percival asked, sipping his wine.

"Just my granddaughter," Ajay said. He held up the glass to Zach. "Is this safe?"

"Granddaughter?" Percival bellowed, seeming surprised. "How old?"

"Thirteen."

"Ah!" Percival grinned. "So, it's her and Burkshire's kid."

"Burkshire?"

Percival waved dismissively. "He's the only man I know who would brag about an invitation to a secret meeting."

"Great." Zach had already moved on, so Ajay risked a taste of his wine. It tasted like wine.

"Rumor is his daughter has been tagging along to social events for the past several years. You know, learning the ropes." He leaned close conspiratorially and whispered, "The girl gives people the creeps, but that's not much of a surprise given who her father is, if you know what I mean."

Ajay did not. "Who else is coming tonight?" He wondered if anyone else would be on Olexie's list.

They strolled past the grasping bare branches of a hawthorn, which stood as the corner piece against the backdrop of a small apple orchard. Its tight, thorny branches extended over the path, and Percival had to duck to avoid them. As they rounded the densely packed trees, they came upon a compact man strolling at a casual pace through the garden. He wore a rumpled brown suit that fit poorly against his broad shoulders. A breeze tousled his thin black hair. He peered at them through thick-framed glasses. Ajay guessed before he heard the man's name that he wasn't going to be on Olexie's list.

"Be careful with this one," Percival whispered to Ajay conspiratorially. Then, louder, he greeted the man, "Declan Bohm, how is business." In three long strides, he closed the distance to the other man and shook his hand vigorously.

Declan Bohm blinked, taken aback. "Percival Trowbridge." He didn't bother glancing at Ajay, as if he didn't dare take his eyes from Percival. "I'm surprised to see you here."

"Well, you know what they say about pending investigations," said Percival.

Ajay said, "They're best avoided?"

"It's not that," said Declan.

Percival clapped the younger man on the back, "Come, Mr. Bohm. Let's call this a truce for tonight and find you a beverage."

When they finally tracked down Zach for another drink—Percival snagged a second, even though Ajay had yet to hazard a second sip of his—Declan said, "I thought I saw a hound sniffing around here."

"Another one?" asked Percival, raising an eyebrow meaningfully. He offered no explanation for the comment.

"A bloodhound, I think," said Declan. "What do you suppose it'll find if it digs in *these* gardens?"

"I'm sure Jocelyn doesn't bury her bodies so close to home," said Percival.

"More likely he'll find snacks," Ajay said. "Garrison is a specifically trained snack hound."

Declan said, "Well, he can have one of those awful sandwiches." He looked at his with distaste. "I always say a person should wear body armor to something like this, but poisoning's not an unreasonable fear, either."

Ajay took a sip of his wine. It was too sweet and made his tongue numb. He held it loosely in one hand and gripped the head of his cane in the other. "Maybe you should hire a taster."

"I'll be the taster," Declan said, tossing the sandwich into the shrub. "This tastes like garbage. Don't bother."

"I should think that would be why one has children," said Percival. Ajay wasn't sure if it was a joke.

"Speaking of which," Ajay said, summoning the most polite voice he could manage. "I believe I should go check in with my granddaughter."

As he left, he tuned his hearing aid so that it picked up the two men continuing their conversation.

Declan said, "Who is that man, Trowbridge?"

"A lower class sort, I think," said the heavy man. "Said his name was Andersen, but he didn't seem very confident about it."

There were a lot of things Ajay wasn't confident about. His name was not one of them.

"Is Lee really coming to this?" Declan asked.

"Wilson?" replied Percival. "I'm sure it'll be a surprise, but I have to say I'm looking forward to hearing what you have to say to him."

"Yeah," said Declan. "Me too."

As Ajay passed a raised bed of the thorniest roses he'd ever seen, he set his wine glass down on the stone wall and strolled forward, tapping his cane lightly on the paver path.

He soon understood the layout of the courtyard. Every path meandered aimlessly, and strategically placed plantings blocked views, lending the space an almost claustrophobic quality. Yet from every location, he could see the steeple set into the center of the mansion and the jagged crenelation running along the roof three stories up. The tower stretched high above the garden, and it was topped by a wide circular room with its windows open to a view of the world in all directions.

To the west, the paths joined into a single stone walkway that plunged straight into a dense oak forest. It reminded Ajay of fairy tales where the deep, dark wood swallowed unsuspecting children.

So, at least he knew where Kylie went. He made his way into the wood and hadn't called her name more than twice before she appeared, standing on a freshly cut stump. Garrison sat several feet away at the base of a burr oak, his leash unhooked.

"I hear there might be another girl coming," Ajay said.

"And what? I'm supposed to be friends with her?" Her tone was a challenge.

"I expect you to be friendly."

She pursed her lips and stared into the depths of the forest.

"What's wrong?"

"I don't like it here," she snapped. "We met grandma, so let's leave."

"We can't leave yet," Ajay sighed. Sometimes her mood changes baffled him, but he understood this one perfectly. She didn't like social situations like this, and she wasn't confident with her ability to meet new people. "Dinner, then we're gone. I promise."

After several long breaths, she whispered, "There's a dangerous person here."

"A few, from what I've met."

"Yeah."

"Don't wander too far," Ajay grumbled. He didn't think he projected the air of authority that might influence Kylie's behavior, but it was the best he could do.

When he returned to the rose wing of the courtyard, he found Declan arguing with a man in a perfectly tailored blue suit in a language Ajay didn't even recognize. Declan gestured wildly and hissed arguments through his teeth.

The man remained calm in the onslaught, without a fleck of emotion passing across his perfectly carved face. His blond hair caught what remained of a ray of sunshine through the growing clouds. When he held up a hand to stop Declan's rant, Ajay noticed that it was missing the pinkie finger at the first joint.

"That's enough, Declan," he said. "This is neither the time nor the place."

"I'm telling you, Robert, I can prove it. I know they were involved." Declan asked. His rumpled suit bunched at his shoulders from all the tension he carried.

A man in black standing a short distance away, watching the two arguing men from behind the jet-black circles of a pair of tech glasses. The glasses flashed blue against the defined orbital bone of his sunken eyes. His suit blended with the shadows in the corner of the courtyard, but after spotting him, Ajay wondered how the man could possibly be missed. A shiver crept down Ajay's back.

"Theodore Parks," Declan said a little later. "He's more of a bad omen than a party guest, but I suppose this isn't your typical social gathering."

"I'm not sure I'd be invited to a typical gathering," Ajay said.

"No, I suppose not." Declan drained his glass. "I'm not exactly on the standard guest list either, but, hey, we can make the most of it, right?" His smile was paper thin.

Zach appeared from nowhere, ready to replace Declan's drink. "Just so you know, gentlemen, the party will be moving indoors soon. We will gather in the ballroom just down the central hall on the left."

"Wonderful," said Ajay. He glanced to the place where the man in black—Theodore Parks—had been, but he was gone. "Have you mentioned this to Kylie?"

"No, sir." A hint of exhaustion crept into Zach's voice. His round cheeks were rosy. "I'm on my way to notify the others right away."

"I'll tell my granddaughter." Ajay nodded to Declan. "I will meet you back in the mansion."

Declan took a glass of red wine from Zach. "Indeed," he said in an imitation of elite snobbery. "Very good." With that, he made his way toward the central door, almost immediately swallowed behind the low shrubs.

As Zach took his leave, too. Ajay chewed on something Declan had said. He wasn't the sort to get invited to a normal party. Ajay wasn't either, and Theodore Parks didn't seem like the typical guest. What was Jocelyn Garver playing at? Why invite all these people on this night to her palace on the shore of Lake Superior? It didn't sit right.

Ajay started back toward the forest where he had last seen Kylie. If something was strange, the least he could do was keep her close by his side.

Kylie didn't like this one bit.

She thought she could handle it. She had dressed for it, but now her bright red outfit and lipstick made her feel fake. Her hair felt funny. It *smelled* funny. She wasn't mentally prepared to meet a whole bunch of new people. That wasn't something a person could just *do*.

I hate it, Kylie texted to her friend Austin.

I'm sorry, he texted back, because of course that's something he would say. He knew just what empathic thing had to be said to disarm her anger.

Disarm it, but not dissipate.

Kylie didn't like how the network here felt. She had learned to test digital communications using the strange modifications in her head, but this network was odd. It grasped at her. It probed her weaknesses, and it made her uncomfortable. It felt *wrong*.

Plus, Papa was on his way to tell her to move into

the house, and she didn't want to move into the house. The network was stronger out in the woods, which was strange. Here at the edge of the forest, she found a tiny shred of peace.

Garrison snuffled her hand the way he did when he thought she needed to be reminded to feed her.

"We fed you on the way here, Gare," she whispered.

He indicated that he did not remember any such thing by snuffling at her purse. She didn't have any treats there.

Kylie didn't like the scary man who had arrived at the party after everyone else. She didn't like the way his personal devices rejected her attempts to passively learn more about them. She got only one good look at him through the bare branches of the bone-white aspens. He wore all black and some fancy sunglasses. His lips were pressed into a thin line as if he were concentrating on something very important.

She wished she could see what that was.

What if I have to be here all night? she texted to Austin using her fidget. The message stuck for several seconds before finally going through.

He took a long time to respond, so she wandered deeper into the forest. Papa was coming to get her, and she didn't want to go into the house. Not yet.

A voice behind her startled her out of her reverie. "Is that your dog?"

The girl was slender, but something about how she stood in her loose black blouse and matching long skirt made her look as tough as the convenience store jerky Papa had eaten on the way over. She was muscled like one of the girls who trained hard at cheerleading or gymnastics at school.

Kylie did her best to bite back the sarcasm in her response. "No, this is a bear that wandered in from the woods."

The girl snorted a laugh, which didn't help Kylie's mood.

"His name's Garrison," Kylie said. "He doesn't like strangers."

Garrison padded over to the girl and sniffed her hand. Finding it devoid of treats of any kind, he licked it just in case.

"I mean, he's not mean or anything," said Kylie.

"I'm Gabby," said the girl.

"Kylie." Kylie still couldn't tell how old Gabby was, but her eyes had an edge that made her uneasy. "Do you get dragged to a lot of parties like this?"

"My dad says I'm his protection," Gabby said.

Kylie clipped Garrison's leash on his collar, leaving her hands draped over the big dog's shoulders. "Papa acts like too much social interaction might make his head explode."

"My dad loves parties. He always needs to show off."

Kylie stood and gave Garrison's leash a little tug. "Come on, Gare." The big dog followed with all the enthusiasm of a bucket of molasses. Kylie could sense that Papa was getting closer, and she didn't want to talk to him yet, even if it meant spending more time with Gabby.

Gabby walked by Kylie's side but didn't say anything. Kylie wondered if the girl just didn't have anything to say or if she'd figured out that Kylie really didn't want to talk. Had she been subtle enough to be polite? It was so hard to tell.

Am I supposed to be nice to people when I meet them? she texted Austin.

Kinda, yeah.

Well, what did he know?

The air was heavy and dull, its humidity making her skin all bloated and warm. There would be a storm soon, she figured. All the forecasts said it would be the first really big storm of the spring, but nobody really agreed on when it would hit or how big it would be. Kylie figured that was because she was pulling information from half a dozen different weather prediction algorithms. None of them had really kept up to the climate changes of the past fifty years, so everything was just a little bit off.

Gabby drew in a long breath. "I love the smell of the leaves," she said.

"Yeah. Rotten leaves. They're great."

"Better than rotten animals," Gabby said.

Kylie didn't ask what Gabby knew about rotten animals because she didn't want the answer. Papa was approaching, so she veered down an extremely narrow side trail. At first, she pushed Garrison in front of her so they could walk single file, but he kept stopping and looking back at her as if she might have gotten lost. After his fifth time doing that, she squeezed in front of him and dragged him along, but then he kept stopping and sniffing her footprints.

"Come on, stupid dog." She pulled on the leash, but he looked up at her with his big puppy dog eyes. "Fine." Kylie crossed her arms in a huff. There wasn't much path left, anyway.

Gabby padded through the forest like a ghost, whispering up behind Garrison. "My dad says that you shouldn't follow deer paths. They tend to disappear."

"This is bigger than a deer path," Kylie said. It was probably a deer path. "Come on, Gare." This time Garrison followed.

The air changed when Kylie pushed her way into the stand of pine. Above, the fluffy tops of white pines danced against the gray sky. They weren't tall—maybe thirty feet. Kylie had seen much taller.

But these were white. Perfect, pure white needles hung like snow above them and dusted the ground below.

"Wow," Gabby gasped.

Kylie picked up one of the needles. "My grandpa says these carry a genetic anomaly that they used to fight climate change."

Gabby raised an eyebrow at that, apparently not convinced. Kylie wasn't sure she believed it, either, but she had never seen pine trees with this modification. She'd also never seen plants this old with the change. If they were here, they must have been some of the first to have been genetically modified with this change. Or maybe this was where it first naturally occurred.

A granite boulder made for a simple seat in the center of the glade, and Kylie scrambled up atop it, followed by Gabby. It occurred to Kylie that this would be the perfect place to spend an evening alone, and that caused other girl's presence to irritate her all the more.

Gabby lay back on the stone. "It's very peaceful out here."

It *was* peaceful. Kylie's sense of background network signals didn't normally irritate her, but when she found a place where she could sense nothing, it struck her how much that sense threatened to over-whelm her. Maybe that was why she had trouble making friends or interacting with the real world. There was just too much. Always too much.

But here, there was nothing. The connections she had sensed at the edge of the forest were completely absent in the pine grove. She closed her eyes and drew a deep breath.

It smelled like the rich stink of dog shit.

"Aw, come on, Garrison!" she cried as the dog dropped a gigantic turd only a few steps upwind from the base of the boulder. Kylie let out a frustrated growl and dropped from her seat. "Let's go."

"It doesn't bother me," said Gabby.

Kylie scrunched up her nose. "Really?"

"You just have to decide not to smell it."

"It'll still be there."

Gabby shrugged.

"Fine. I'll see you inside." Kylie led Garrison back through the narrow path, dragging him along every time he stopped to sniff something interesting. *Everything* was interesting.

When she reached the edge of the forest, Papa was there with his arms crossed and a scowl on his wrinkly face.

"I know, I know," she said. "It's time to go inside to the party."

Thankfully, he didn't need to mention that he had said not to wander into the forest. She could read his disappointment on his face, and it only made her feel another wave of guilt.

And she didn't like it one bit.

CHAPTER FOUR

"Shush," Ajay said. He was trying his best to be sympathetic to Kylie's situation, but she was ramping up to cause trouble, and he simply couldn't think of anything better to say. He could feel her frustration mounting in the prickle at the back of his neck, and he couldn't deal with that and his own growing impatience at the same time.

They were lost in the damn mansion.

Kylie led a stubborn Garrison down next to Ajay. "I think it's more of a palace."

"What's the difference?" asked Ajay.

"I don't know, like a thousand rooms, maybe?"

The high arched ceilings disappeared into the dark above, and the hallway stretched forever into the dimly lit distance. Automatic lights activated wherever they stepped, but that only blinded him to the expanse that stretched out ahead.

"Who needs a house this big?" Ajay grumbled.

Kylie peered through an open door into a library. "People who like to explore?"

"Sounds awful."

"We could just stay here," Kylie said. "This library looks nice."

All Ajay ever wanted was two bedrooms, a bath, and an unfinished basement that he could talk about finishing but never actually finish. Anything more just meant more maintenance and more cleaning, even if it was a giant library.

The Garver mansion was ridiculous. They passed a room with rugs on the walls. They were nice rugs. Probably. How would Ajay know? Maybe that was the point. The central hallway was lined with alcoves where old, chipped vases stood on pedestals.

"Are these Ming vases?" Kylie asked.

"Shush." They probably were. Ajay didn't know.

"Because I've heard of Ming vases, but I've never seen one." She flashed through the controls of her fidget, zipping through the holographic display faster than Ajay could follow. "How come there's no network signal here?"

"Privacy, probably," Ajay said.

The tip of Ajay's cane pressed circles into the sprawling rug as they continued to walk the length of the building. The massive rug displayed an epic battle in a valley, with bronze swords flashing in the moonlight in front of a huge black tower. If he could see it from above, it would probably be beautiful. Stunning, even. Up close, the fibers made his nose itch. A quick movement to one side caught his attention. A crab-shaped cleaning bot the size of a football skittered away. Ajay gestured for Kylie to follow. Where was that damn ballroom?

They approached the end of the long hall, and Ajay's extra-sensitive hearing aid picked up voices. Relief unclenched his chest and he plodded forward a little faster. Kylie lagged behind, but only because Garrison refused to walk faster.

He gestured to Kylie for her to stop when he heard the words.

"I need to see him, Jocelyn," said a gruff voice.

"Then do come in." Jocelyn Garver's calm brought a cold threat that sent a shiver down Ajay's spine.

"Bring him out here," said the man. "If I set one foot in your mansion, it'll be with an army at my side."

"It's time to let our differences go, Mr. Parks." Jocelyn said. "Theodore has seen fit to accept my invitation and a truce."

"A truce?" roared the man. "I'll show you a truce."

"Leave the weapons, Alex," said Jocelyn. "You know the rules here."

Ajay clicked the top of his cane and extended it around the corner. Through a camera on its head, he projected an image through his cheaters to see who would dare argue with Jocelyn Garver. The adjacent room was the foyer, where the three main hallways met in the front of the building.

The man stood a head taller than her, with a lean, muscular frame and a jaw so square he could use it for carpentry. He wore fatigues as if he might be heading off to combat. Maybe he wasn't bluffing about his army. On his shoulder was a Frontier Arms logo.

Frontier Arms. Ajay had tangled with them before. Kylie's sister, Isabelle, had worked for them, but they were as tough a mercenary group as Ajay had ever seen. If they were involved, there would be violence.

The man jabbed a finger at Jocelyn, but he didn't step forward past the threshold. "You bitch. You *knew* I was on deployment when you sent that invitation."

"Leave," said Jocelyn, ice in her voice.

Parks grabbed her wrist and pulled her close. He growled something Ajay couldn't quite hear, even with the enhancements on his hearing aids.

"We have to help her," whispered Kylie.

Ajay shook his head. "It's not our place."

"Papa."

Now it was Ajay's turn to feel like he had disappointed his granddaughter. But when powerful people quarreled, his instinct had always told him to stay out of the way. It was like King Kong fighting Godzilla. Maybe the big guys got hurt, but everything around was dust for sure.

Jocelyn pulled away from Parks. "He doesn't want to speak with you."

"He doesn't *know*." Parks took a step back.

"Then come inside," Jocelyn said with a wicked smile. "You may, of course, join us for dinner as soon as you drop off all your weapons."

Parks's jaw hardened. "That won't be happening."

Jocelyn made a gesture, and a light near the door flashed red. "And I won't have you wandering the grounds."

Fists clenched at Parks's sides. "You have no right."

"I have every right," said Jocelyn. "This is my house. My property. My party." She gestured at the hallways leading from the foyer. "These are my guests."

Parks stepped outside into the gloomy daylight. He spread his hands wide. "Until they leave."

"I'll tell him you graciously refused the invitation, and that you'll wait for him outside of my property," she purred.

Before the man could respond, the doors slammed shut. Even from the hall, Ajay could hear a heavy bolt grind into place.

Jocelyn slumped, letting out a gasp of air and clutching her chest. "Oh, to not have to deal with men like that."

Ajay stepped around the corner and into the foyer. "Trouble?"

"I'm sorry you had to hear that, Ajay," Jocelyn said, gathering herself. "It wasn't pleasant, and *I'm* never pleasant dealing with such people."

Kylie stepped from her hiding place. "You were a stone-cold bitch, grandma."

Jocelyn offered a weak smile. "I was, wasn't I?" She stalked to her granddaughter, but instead of stopping in front of her, continued past and opened the gray box on the wall. She punched in a long code.

A smooth male voice spoke through the walls. "Perimeter security armed."

"There," she said. "That will keep him away."

Ajay leaned on his cane. "Who was that man?"

Jocelyn led the way out of the foyer and into a long hall that ran the length of the east wing. The art that lined this hallway was a series of twisted and surreal paintings, making the space uncomfortable and strange.

"You're a fan of Salvador Dali?" Ajay asked as they passed a painting in which a disembodied head sat in a desert with horrified faces in its eyes and mouth.

A thin smile touched her red lips. "I like to think that it reminds us of the consequences of our actions."

"It just shows suffering."

"Yes, well, that's war for you, isn't it?" Jocelyn said.

Kylie frowned at the painting. "It's infinite. The faces in the eyes have faces in their eyes."

They passed another painting in which distorted figures attacked each other with forks and spoons. Ajay shuddered. He put a hand around Kylie's shoulder and guided her away, but she seemed fascinated.

"I prefer my art a little more abstract," Ajay said.

Jocelyn scoffed. "How so?"

"Well you know," said Ajay. "Giant squares. Paint spatters. That kind of thing. I like my art open to a little more interpretation."

"You don't think Dali is open to interpretation?"

"It's all melting clocks and cannibalism. Not much to interpret."

Jocelyn scoffed. The conversation had taken the edge from her voice, and now she considered each work as they passed.

"Will you be sending your guests home?" he asked as they neared the end of the hall. "If that man out there is a threat."

She stopped and looked at each of them in turn. "I don't see how I can." She drew a long, slow breath, and Ajay saw that his question had upset her again. "No, Mr. Andersen, nobody will be leaving anytime soon. This meeting will take place as scheduled."

Kylie picked up on a change in the woman's tone. "I thought this was a dinner party."

Jocelyn spread her hands. "Why not both, my dear?"

The hallway was plunged into darkness. Kylie gasped. Down the hall, the front lights went black, and Ajay's ears rang with the emptiness that came with a total loss of power.

Jocelyn said, "Melinda, dear, what is the meaning of this." When there was no response, she stalked to the wall. "Melinda?"

"Power's out," Ajay grumbled. "She probably can't hear you."

"My power doesn't go out," Jocelyn snapped. "Melinda, what is wrong with the automated lights in the center hall?" She listened for a moment, then said to Ajay and Kylie, "Melinda tells me that lights are out everywhere. Backup systems running soon. I knew I shouldn't have trusted her with tonight."

"I'm sure she's doing her best," Ajay said.

"Stay here," Jocelyn said.

Ajay placed his cheaters on the bridge of his nose. They couldn't let him see in complete darkness, but they could catch the faint ambient light from the adjacent room that had windows. As his cheaters adjusted to the abysmal light conditions, he heard the scuff of movement where Jocelyn had been, but when the image finally resolved, she was gone. His indicators didn't detect a network on any of the standard channels. He looked to Kylie, who shrugged.

"Maybe she was talking to herself," Kylie said.

Ajay pressed a hand on the wall where Jocelyn had been. "This is why I normally avoid social engagements."

"This is why I love palaces," said Kylie. He could hear the smile in her voice.

"Don't get used to it," he said.

Kylie let out a frustrated noise, and Ajay didn't blame her. After all, she really only wanted as normal a life as possible, and this wasn't it. It wasn't her fault that things were always complicated. He knew there would be issues dealing with her father's side of the family. When he thought about it, a single angry mercenary and an engaged defense perimeter didn't sound too bad. If he was careful, they could navigate this party, maybe get the power back on, and leave with a fascinating anecdote about the fraught complications of being wealthy in America. Mercenaries at the gate? Well of course. That's just how things are for multi-trillionaires.

"This Parks guy isn't our problem," Ajay said. "Your grandmother probably has something she needs to deal with, but it doesn't involve us."

"Are you sure?"

"How could it? We don't know any of these people."

"Yeah."

"As long as nothing else happens, we'll still be able to leave right after dinner."

Two gunshots rang out from somewhere down the hall, and the evening pretty much went downhill from there.

CHAPTER FIVE

"Stay close," Ajay said when the lights flickered back to life. They had only been out for a minute that stretched somehow into an eternity.

"Fine," Kylie sighed.

"Very close."

She rolled her eyes, but Ajay pretended to be unaffected by the sentiment. The commotion came from a door down the hall. He pushed through the door and was met with the chaotic clucking of upset rich people.

Robert Burkshire held Declan Bohm's wrist in an iron grip and dragged him through the hall.

Declan struggled against the bigger man's grip. "Let me go, Burkshire."

Robert pulled harder. The man's muscles flexed against the shiny fabric of his suit. "You'll come with me, Bohm. This time we've finally caught you in the act."

Declan dropped his weight, shoved hard against Robert, and twisted himself away from the man's grasp. He raised his fists as if to continue the fight.

"Stop," Ajay said, thumping his cane on the floor. "Stop!"

Declan took a step back.

"Tell me what's happening here," Ajay said, getting between the two men. Kylie wisely stayed at the edge of the room. "What were those gunshots?"

"This idiot attacked me," cried Declan.

"I did nothing of the sort." Spittle flew from Robert's lips. He moved forward, but Ajay stepped between the two men.

"That's enough!" Ajay jabbed the tip of his cane at Robert. "Tell me what happened."

Robert gestured at Declan. "I was waiting for my daughter when I heard the gunshots, and when I opened the door, I saw Declan Bohm here. The gun was on the floor, and there was nobody else in the room." He swallowed.

"Did you pick it up?" Ajay asked.

"Of course not," said Robert. "I don't want my fingerprints anywhere near the murder weapon."

"Murder?" said Ajay.

Declan said, "There was so much blood."

Ajay stared at Declan, not knowing what to say.

Declan said, "I entered the room when I heard the shots. Burkshire here came in only a moment after me." His shoulders deflated. "It happened so fast."

Ajay waved his cane until Robert started to move toward the door. To Kylie, he said, "Stay back, but stay close."

Kylie nodded and kept a close hold of Garrison. The big dog took the pause in movement as an indication that it was time for a nap.

"I was there right after the gunshot," Robert said. "There was no time for anyone else to leave."

"I'm sure you're right and you've observed everything there is to observe," Ajay deadpanned. "Who's the body?"

"Excuse me?" Robert huffed.

"The body. It must have been someone. Are you sure they're dead?"

It was Declan who answered. "I think it was Theodore."

"You think?" spat Robert. To Ajay, he said, "He's the one with reason to assault Parks. Ask him!"

"Now settle down," said Ajay. He let out a shuddering breath. "Let's go have a look first."

Kylie walked with Garrison behind the group, silent as a ghost. Theodore was the man she had thought was scary. Ajay would have to talk with her about that later, but he didn't want the others to know about her special senses. There was enough trouble here already.

They passed several rooms before coming to a recessed doorway. Their footsteps were muffled by elaborate rugs, and the walls were all covered in paintings and tapestries. Ajay ignored it all, following Robert to a tall mahogany door.

"In here," the man said. He had an east coast accent, Ajay realized. Something like Boston, but not quite.

Ajay nudged the door open with his cane.

A woman stood in the far corner, her hand pressed to her mouth. She had skin so dark and smooth it glowed, and her hair hugged her skull in tight curls. A red dress clung to her shapely body like the wash of blood covering the floor. She drew a deep, steadying breath and tore her gaze from the corpse to meet Ajay's eyes. He got the impression of a model posed specifically to evoke a response, but he didn't know what that response was intended to be.

Ajay recognized the corpse immediately. Declan had been right. This was the man in black he had seen in the garden. The man who had drawn Kylie's attention and who had given Ajay the creeps. This was Theodore, the man Alexander Parks was looking for. Here he was, clearly dead on the floor, his blood still seeping into an elaborately woven rug depicting the battle of Gettysburg in stark gory detail. The wounds in his torso stained his black suit, but the cuts in his face and neck oozed directly onto the floor. Next to his head lay his tech glasses, crushed beyond recovery.

Civil War art decorated every inch of the walls in the long room, from the swords bolted to a plaque above the door to the oil paintings lit by the glow from the gloomy sky outside. The only other source of light was two standing lamps shaped like standing gas lanterns lit with the flickering glow of antique incandescent bulbs. Outside, the view ended almost immediately, choked by a tight knot of lilac.

The only other door to the room opened, admitting Loretta and Percival Trowbridge.

"I say," said Percival. "What is the meaning of all this?"

"Murder," said Robert stepping into the room. He held Declan's wrist in his iron grip again. "And this is the man responsible."

Percival blinked and took a step back, but his eyes weren't on Declan. He watched Robert the way a mouse watched a cat. "Is that really so?"

"Now, hold on," said Ajay. "Normally, I wouldn't care who of you all killed each other. The more the better far as I'm concerned, but since we're stuck here, we're going to get a few things clear."

"Stuck here?" said Loretta. She turned to her husband. "Whatever does he mean by that?"

"This isn't what we signed up for," huffed Percival.

"Kylie." Ajay pointed at a discreet box outside the door. "Get Zach on the intercom and tell him to bring the kitchen help up to this room." He looked at the worried expressions on all the guests' faces. "And tell him to bring another round of drinks. We're going to need them."

She did as asked, using the intercom box to send messages down to the help.

"Can someone tell me what's happening here?" asked Loretta. "And who is she?" She pointed to the dark-skinned woman in the corner.

"My father sent me," said the woman.

Loretta swirled the wine in her glass. "And he would be?"

"Wilson Lee," the woman said, bringing a heavy hush to the room.

"That bastard," whispered Loretta.

"My sentiment exactly," the woman said. To Ajay, she said, "My name is Nailah. It is my job to oversee my father's account and attend social gatherings."

"Thank you," Ajay said. "That doesn't help me at all."

It was Percival who took mercy on Ajay's ignorance. "Wilson Lee is the greatest investor of our times. His predictive logic drives a large percentage of the wealth in this part of the world."

"I see," said Ajay. "Kylie?"

"They're coming," she said. "And bringing drinks."

"Wonderful." Ajay stepped closer to the body of Theodore Parks. Next to the body lay a silver revolver elaborately decorated with scrollwork and an ivory handle. "Robert, you can let go of Mr. Bohm."

"Why should I?" Robert said through tight lips.

Ajay picked the gun up by hooking it with the tip of his cane. "This is not the murder weapon."

A murmur passed through the crowd. Ajay knelt close to the body and touched the blood. Fresh, of course. It had soaked into the rug at the base of Gettysburg where heroic-looking Confederate soldiers rallied against a final onslaught. He held the gun up carefully to peer at it. Several fingerprints were visible on the gun, imprinted with dried blood. He lowered it and placed it next to Theodore's big hands.

"This is the murder victim's weapon," he said.

"Impossible," sputtered Robert. "Jocelyn's guests are not allowed to bring weapons past the foyer."

"And yet, here is a gun," said Ajay. He looked to each of the guests. "And it isn't the murder weapon because, as you can see, the victim was not shot."

Ajay nudged the body's head to one side, revealing a long slash along the base of his neck. Another ran along his cheekbone. Two smaller holes perforated his torso near the lungs. Ajay didn't know which wound killed the man, but none of them had been caused by a gun.

Zach cleared his throat from the doorway. He held a tray of tall champaign flutes in a shaking hand. "Excuse me, I—" Then his eyes rolled to the back of his head. His tray tumbled. With a quick step from behind him, Gabby Burkshire swept in, caught the tray, and steadied it without dropping a single tall glass. The girl sheepishly stood in silence with the drinks, while Zach collapsed at her feet.

Percival broke the silence with a clap. "Good catch!" Loretta nudged him into silence.

"Some would have caught the boy and not the drinks," said Declan.

"Good to see her priorities are in order," Percival bellowed, taking a glass from the tray and emptying it, earning a scowl from his wife.

At Robert's beckoning, Gabby crossed the room and stood at his side. He whispered something in her ear. A subtle blush rose to her high cheeks.

"What is this about?" said Melinda, stepping into the room from the same door Loretta and Percival had used. When she saw the body on the floor, she bit off her next words with a sharp intake of breath.

"Murder," said Ajay. "Where's your boss?"

"Upstairs in her room." Melinda slipped a pair of slender glasses on. With a gesture of her slender fingers, a blue holographic display danced across the lenses. "Everybody out. I'll lock the doors and call the authorities."

Zach recovered quickly and agreed to lead the way to the ballroom. "This way, folks!" His voice was full of false cheer as if he might startle the terror away with obviously false bravado.

The guests bustled out of the sitting room, and Melinda sealed both doors with a physical lock, stowing the key in her pocket. She rested with her back to the heavy double doors and stood in the recessed entryway for the span of a slowly released breath. "Well," she whispered. "This evening not going well."

Gabby Burkshire took her father's arm as they waited, and Ajay, seeing this, sought out Kylie to stand by her side. She sulked, as usual, but allowed him to be nearby.

"How are you handling this?" Ajay said.

She didn't answer, so he assumed she was handling it just fine.

"I need to get back to the kitchen," sputtered Zach, as if he just then remembered his other duties.

Ajay took hold of the boy's elbow. "You were supposed to bring the rest of the kitchen staff."

Zach said, "I'm sorry. Ben—Mr. Hale—our chef, was busy with the appetizers. Olexie was helping him, if you can call what he does helping."

Ajay thought of Olexie working in the kitchen. No wonder the sandwiches were so bad. Olexie had been gathering data on Jocelyn Garver for several weeks, and Ajay didn't want to break the Russian's cover. "You were all three together when the lights went out?"

Zach furrowed his brow. "Yeah."

"You don't sound convinced."

"No, I am. I mean, it's a big kitchen, but we were all there."

"I'll lead them the rest of the way," Melinda sighed, rejoining the group.

Zach ducked down a side passage and left the group.

"Well," Melinda added. "Come along, then."

She led them to another enormous door, which opened to reveal the opulent ballroom. Gold-trimmed walls framed a gorgeous inlaid roof. The parquet floor was an interwoven network of oak and mahogany, matched only by the intricately carved framing for the double doors they had just passed through. To one side of the sprawling dance floor sat a single long table set with eight high-backed chairs, arranged to one side like Michelangelo's Last Supper. Above the dance floor hung a delicate spiderweb of a chandelier, the crystalline network of connections sprawling twenty feet across.

"Shouldn't we do something with the body?" asked Percival.

"No," snapped Ajay.

"Put it in the refrigerator or something?"

"No."

"Cover it with a sheet?"

"No." Ajay looked the man in the eyes. "We don't interfere with the body. When the police arrive, they will find an undisturbed crime scene."

"Police," scoffed Robert. "As if they'll be anything approaching worthwhile."

"They're the best we have," said Ajay.

"We already know the killer," said Robert. "Declan was at the crime scene."

"Without a murder weapon."

Robert licked his lips. "Have you searched him? Or for that matter, he could have hidden it somewhere in the room."

"I haven't searched anybody." It only then occurred to him that he had inadvertently put himself in charge. He'd spoken up at the wrong moment, and now he'd have to deal with it. Fine. He could be the asshole in the room. He thumped his cane on the floor to get everyone's attention. "Listen up, folks." Ajay peered at each in turn.

Melinda stood tall and aloof with pride only a leader could have. Loretta and Percival Trowbridge looked on. The elderly woman clung to her flustered husband as if she were providing him physical support. Robert Burkshire crossed his arms, keeping Declan Bohm in his sight at all times. Gabby Burkshire, conversely, had already found a distant corner to lurk in, apart from the crowd. Kylie lingered nearby. Her beautiful red suit was already rumpled and covered in leaves. Her clutch purse was missing, but she hadn't had anything in it anyway. She was a stark contrast to Nailah, whose dress was still as perfect and unblemished as a sunset on a clear summer eve.

Declan had claimed the whole dance floor as his own. Nobody stood near him in his rumpled suit, but Ajay couldn't tell if that was due to Robert's accusations or some previous sin. The closest to him was Nailah Lee, the daughter of powerful magnate Wilson Lee. Her role here was unclear, but her status was not. She was wealth personified, and if anything she stood above the sniveling upper crust that populated the rest of the party. She appeared like royalty with her perfect skin and perfect posture and perfect eyes.

When he had everyone's attention, Ajay said, "There's a murderer among us, and we're not leaving any time soon."

Every guest started talking at once, their words joining in an ever-rising crescendo approaching panic. Ajay silenced them with a loud thump of his cane on the floor that echoed in the enormous ballroom.

"Why can't we leave?" asked Robert.

He didn't get a chance to respond, because the double doors swung wide again and Jocelyn Garver stepped in. She wore a different gold dress and carried a smoldering cigarette in a long black holder.

"Well, my friends," she said, her voice resonating in the gigantic room, "it seems Mr. Andersen is correct. One of you is a killer."

"But what's this about not leaving," growled Robert.

Jocelyn fixed him with a serious gaze. She appeared calm and controlled, but a muscle on her neck twitched with tension. "Alexander Parks is waiting for you to leave."

"Alexander!" Percival exclaimed. "What has that ruffian got to do with any of this?"

Loretta placed a calming hand on his elbow. To

the rest, she explained, "We tried to hire him once, but it didn't go well."

"Alexander Parks doesn't know about Theodore yet," Jocelyn said. "But he is outside waiting for you if you decide to leave."

Robert shot a glance at Gabby. "We'll stay for now," he said. "But I want a guarantee of safety for my daughter."

A wicked smile sliced across Jocelyn's face. "Alexander is one of the cruelest men I know. If we can't prove who killed Theodore, then we are all in danger."

"This is preposterous," Percival blurted.

"We *know* who killed the man," Robert said, pointing at Declan.

Declan took a step back and raised his hands in surrender. "It wasn't me, I swear."

Ajay clapped his hands once and stood as tall as his old back would allow. He met gazes with each guest in turn. "We'll figure out who the murderer is. I promise." It was a lie. He had no idea if they could prove anything. He walked to the table and noisily pulled out a chair. "Until then, I believe we were promised some dinner."

CHAPTER SIX

"I need access," said Ajay to Melinda a few feet from the table where the rest of the guests sat and picked at some kind of fish puff appetizer that smelled like pickles.

Melinda shook her head. She had pulled her dark hair back into a tight ponytail, which made her look even younger than she had before—a woman out of her element in a difficult situation. "We don't give out credentials."

"You've done your research on me," he said. "I know you have. You know I could take access with two hands tied behind my back."

"Not likely." Melinda's glasses flashed. "If you even tried, our automatic EMP response would toast every networking device in the room. It would be inconvenient for us all."

Ajay blinked. He didn't want to think about what that might do to Kylie. "You're right. I don't want to get into that here. Give me read access. I can help."

"No," Melinda said.

"Melinda." Jocelyn's voice was laced with warning.

"It's a security risk, and I don't like it," said the butler. "You put me in charge of this. If he has read access—"

"Then he'll be able to find his way around the house. Nothing else." Jocelyn's facade cracked for a fraction of a second, and something like an understanding passed between the two women. "I understand your concerns, my dear," she said, placing a hand atop Melinda's. "Ajay was with me in the far side of the house just before the murder happened, so I know he isn't the killer." She spoke loud enough for the others to hear. "In fact, I'm putting Mr. Andersen in charge of the investigation."

Melinda's brow creased. "Yes, ma'am."

Jocelyn continued, "Your job is to keep Alexander Parks from learning anything about my guests and keep his drones off my property. The perimeter defense will do most of the work."

"Perimeter defense," Ajay mused. "Were you expecting an invading army from Canada?"

Jocelyn fixed Ajay with a look that told him that yes, she understood that he was joking, but no, she didn't think it was very funny.

Melinda pressed her lips firmly together but didn't offer any more protests. "Fine, I've created read-only credentials." She swiped across her display and Ajay received the key in his cheaters. He copied it to a safe place. "That'll only work for tonight, but you'll be able to see the surveillance system and everything connected to it." She gave him a plastic widget the size of a golf tee. "And you'll need to pipe your network through this."

"Thank you," Ajay said absently, plugging the widget into his cane. He ran the key through the device's network layer and found the information he wanted masked under the rolling wall of background noise. "Clever."

"You'll only see the surveillance network through that device. Nothing else."

"How does it work?"

"That's not necessary information."

The engineer in the back of Ajay's brain tried to pull apart what he saw, but it didn't quite figure. Where were they hiding the network? What were they doing on the protocols that kept him from finding it without the widget? Keeping the network non-standard meant it was difficult to find and therefore hard to hack. It also meant that the noise it created would interfere with other devices, which was probably why their connection outside wasn't working.

Inside the house, eyes were everywhere. He saw everything. At the edge of the forest, the stationary systems were readied against a wave of approaching drones. The drones tested each point in the barrier, only to retreat when perimeter warnings flashed before them. Ajay watched as Melinda adjusted the defenses to adapt to Alexander Parks's changing techniques.

"Just until the reinforcements arrive," Melinda whispered in his ear. She had taken the opportunity to connect her comm unit to his hearing aid. Wonderful.

"What reinforcements?"

"Police. Mercenaries."

"They've been called?"

"Things will go much better for everyone if you figure out who the killer is before they arrive."

Cameras flooded the courtyard, and Ajay found recordings of the early minutes of the party. He saw himself chatting with Declan and noted that audio recordings also existed. That might come in handy.

Inside the house was another matter. He had access to the cameras and current surveillance, but no recordings existed.

"Gone," Melinda said when she noticed that he was looking for the most useful recordings. "Wiped from the drive before they could be backed up offline."

"Damn."

"You're telling me."

Ajay scowled at the empty recording logs. "Who has access to that?"

"Me. Jocelyn. Anybody with the ability to crack heavy encryption."

"Someone's carrying around a quantum computer?" Ajay mused, knowing that Kylie could probably have cracked that encryption if she'd tried hard enough. If she was interested. It got harder and harder to get her to do anything these days. She would have needed access to a wireless network for that, anyway, and as far as he knew the only way to get that was through Melinda's decoder.

"Or they're very good at guessing," Melinda said.

"That's something I've always been pretty good at." He shot her a sideways grin.

"What else can you do?"

"I'm the best in town at hacking drones."

"That many?" Melinda indicated the swarms outside.

"Probably not."

"Pity." She'd come across as stiff and formal before, but whispering through comms made her seem almost personable. Friendly. Maybe she finally saw what kind of help he could provide.

"All right," he said, "so we're looking for a quantum computer, a murder weapon, and a murderer."

"But not necessarily in that order."

"Right."

Ajay clicked through his options. Robert was watching him from the table, and he wondered if the big man had been listening. Then Robert went back to telling Jocelyn a story that involved Gabby being exceptionally clever. It made Ajay want to strangle him, but Jocelyn gave every appearance of thoroughly enjoying it.

His read-only feed couldn't affect anything, but it gave him a visual of the entire mansion. He looked at the building as a whole, its networks of hallways and rooms spreading before him in a wireframe diagram. His attention was drawn to a room deep in the basement level.

"What's this?" he swiped the image over to Melinda.

Melinda said, "A maintenance room."

"Looks like a panic room to me."

"It's barely big enough for two people," she said, looking down her narrow nose at him again.

"Perfect."

"We are more than two people, Mr. Andersen."

"Call me Ajay." He swiped the surveillance maps away.

He couldn't tell if the twinkle in her eye was amusement or because she was still running the optical display through her glasses. "Just find the murderer, Mr. Andersen."

"I will," he said, "But I'm—"

"Percival, stop!" shouted Loretta to a clatter of silverware. She pulled her husband's arm.

The older man lunged at Declan, swinging a clumsy fist. "Take it back, Bohm."

"I'm sorry," said Declan, stepping aside. "It's the truth. You would have been convicted."

"This is an attack on my person. I'll not listen to this," shouted Percival. "We did nothing wrong."

Declan held his palms forward in contrition. "I'm not saying that you killed him, old man, only that you have as much a motivation as any, and his death certainly saved your case."

Percival's face was as red as Nailah's dress. "You have no reason—"

"I have every reason!" Declan snapped.

Ajay folded both hands on the top of his cane and watched. The two men were red with the heat of their anger. Fists clenched. Teeth ground. He didn't know where it was going, but whatever happened might give him some information.

"You don't have a lot of friends here," Robert said to Declan.

Trembling tension shook Declan for a moment longer, then dissipated. "I'm sorry." He swept his thin hair to one side using his fingers. "I take it back."

Percival rubbed his elbow. "I've had enough of this. We're leaving."

"You can't leave," sighed Melinda. "Help is on the way."

Robert caught Ajay's eyes and frowned. Ajay wondered what the man was thinking.

Percival offered a hand to his wife, who took it and followed him to the doors of the ballroom.

Melinda's delicate fingers danced across her controls, and a mechanism in the doors let out a loud thunk. "I don't think you understand me," she said calmly. "You *can't* leave."

Percival turned toward them, his face red with rage. "You wouldn't *dare* lock us in."

Ajay glanced at Jocelyn where she stood by the wall, and for a fraction of a second, he thought he saw a hint of amusement there. Then it was gone, replaced by something that looked like worry.

"Honey, it's fine," said Loretta to her husband. "We're safe here." She watched Robert as she spoke.

"Safe?" sputtered Percival. His eyes darted to the dark corners of the room. "With a murderer?"

"With a group, dear," Loretta said, hanging on his arm.

Percival shrugged her off and roared at Melinda, "Let us go this instant. We won't leave the premises, but we won't stay here with these—" he sputtered for a moment "—people."

Melinda's shoulders tensed, but before she could protest, Ajay cut her off. "Let them go. We'll keep an eye on them." He glanced to Kylie, who sat against the wall with Garrison. His surveillance feed showed that nobody else was in the mansion. The grounds were silent as a grave except for the kitchen. "I need you to let me out, too."

"Where?" asked Melinda.

"Jocelyn," Ajay said, but the woman had disappeared again. "Where did she go?"

Melinda shrugged. "She's a very busy person."

"Did anyone see where she went?" Ajay asked.

The guests couldn't bother to meet his eyes. Nobody had seen her leave, or at least they weren't going to admit to it.

"Robert, you're coming with me," Ajay said. "We need to talk."

CHAPTER SEVEN

SOMETHING CLENCHED in Kylie's chest so tight that she couldn't talk. She could hardly breathe. The tenuous remains of her connection to the outside world died when Grandma Garver enabled the security perimeter. Papa hadn't even noticed. She wondered if she could break through if she used the tech in her head, but Papa had warned her against that. The warning probably applied doubly so now, but how was she supposed to know?

She swallowed back a wave of bile. This wasn't happening.

Garrison nuzzled his nose into her armpit, interrupting the vortex of doom forming in her brain.

With the wall pressed firmly against her back, she watched the adults bicker. Two of the men fought, but she didn't twitch a muscle. Let them fight. One of those adults was a killer, and she wanted to know which one.

But she didn't want to *see* which one. She had seen enough death already. She knew she'd need to see more one day. She was meant for it. Isn't that what her father had thought? The truth of it lingered as a slow-burning ember in the edge of her vision, but usually, she was able to deny it. Usually, she was able to rely on her friend Austin for support, but without a connection, he was gone.

"Whatcha doin'?" Gabby asked, suddenly sitting next to her.

"Brooding," said Kylie without thinking.

"My dad says I'm not supposed to be the kind of person who broods."

"My grandpa says I can be whoever I want."

"Sounds nice."

"He doesn't mean it. It's horrible." If she could be whoever she wanted, why would she be who she is? Nobody ever wanted to be a broken, traumatized thirteen-year-old girl. Ever. It was basically the lowest ranked of all the potential people anyone could be. No wonder Isabelle decided to be someone else. Someone older. More competent. Kylie glanced at Gabby. The girl had a frown on her face, and her brow was crinkled. How old was she? Eleven? Twelve? Kylie couldn't tell.

Garrison whined, so Kylie rubbed behind his ears. She wasn't supposed to reward his whining, but she didn't care. Kylie wanted to talk to Gabby about as much as she wanted to be at this party.

"C'mon, Kylie," Papa said. "It's time to go."

Kylie blinked. "What?"

Mr. Burkshire beckoned Gabby with a quick gesture and the girl hopped up to attention. "We've come to an agreement," he said. "You two will be taking the panic room for a while."

"But I can panic out here," Kylie muttered.

"It's the only way to keep you safe." Papa tried to take her hand, but she pulled away.

"I'm safe here," Kylie said, but she knew it wasn't true. "I'm safe at home."

Meanwhile, Mr. Burkshire whispered in Gabby's ear. Kylie didn't like the way the girl's eyes tracked her as she crossed the ballroom with Papa. After a few exchanged words, the Burkshires followed, passing through the big double doors and leaving the party.

"What's a panic room?" Gabby asked.

"You'll see," said Mr. Burkshire, placing a hand on her small back. "It's a room where people can go to be safe in case of an emergency."

"What if the house burns down?" Gabby asked.

"You'll be safe."

"What if bad people attack?"

"Safe."

"Tornado?"

Mr. Burkshire gave her a stern look.

Gabby nodded, apparently mollified, but Kylie didn't buy it. She got the distinct impression that Gabby was phony-playing a part for her father's benefit. Papa didn't seem to notice any of this.

Papa said, "Once engaged, the room will only unlock from the inside. It would take industrial strength cutting torches or a top-notch safecracker to find their way into your vault, and the environmental systems are all self-sustained." He shot a glance at Kylie. "You'll have all the food and supplies you need, and hopefully some entertainment."

And it meant she didn't need to be at the party. Kylie weighed her options, not really liking any of them. It was either hang out with a bunch of stodgy adults and be in danger, or hide with Gabby and be safe.

"It'll be fun!" said Gabby, because of course she did.

"Down here," said Mr. Burkshire. He pressed on a wood panel in the hallway wall, and it opened to reveal a service elevator. "We'll take this to the basement level."

They crammed inside. The elevator felt like it was built for a single person, not four plus a huge dog, two of whom were smelly and old. One of which was a dog whose main response to the stress of new situations came in the form of noxious gas. Kylie tried her best not to touch anyone, but as the elevator rumbled downward, she bumped into Papa.

She wasn't even mad at him. He was doing everything he could. She was mad at the situation. Why would Grandma put her through this? Even before the murder and that horrible body on the floor, she'd been uncomfortable, and it wasn't going to get any better. She felt like Grandma Garver watched her every move, and it made her spine itch.

The elevator thunked to a stop, but the doors didn't open.

Several long seconds passed. The air grew stuffy and hot.

"What's happening?" squeaked Gabby.

Kylie longed to hack the elevator's systems. She knew she could do it in seconds if she wanted. It wasn't hard. There was a real network signal in the tiny space. But Papa had made her promise to stay silent, so she did nothing.

Then again, that was when he thought they were going to a plain old dinner with Grandma. This was different. This was something important. The weight of their confined space pressed in on her from all sides. She choked on the hot stink of the people around her.

Kylie reached her senses out, ever so carefully.

"I've got it," said Papa. He manipulated the controls of his cane-mounted computer and attached a universal connector to a data port. Lights flashed in his tiny half-moon glasses. "Hold on, what is she doing?"

"What is it?" asked Mr. Burkshire. "What is who doing?"

"Something's changed," said Papa.

Mr. Burkshire swore.

"There," Papa said. The elevator lurched

upward. To Robert, he said, "Jocelyn is going to the panic room."

Mr. Burkshire said, "We need to get there first."

All Kylie wanted was *out*.

Gabby took hold of Kylie's hand, as if for comfort, but Kylie pulled away. She placed a hand on Garrison's head instead, drawing comfort from the big dog.

The elevator stopped, and the door opened to reveal the same hallway where they had left.

"So much for our shortcut," Papa said.

"Dammit, we need to get there before she closes the panic room." Mr. Burkshire practically shoved Gabby out in front of him. Together they raced down the long hall.

Papa stepped forward. They were too fast.

"Why is she going there?" Kylie asked.

"I don't know," said Papa, "but I suspect she's starting to lose interest in attending to her guests."

Kylie grabbed Papa's arm and pulled him to a stop. "We won't make it running after them."

"The elevator won't go down. There's a block."

Kylie drew him back toward the elevator. "Let me do it." Her eyes pleaded for him to just trust her to do it.

He seemed to think forever on the decision. She knew what he must be weighing. If she hacked the elevator, she'd be able to get it to work, but she would also be revealing a little bit of her abilities in a place where it was probably smarter to keep everything a secret. Just this once, though. One little hack to get the elevator to the right place.

Papa gave the tiniest nod.

She took his cane and plugged its universal connector back into the elevator. With a quick dance through the menus, she routed the elevator's operating controls through the cane's local wireless network signal.

Then, Kylie was in. Waves of code flowed through the computer half of her brain. She picked apart the security blockade and wiped the lingering status alerts from the logs. As Papa shoved Garrison back into the tiny box, she overrode the safety mechanisms and took full control.

The elevator plummeted even before the doors fully closed.

CHAPTER EIGHT

AJAY'S STOMACH punched the back of his throat, and his knuckles turned white from gripping the handrail. His feet felt like they barely touched the shiny linoleum floor, and the lights above flickered.

The elevator ground to a stop. Kylie fixed her flat gaze on him.

"Kylie," Ajay said, a spike of worry bristling at the back of his neck. "Come back to me, dear." She had done too much. This was the first sign of trouble, and she'd already tossed out the idea of staying hidden. Ajay only hoped she wouldn't be noticed before she got herself under control.

Kylie blinked. "I'm fine," she rasped.

The elevator revealed the utility corridors under the mansion. Dull white walls were lined with storage racks containing dusty bins and old equipment. Flickering lights ran the length of the ceiling.

Odd shadows danced across the concrete floor. Shouts came from down the hall.

Ajay hurried as fast as he could. His hip would ache later, but he could almost run for short periods without causing himself any real trouble. Already, the ache in his joints flared. Make that very short periods.

Jocelyn stalked down the hall from the other direction.

"Jocelyn," he called to her.

She turned around the corner into an unlit basement room. When Ajay reached the room, he saw her step into the black maw of a vaulted doorway. The massive door started to slide closed.

"Oh no you don't," he said. He jabbed his cane out as the door closed, and it wedged in the heavy door's track, stopping it. "Jocelyn, what are you doing?"

Jocelyn stared at him as if he'd committed the greatest faux pas she had ever seen at one of her parties. She grasped his cane, trying to dislodge it. Behind her, the panic room lights slowly flickered to life. The tiny room had a bank of computers along one wall and a packed shelf opposite. A single rickety chair sat in the center of the room, and a doorway on the far side opened into another room that Ajay couldn't see.

Ajay punched the controls, and the door slid open. His cane clattered to the floor. Jocelyn snatched it up before he could grab it.

She waved the cane at Ajay. "You don't understand, Ajay. Guests aren't meant to come down here. You just don't understand."

"Tell me, then."

She sputtered. When she spoke again, her voice was artificially light. "Well, let's at least make things presentable." She turned around and punched the power switch on the vault's computer.

"Jocelyn, we're going to keep the girls safe here while we figure things out. That's all," said Ajay with as much calm as he could muster. He turned around to see Robert and Gabby standing in the doorway. "Isn't that right, Robert?"

The big man's chest heaved with heavy breaths. "I've had about enough of this." He pushed past Ajay and took Jocelyn by the arm.

"Robert," Ajay said, stepping forward to stop him.

But the big man yanked the old lady out of the panic room and threw her to the floor. She yelped in pain. Ajay's cane clattered at her feet.

"Gabby, come," Robert said. "Ajay, we're taking the panic room. We'll be safe while they figure this out."

Gabby crossed the room to stand at his side inside the safe room. Robert punched the controls and the door started to slide closed.

Ajay let out a growl of frustration and shoved hard against the closing door. Its safety systems wouldn't let it close as long as he was there. Hopefully. "You're not doing this, Robert," he said.

"She knows something, Andersen," said Robert, pointing at Jocelyn. "Ask her what she saw that's making her so excited to hide."

"Jocelyn?" Ajay asked of the woman.

Jocelyn stood against the wall and hugged herself close, rubbing a bruised arm. "There's someone else in the house."

When Jocelyn didn't continue, he said, "Who?"

"A killer," Jocelyn said.

"Who?" Ajay repeated.

Jocelyn shrank into herself. She stared at the far wall, her eyes glassy and unfocused. "Quinn."

The name felt like snow dumped down the back of Ajay's coat. He had watched Quinn casually kill before, and he was hoping to never repeat the experience.

Jocelyn took a step back, but she was against the wall. "Parks must have just sent her. She'll find Theodore. She'll find all of us." Her eyes darted to the safe room, where an array of screens flared to life a short distance from the vault door.

Percival burst into the room behind Ajay, followed by Loretta. His jowls were rosy from anger and he frothed at the mouth. His breaths came in deep rasps.

"Get that coward out of there," growled Percival, pointing at Robert. "I will not stand for this."

Ajay held up his hands to prevent Percival from shoving past. "Hold on, now."

Robert punched the controls on the computer inside the panic room. Screens flashed, showing the surveillance grid of the surrounding areas. A drone system showed flashes of movement through the edge of the forest. In one corner the shadow of a figure moved through the video feeds inside the mansion.

"The killer," Robert said.

Gabby blinked silently.

Jocelyn brushed off the front of her dress but failed to regain any shred of dignity. "She's not after you, Robert."

"No, I imagine she's not," Robert said to Jocelyn. "She's one of yours, isn't she?"

"He's afraid for his daughter," whispered Kylie. She stood in the darkest corner of the room, and Ajay wouldn't have heard her if not for his tuned hearing aid.

He met her gaze, catching her eye for a second until she nodded. She knew what he wanted, and she agreed to it. He made like he was trying to move away from the door, but acted as if his hip hurt more than it really did.

"He needs his cane," Kylie said, speaking so everyone could hear. "Just give it to him."

Jocelyn looked at the cane on the floor like it was a snake. When she didn't move to pick it up, Kylie crossed the room and plucked it up. She turned it over in her hands, carefully rubbing the marks where it had taken some damage when the door closed on it. Seemingly satisfied, she pulled Garrison with her and handed the cane to her grandfather.

He took it, gave it a twirl, and hit Robert with a searing jolt of electricity.

Gabby's tight fist struck Ajay first in the head, then neck, then pounded his kidney. He was on the ground, fending off the attacks as best he could— which wasn't very well. The girl was so fast. She howled in rage and pounded on him, each strike a shot of liquid fire through his muscles and bone. Something ground in his chest when she hit him with both fists.

A massive form struck Gabby from the side. Robert.

Kylie had thrown the man out of the panic room, leveraging his weight against him.

But it didn't stop the younger girl. Gabby recovered from the blow, got her feet under her, and launched herself at Ajay. He blocked her away with his cane, but the taser hadn't recharged. Her blows came lightning quick, jabbing at his legs and face and hands. He couldn't keep her at bay for long.

Percival stuttered, absolutely worthless in the fight. Jocelyn tried to circle around, but Gabby was too fast. Too dangerous.

Ajay snapped out with one hand, trying to grab her wrist.

Missed.

She struck him in the side of the head, and flashes

of light burst in his vision. Another blow to his gut bent him over. He collapsed in a heap, and she stood over him, her breath heaving.

"Stop, Gabby," Robert barked.

The girl snapped her head over to look at him, her expression completely blank.

Robert stood and brushed off his suit. Ajay took the opportunity to crawl a few feet away from the vicious girl. Any distance helped, he figured. Percival only stared at Robert.

"I apologize for the inconvenience," Robert said to Ajay. He shot a glance at Jocelyn. "She's had quite a bit of training in the martial arts and takes it very seriously." He smiled at his daughter. "I'm very proud of her, actually."

A hint of a smile crossed Gabby's lips.

Robert offered Ajay a hand up, but Ajay refused, instead using the wall to steady himself. He leaned heavily on his cane.

Kylie stood inside the panic room, its bright internal lights making her a frayed silhouette at the edge of the otherwise dark room. Her hair tumbled in a mess against her shoulders, curling and twisting in the still basement air. At her side, Garrison sat at the most attention Ajay had seen from the lazy dog since nacho night at the Andersen house. A few steps away from Kylie stood Gabby, in a similar pose but darker against the bright backdrop. She lingered in Kylie's shadow the way Kylie had once stood before her sister Isabelle. It struck Ajay how similar they were. Terrifying, the whole lot of them.

But, then again, teenage girls had always been a little terrifying.

He met Kylie's gaze and gave her the tiniest of nods.

Kylie lunged forward, grabbed Gabby by the arm, and pulled her back into the panic room. With the swipe of her free hand, she triggered the door.

At the same time, Ajay stuck his cane out to hinder Robert. It caught his ankle and slowed him just enough that the man reached the door too late.

The panic room closed.

CHAPTER NINE

Kylie had never seen a girl so angry.

Gabby spun on her when the door closed, fists balled at her sides. Her teeth were bared and her pupils were pinpricks. Seeing Gabby's anger made Kylie angry. A flush of rage burned at the base of her neck.

Kylie had *been* that angry before, and the realization came at her with a warm flush of embarrassment.

"Open it," Gabby growled.

Kylie forced her anger down, burying it deep inside her chest. "They'll be fine," she said, wishing she knew the right thing to say. "And we're safe." That wasn't it.

"Open. The. Door," Gabby hissed.

Kylie glanced at the controls. It would be easy to open the door again, but then what would happen? Papa was probably right that she should stay down here where it was safe. And Gabby had been so furious at him that Kylie had feared for her grandfather's life.

"No," she said.

Gabby lunged, but Kylie wasn't ready for it. She had been working on her self-defense classes, and she knew how to stop the smaller girl's wild attacks, but it didn't help. She stumbled back, blocked absolutely nothing, and grabbed Gabby's wrist.

Gabby wailed and gnashed and screamed. Garrison watched the entire exchange with passive indifference. Thanks a lot, guard dog.

"Stop," Kylie shouted.

It worked. Gabby froze, fists balled into jagged stones.

"Stop," Kylie repeated in the calmest voice she could manage. "We can do this."

Gabby's gaze went to the switch that would open the door. Kylie could almost see the plan clicking into place in the other girl's head.

"I'm sorry," said Kylie. "We can't go out there."

"Why not?" Gabby said. Tears beaded in her eyes.

Kylie swallowed hard. Her mouth was dry and her throat felt like sandpaper. She extended her senses an inch at a time, reaching out to sense the flow of information touching the deep recesses of their hidden panic room. There wasn't much. The local network had a weak signal that barely covered the tiny room.

But she sensed something. A lingering echo

danced through the chamber. It skirted the edge of Kylie's senses and avoided a direct link, but she knew it was there. Slowly, carefully, she allowed herself a minute signal and watched as Gabby's eyes grew wide.

"Because you're like me," Kylie said, sensing the network signals blossoming like roses from the other girl's brain. "We're the same."

CHAPTER TEN

"WHAT DID YOU DO?" Robert roared at Ajay. He wrenched the cane from Ajay's hands and threw it to the floor, where it landed next to Jocelyn. The old woman stood, staring out into the vast beyond without blinking.

"I've made sure our girls are safe," said Ajay, stepping forward. His hackles raised at the thought of being intimidated by this blowhard. "You should be thankful."

"Open it," Robert growled, clawing at the door.

"It's not going to open," said Percival. He stood in the doorway, shadows covering the expression on his face. "Not unless one of them opens it from inside."

"They're safe," said Ajay.

Robert spun back on Ajay. "Your daughter attacked mine. How do I know my girl is safe?"

A flash of anger boiled in Ajay. He jabbed Robert

in the chest. "You go accusing my girl one more time, Burkshire. See where it gets you."

Robert towered over Ajay, his body a powerhouse compared to the weak old man. Without his cane, Ajay had no advantage at all. Even with it, he probably wouldn't be a match for Robert. Not without the element of surprise. Up close, Ajay could see the man was in exquisite shape. The bigger man's knuckles popped when he clenched his fists.

"That's enough," said Jocelyn, stepping forward from the shadow. She smoothed her dress and drew a long, steadying breath. Something clicked behind her eyes, and the facade of quiet authority snapped back in place. "This whole thing is a waste."

"What do you mean?" asked Percival.

"You know exactly what I mean, Percival," the old woman spat.

Percival flinched. Loretta took his elbow and held him close. Ajay noticed something that looked like communication between the two. Whatever their nonverbal message was, it placated the old man and he backed down.

Robert let out a sigh of disgust. "This isn't over."

"No, I expect not," said Ajay. "But I for one would like to know why Chay Quinn is wandering the mansion."

Jocelyn said, "The children are safe in the panic room, and they are both critical to the reason I brought you all here tonight." When nobody responded, she said, "We're here for dinner, of course. There is a meal ready in the ballroom."

Percival said, "There's a murderer."

"And this Chay Quinn," said Robert.

Jocelyn waved it off as if a paltry little murder was nothing in her hectic life. "Of course, we'll take that into consideration." She turned to Ajay and Robert. "Can you two behave?"

"Not likely," said Ajay before he could stop himself.

Robert straightened his suit coat. He shot a glance at the panic room door. "Well, the only way to get those girls out is for them to open the door themselves, so I suppose there's no use in fighting about it."

"Fine," said Ajay. He picked his cane up and brushed it off, making sure it wasn't broken before putting it to use again. He found no local network, and his computer flashed an error when he tried to locate Kylie. Good.

Jocelyn waved the group out through the dim basement hallways. The decor in the basement was surprisingly spartan, considering the elegance above. Painted concrete walls gave way to the steel beams that supported the ceiling. Unlabeled doors led from hallways to other hallways in a vast and seemingly endless maze. They walked the long route around, avoiding the elevator that Kylie hacked for their way down. Eventually, they came to a wide staircase that led up through a pair of metal double doors. When they stepped through, they stood on the stone floor of the mansion. The door behind them appeared like any other ornate wooden door in the mansion.

When Percival and Robert were a few steps ahead, Jocelyn whispered to Ajay, "The murderer is one of the guests."

Ajay took a few steps before responding. "What about Quinn?"

"She wasn't here when Theodore was killed."

"You're sure?"

"Melinda is certain." Jocelyn placed a hand gently on Ajay's elbow and he stopped walking. "I still need you to discover who the murderer is."

"Fine," he said. "I'll see what I can come up with before the authorities arrive."

"Of course," Jocelyn said.

Ajay started walking again, his cane tapping against the carpeted floor. Already, he was lost in thoughts about how he might approach the mystery. "Parks is going to be upset."

Jocelyn said, "Melinda is almost certain he will breach our defenses, and there is a significant chance he will arrive before any reinforcements. This Quinn woman managed to get inside the mansion and will no doubt feed him information on how to breach our walls."

"How did she get in?" Ajay asked, but he already suspected the answer.

"Ms. Quinn has worked for me in the past," said Jocelyn. "Her access was never revoked."

"That doesn't seem like an error Melinda would make."

Jocelyn pursed her lips. "Melinda has made plenty of mistakes in her time here."

They walked in silence until they reached the door to the ballroom. Ajay turned to Jocelyn. "Does he know?"

"Know what?"

"About Theodore. The murder."

"If he doesn't know already, then he will soon enough. We have to assume that every system is compromised."

"So you want me to tell him a story when he shows up," Ajay said. "Give him a murderer other than you to be angry at."

"I want the story to be true."

"You want the story to be convincing."

Jocelyn took one of his hands in both of hers. "We are all in danger, Mr. Andersen. It is admirable that you were able to get your daughter to safety, but that means the rest of us must face what comes, and it won't be pretty."

"Avoiding the consequences of our own actions is often an ugly prospect." Ajay didn't look at her as he spoke. "I know a little something about how that works."

"I'm sure you do."

It was minutes later before Ajay started to wonder what she actually meant by those words.

CHAPTER ELEVEN

"THERE WERE to be dancers for entertainment," Jocelyn said, gesturing at the ballroom floor before them. To Ajay, she appeared diminished from her previous self. The stress of the evening was eating at her. "But of course, they have been canceled."

"Well," said Loretta, "I suppose we must provide our own entertainment."

The two women laughed as if there had been a mildly amusing joke, which there had not as far as Ajay could figure. The women sat in the center of the long table, still facing the broad and empty expanse of the dance floor. Behind them, Zach and an older server with a well-trimmed beard and quick eyes arranged bowls of soup in preparation for distribution. To Jocelyn's right sat Ajay, then Declan, and the tall beauty Nailah Lee. To Loretta's left sat her husband Percival, displaying a somewhat peeved affect, then Robert.

Ajay took a roll from the basket at the center of the table, broke it, and took a bite. He seriously considered making a joke about Jesus breaking bread, but he wasn't sure if it would be considered polite.

"It's good you got your daughter somewhere safe," whispered Declan.

Ajay chewed the roll.

Declan said, "I mean, I never figured this group to be the murdering type, but they're *definitely* not the leaving witnesses type. Do you think she'll stay put?"

"She's not Nancy Drew." She definitely would be. The idea made Ajay want to figure out how to lock the panic room from the *outside.*

"Well, girls of a certain age, you know."

"You have a daughter?"

"Two, actually." A flash of pride danced over Declan's dark features, erasing the worry lines for a brief moment. "They were good kids. Better adults."

"So, you knew what you were doing?"

Declan slumped into his brown suit. "I think they did well *despite* me. I was the kind of dad who thought working harder made their lives better."

"I know how that goes."

"Not well, it turns out." Declan let out a long sigh. "I missed too much of their lives, and there's nothing to show for it."

"You're talking about Percival."

Declan's jaw hardened. "Yes, well. Sometimes I wish men like him would at least use their wealth to make the world a better place. It would make failing to prosecute them a little easier to bear."

"What did the old man do, anyway?" Ajay asked.

Declan leaned close. "The age-old mix of real estate and insider trading, if you ask me. An interesting mix for a man who never leaves the house and despises risk, but I guess you do what you can when you want to hold onto as much of daddy's money as possible."

Zach and the other server placed bowls of soup in front of the guests. The soup was a thin broth that smelled of chives, mushrooms, and gym socks. When the old man placed a bowl in front of Ajay, he whispered, "We should talk," in a thick Russian accent.

Ajay didn't turn to look at the older server. He barely recognized Olexie dressed in his immaculate whites, but the voice was unmistakable.

The servers disappeared, leaving only Melinda leaning against the wall in one dark corner of the ballroom as the guests endured their tepid soup. Lights flashed across her eyes as she surveyed the security system input. At one point, Nailah waved her over and whispered something in her ear. When Declan saw this, he blew out a puff of air, but Ajay couldn't tell if it was a sigh or a show of frustration.

Ajay said, "I need to conduct interviews with everyone. Get to the bottom of all this."

"They'll lie," said Declan. "Trust me. They always lie."

Ajay gestured with his spoon, sending drops of

soup to soak into the smooth tablecloth. "I believe only the guilty lie."

Declan barked a bitter laugh. "They're all guilty, Ajay. Guilty of something." This earned him a dirty look from Percival. "What, it's true."

"I'm starting to understand why people don't like you," said Ajay.

"I investigate for the Securities and Exchange Commission. These people are never going to like me."

"You're an investigator?" Ajay said. "Maybe you should be in charge of this."

Jocelyn placed a hand on Ajay's arm. "If I didn't appreciate his company, I wouldn't have invited him tonight, no matter what he does for a profession."

"I usually have to invite myself," Declan said.

"And this is much nicer, isn't it?" Jocelyn said.

"My father still dislikes you," Nailah said to Declan. "But I have not yet formed an opinion."

Declan replied, "Good. There have been enough fistfights for one night." He straightened his brown tie.

Her laugh was like the tumbling of church bells. Beautiful almost to the point of sounding false. "Enough murders, too," she said. When nobody responded, she added, "Well, it's true."

Ajay stood, his chair loudly scraping against the parquet floor. He dabbed the corners of his mouth with a napkin. "Excuse me," he said, addressing Jocelyn, "but I need to use the restroom. Old man bladder, you see."

Jocelyn gestured with two fingers, and Melinda jumped to attention.

The butler crossed the floor and stood next to Ajay. "This way, sir."

"An escort," Ajay said. "How fancy."

This, he decided. This right here. This was the limit to his tolerance for fancy. He'd been amused at first. Then morbidly curious. Finally, he had tolerated the odd ways of the ultra-rich.

But he'd had enough. A butler to escort him to the bathroom was too much. "I know where it is," he said, tapping the corner of his cheaters where a map was already hovering in view.

"Yes, I know," said Melinda. She stayed at his side.

"You could watch me pee on the surveillance video."

"Oh, but sir, how would I know that you only need to pee?"

Ajay opened his mouth to protest. Closed it again. Looked to Melinda. She watched him with an amused expression. He walked the rest of the way in silence.

"I'll wait out here," she said when they reached the restroom. "Let me know if you're being murdered or something."

Ajay did his best to stay grumpy, but the more he thought about it, the more he liked Melinda Yaris.

Why was it he could come to a fancy party and only get along with the guy everyone hated and the servants? He wasn't cut out for upper-class lifestyle.

He pushed through the door, unsurprised to find a tall Russian standing by the frosted glass window in the ridiculously large restroom.

"Olexie," said Ajay. "Murder anyone lately?"

"You know that wasn't me," said Olexie Sokolov. Olexie was involved in a countercapitalist movement which sometimes almost earned its reputation as a terrorist group. There could be no innocent reason for him to be employed by the ultra-wealthy Jocelyn Garver, but Ajay knew the man wasn't there to kill anyone. Ajay had made the man promise not to act until there was evidence, and even then the solution wasn't going to be violence. "I would not do that."

"I've seen you kill people before."

"They were very bad people."

Ajay sighed. "Do you think the dead guy wasn't a bad person?"

"He tipped me when I took his weapons."

Right. The weapons. Ajay wondered how many weapons had been taken from the guests. "You missed one," he said, remembering the pistol the man had fired before his death.

"Well, he tipped very well," Olexie said.

"You're a pain in the ass, Olexie," Ajay said.

"The boss said not to check him too close."

"Him specifically?"

Olexie gave a noncommittal shrug. "I'm mostly kitchen staff."

"You may need to branch out," Ajay said. "Word is Alexander Parks sent Chay Quinn."

"We had a chat," Olexie said. "She is still not very nice."

"I've been over the surveillance feeds, but I can't find her."

"The feeds don't cover every corner of the property. Even I know that." Olexie slapped Ajay on the shoulder. "Don't worry. She will find you. Just say her name three times and she'll appear."

"Yeah, that's what I'm worried about." Ajay didn't want to linger on the topic. "What do you know about Parks?"

"Drone and robotics expert. Works for Frontier Arms."

"Is he really working with Quinn?"

"Who knows?"

Ajay growled, "I was hoping you had something useful for me."

"What? One of the rich bastards was assassinated. I'm telling you the assassin was Chay Quinn. Problem solved."

Ajay wasn't convinced. "I don't think she did it. The timing's wrong."

"You should arm yourself," Olexie suggested. "You know where the weapon check room is, right?"

"If we arm ourselves and group up in the ballroom, you think we'll be safe?"

Olexie shrugged. "What is safe?"

"Thanks, asshole." Ajay ran some water at the sink. "Do you have the code for the safe?"

"You are a hacker. It should be no problem for you."

"Anything you'd like to report?" Melinda asked with a quirk of a smile when Ajay exited the bathroom.

"Yeah," said Ajay. "I left a massive turd back there."

Back at the table, someone had cursed his place setting with an arugula and pickled beet salad, and the dressing that sat in the little bowl next to his place was filled with a congealed oil mixture. He figured it was fancy enough, but he wasn't sure it was food. He leaned his cane on the table, settled himself into his chair, and folded his napkin on his lap.

Declan said, "May I ask what you did for a living, Ajay?"

"I'm too old for small talk, Declan."

"Maybe I'm trying to assess your skill set since you're running this investigation instead of me."

"Before I retired, I had a full career investigating murders in big spooky mansions."

Declan made a show of looking around the well-decorated ballroom. "I would hardly call this spooky."

"I would think a man like you would understand how many people needed to be stepped on to accumulate this much wealth."

"You think their ghosts haunt this place?"

"The dead don't leave ghosts, but the suffering do." He considered his options. He could tell Declan about what Olexie had told him, or keep everything a secret. But, then again, what were the chances Declan was up to something bad? Robert had found the man near the corpse, but there wasn't hard evidence Declan was the killer. "We're not the only people here."

Declan glanced behind him. "Are you referring to the help?"

"No, someone else." Ajay pushed his salad plate away. He had better things to do to his taste buds than that.

Loretta laughed at something Percival said, and that whole side of the table burst into amused chuckles. When Ajay turned their direction, they dropped into silence.

"I feel like I'm in middle school," Ajay muttered.

Nailah, having finished her salad, said, "You're telling me."

Ajay realized that by quietly conversing with Declan he had stranded Nailah on the end of the table. He leaned forward so that she could see him, and said, "Nailah, what brings you to this party?"

"Small talk?" said Declan.

"I'm grilling her for relevant information," Ajay said.

"I've told you," Nailah said, "my father sent me as

a proxy. He didn't want the business to miss out on any opportunities, but he also didn't want to be here."

"Some reason he doesn't like our host?" Ajay felt Jocelyn's attention on him like the chill touch of death.

"No, of course not," Nailah said. "He's a very busy man. He needed to go to Duluth at the last minute and handle some business."

Ajay opted for a direct line of questioning. "What were you doing in the room with the corpse?"

As Zach collected her salad plate, Nailah said, "I was busy being shocked that there was a corpse, and then I was shocked that it was someone I knew."

"You knew him?"

"Theodore Parks had done work for my father. Clandestine stuff mostly, but he had a line on the budget and it was all above board." This last part she directed toward Declan, who was pretending not to listen.

"Above board clandestine work. Got it," Ajay said, remembering how Declan accused Percival. Ajay leaned back as Zach collected his completely full salad plate. "It was great," he told the server. "Just great."

"I'm glad you enjoyed it," said Zach with a hint of amusement in his voice.

When Ajay turned back to Nailah, she was already occupied by the next dish, which appeared to be a rectangle of tofu dressed up with an array of herbs and spices. Ajay's version of it appeared seconds later, delivered by Olexie.

"Thanks," Ajay muttered despite himself. He wasn't sure if he was supposed to thank the staff. In fact, there might be an etiquette rule that said he wasn't to talk to them at all. He didn't really care. "It looks wonderful."

It wasn't. He took one bite and realized that it wasn't tofu, which would have been non-offensively terrible, but it was a kind of spicy cheese. The kind of cheese that happens when good cheese goes bad. Ajay wondered if the entire meal was some kind of joke. If it was, it wasn't funny. At least the bad cheese ruined his appetite, so he wouldn't be hungry for whatever monstrosity they served next.

Ajay leaned forward to ask Nailah more about Theodore Parks but was interrupted by a wave of harsh whispers coming from the other end of the table. The argument culminated with Robert standing, tossing his napkin down onto his cheese rectangle, and stalking out of the room. Jocelyn gestured to Melinda, and the butler followed the raging entrepreneur.

"What got his goat?" Ajay asked.

Percival plastered a look of intense innocence on his face.

"He's an angry man," said Loretta, placing a hand on Percival's arm. "Maybe we should leave him be."

Ajay took up his cane and stood. "Listen up." When the others failed to pay attention to him, he spoke louder. "I don't want anyone wandering off on their own."

Loretta pressed her fingers to her chest, offended at the suggestion. "Why ever not?"

"There is a trained assassin in the building."

"I won't stand for this," said Percival.

"Shut up, Percival," Ajay snapped, taking absolutely zero satisfaction in the way Loretta gasped. "There's a trained assassin, and we're trapped here. We need to start working together."

"This is unacceptable," sputtered Percival. He stood and pulled his wife back from the table. "What do you mean we're trapped here?"

"I mean, if you try to leave, you'll likely get yourself killed." Ajay didn't have much patience to begin with, but now it was gone. "Why did you think Robert wanted access to the panic room?"

Percival's jowls went stiff. "You think Robert killed that man."

"No," Ajay said. "I don't know. Maybe."

Loretta pushed her plate away. "This is a waste of time."

"Look," Ajay said, "all I want is to keep us all safe. We should move around in threes, at a minimum. Always stick with two partners and you should be safe."

Loretta said, "Not if there's a trained assassin."

Jocelyn was the only one not standing now. Her shoulders shook slightly, in the manner of someone sobbing but holding it back as much as possible. Ajay placed a hand on the back of her chair, but she flinched away.

"We're going for a walk," said Loretta, to Percival's apparent shock.

"It's safer to stay together," Ajay said.

"We will," said Loretta. She half led, half dragged Percival to the door. "But not with you."

The two disappeared out of the ballroom, leaving Jocelyn, Declan, Nailah, and Ajay to stare blankly after them.

"Groups of three," muttered Ajay. "For safety."

Declan slumped back into his chair. "Well," he said, "more supper for us, then."

CHAPTER TWELVE

Gabby settled into an eerie calm, and Kylie felt like she was sitting in the poised jaws of a bear trap. She couldn't trust the girl. Couldn't turn her back—not after the ferocious attack on Papa. What else was Gabby capable of?

The girl stared at her, tension hunched in her shoulders and nervous energy twitching in her lower lip.

And still, Kylie felt Gabby's signal, as clear as a spoken voice in a library. Now that she'd located it, she understood the strange feeling she'd gotten from the other girl when they had first met. Her head pounded with a low-level thrum that itched all the way down to the back of Kylie's neck. A lingering tickle in the spine. She didn't like it, but it hadn't been clear until Gabby fell into that rage.

Then, the signal had been amplified a thousand times. Gabby had hidden herself before, and then she unfurled in her full glory to attack. It was like a predatory spider that Kylie had seen in a nature video. She had even witnessed geese do a similar thing the previous summer when she walked too close along the shore of Lake Bemidji. Wings spread, mouth open, full fury on display.

Geese were vicious monsters, but was Gabby?

Hiding made sense, and Kylie wanted to be better at it. She shrank further into herself, locking away her senses until she was sure Gabby wouldn't notice her. She focused her attention on the computer without letting Gabby out of her peripheral vision.

"We're not the same," Gabby muttered as she backed away. A little of the tension eased from her posture.

Garrison loped to the corner and lay on the hard concrete floor. Kylie scratched him behind his ears and tried to absorb some of his chill nature.

The panic room was actually two rooms in an 'L' shape. Kylie plucked a package of crackers off the shelf. It looked new. Not dusty and old like she had expected. She opened the package and tried one. It was dangerously bland but better than anything else they had been served at this stupid party. She found a bottle of water and washed it down.

The second room was wood-paneled and contained a soft bed and virtual reality rig. Kylie recognized the VR model as one that had come out before she was born, but it looked like it had been well cared for. The controls weren't worn from ages of use, and the color on the outside of the visor hadn't worn off. Kylie had never really liked VR—it mostly reminded her of school—but this one looked nice enough.

She was more interested in the wall of displays flanked by two old-style keyboards in the first room. With a few keystrokes, Kylie brought up security footage throughout the mansion and surrounding grounds.

Gabby wandered up next to Kylie, staying a few steps back. "Where is my father?"

"He's fine," Kylie said. She manipulated the controls and brought an image of Robert Burkshire to the big screen. He desperately mashed at the controls of his personal device, no doubt trying to communicate with someone. Based on the frustration on his face, he wasn't making much progress. "Is he calling you?" Kylie tried to remember if she had seen a device on the girl.

Gabby shook her head. "He has people who fix problems, but there's no signal to the outside right now. There hasn't been since before supper."

"Grandma's security system?"

"Maybe," Gabby said. "Why do you think she's doing this?"

"She's trying to keep us safe," Kylie said, but she didn't believe it. "Or maybe something more interesting is going on."

Curious, Kylie tapped through the menu options.

There was a screen that interfaced with the security network and contained loads more data, but it required extra credentials. She might be able to hack it, but Papa had been sure that hacking was a bad idea. He didn't want anyone knowing what she could do.

Then again, she had already revealed her identity once in the elevator. What more could this hurt?

"Password," she said, reading the screen. Maybe she didn't need to use the tech in her head to hack past this. If she could guess the password, she could get in almost as if she were a legitimate user.

"What is this?" Gabby asked, taking a tentative step forward. Light from the screen danced eerily over her pale face.

"My grandpa always says that passwords are a useless security mechanism," Kylie said. "You could usually guess them if you had a good idea of who set it."

"Can—can we do that?" Gabby swallowed loudly. "I don't think we should."

A rule follower. Kylie tried very hard to bite back her retort. "Rules are stupid."

Gabby's brow furrowed. "They're not stupid. My dad says rules keep us safe."

Robert, the guy who walked through life expecting everybody to do everything his way. Of course, he told Gabby that rules were important. *His* rules.

"Rules are only important if they keep you safe,"

Kylie said, remembering something Papa had told her. "Rules that don't are stupid and should be ignored."

Gabby chewed on her lip.

"If we could get control of security, we can use it to better protect your father." Plus, the data repository might be interesting.

A breath escaped Gabby. "What do you know about Ms. Garver?"

"Almost nothing." Kylie made the screens dance between rooms. "But maybe we can learn."

"I still don't know—"

"Shoosh." Shoosh? When had she picked up that word? Kylie sounded just like Papa, and she hated it. "Go in the other room if you're going to be stupid." That was *way* meaner than she meant, but she couldn't take it back.

"I'm going to use the VR rig," Gabby sighed. "I've never used one like that. Have you?"

"Not really. They're old."

"This one doesn't look old."

Kylie wheeled her chair over so that she could look at the rig again. "It's old."

The rig was a standup suspension system. Properly configured, a person would have full range of movement. Bands dangled from the low ceiling, and a suit sat folded neatly on the ledge of a protective ring. It took up nearly half the room, including the accompanying control display.

Gabby touched the system and it came to life. "Do you think Ms. Garver is into video games?"

Jocelyn didn't strike Kylie as much of a retro gamer, but if this thing could keep Gabby occupied, maybe it didn't matter.

Kylie wheeled back to the surveillance screens. She clicked through images. The million rooms of the house—who needs this many rooms—scrolled before her. Almost all were empty. She saw the sitting room with the body where Papa and some of the other guests poked around the crime scene. That woman, Nailah, was there, and Kylie's heart ran a little faster when she saw her. Nailah was what Kylie wanted to be someday. Confident. Beautiful. Intelligent. Kylie swiped across the screen and switched to a room that she thought might be right below Jocelyn's central tower. She would have to come back to that one later.

Garrison let out a big snore, and she rubbed his head. He looked up at her, blinked, then lay his head down on her foot. She figured that was good enough reason to stay stuck there while Gabby occupied herself in the other room.

Then, she clicked the next image and saw the outside of the house. A white flare exploded over the tops of the barren trees. She almost felt the impact as the camera wobbled from a wave of force.

"Damn," she muttered to Garrison. He didn't seem upset by it, but he lifted his head to look at her again. "Damn."

Something was happening at the edge of the forest. It was coming.

And soon.

All of the cameras on that side of the house went black.

CHAPTER THIRTEEN

"I NEED TO USE THE BATHROOM," Ajay lied.

"You just did that," replied Declan.

"I'm old."

Declan seemed to consider it for a long while, then shrugged. "I think you're right that we should stick together."

Ajay scowled. "I'm fine on my own, thanks."

Declan turned to Nailah. "Care to join us?"

She raised one immaculate eyebrow. "To the bathroom?"

Jocelyn drew a deep breath. "We'll all go together."

Ajay blinked at her for several seconds. "Good," he said, "that means you can take me to the room where the body is, because I get lost pretty easily in this place."

Nailah tucked a purse under her arm. "I thought you were going to the bathroom."

"I was obviously lying," Ajay muttered. "I need a better look at the body if I'm going to figure out who murdered him."

Jocelyn led the group out of the ballroom, leaving Zach and Olexie to clear the rest of the awful salad from the table. No doubt they had some similarly terrible course to plate next, but it would need to wait. Ajay kept track of the path through the mansion using the security footage. If Chay Quinn was out there, she still wasn't showing her face on the surveilled footage, but the more Ajay looked the more he thought there were gaps in coverage.

"What about our access to the network?" Declan asked Jocelyn as they walked through the quiet hall. "It would be nice to get a signal out."

"Melinda tells me that if we allow you a way out, then we allow him back in," Jocelyn said. "And that is *not* acceptable."

"She has a good point from a sec-ops perspective," Ajay sighed. "It's best to wait. There will no longer be a threat when Alexander Parks learns who killed his brother."

"Husband," Jocelyn said.

Ajay drummed his fingers on the head of his cane. "Oh, that makes sense, too."

Declan smiled. "First rule of investigating is that you must resist the temptation to make assumptions."

"Thanks," deadpanned Ajay. "I didn't realize men took the names of their husbands these days."

"They're very traditional," said Jocelyn. "And extremely Catholic."

"You know them well, then?" Ajay asked.

"In passing," said Jocelyn. "You know how things are."

Ajay did not know how things were, but he decided not to press the point.

Out of curiosity, he found Robert on the cameras. The man had found the lockbox where their weapons had been stored, but so far his attempts to open it had been fruitless. A broken wooden chair lay in scraps at his feet, shattered in his attempts to bash open the safe. Because, of course. Sometimes Ajay wondered how rich people could possibly think of themselves as more worthy than their lower-class brethren.

Ajay saw no sign of Melinda, which was another hint that places were missing from the camera footage. He scrubbed the video back to the point where Melinda left the ballroom. He watched her step through the door.

Then disappear.

Great.

She hadn't gone to a secret passage or into a room uncovered by cameras. She had simply stepped out of the range of one camera and never shown up on the overlapping footage.

He rewound again, but the footage was gone, erased from memory. Had she noticed that he was looking for her and deleted the footage? What did it matter if he knew where she was?

It mattered plenty if she was the killer.

"Everybody's so goddamn suspicious," he mumbled too quiet for anyone to hear.

"I think they have a right to be," said Declan.

"Why's that?" Ajay snapped, a little offended at the investigator's eavesdropping.

Declan watched Jocelyn and Nailah walking ahead of them. He dropped back a few more feet. "There's not a great reason for us to trust anyone, you know. We all have our issues with Jocelyn, especially Robert."

"Especially, especially." Ajay thumped his cane with each step. "Robert has the right idea. He's prepping for Alexander Parks's drones breaching security."

"That might be what he's doing," said Declan. "Or maybe he's arming himself because he knows you'll figure him out."

"Why were you in the room when Robert got there?"

"We arrived at the same time," Declan said.

"He wasn't there first?"

A line formed between Declan's brows. "Maybe."

"I'm pretty sure it's the drone thing," said Ajay.

Declan said, "You really think it's going to happen?"

"Sure as cancer and taxes."

Declan ran his fingers through his thin hair. "What do we do about it?"

"Son, where I come from, we call that line of thinking a waterfall."

"Wh-what?"

"Waterfall. The waterfall method of software development was a system where people tried their best to figure out every single roadblock and solve every problem before the project ever put code to screen. It was like a waterfall. Slow at first, then a huge, thundering cataclysm when the product landed."

"Did it work?"

"As a metaphor? Yes. Every project ended up dashed against the rocks and smashed to smithereens." They rounded a corner and Ajay recognized the recessed door to the sitting room. "That's why we're not going to plan that far ahead. I'll focus on what comes next, and we can figure the rest out later."

"What comes next?"

"I have no idea," said Ajay. "Wait here. I want to go in alone."

"I don't think that's a good idea," said Declan.

"Why ever not?" asked Jocelyn.

"Trust," said Declan. "If he goes alone, it looks like he's covering something up."

Jocelyn's expression hardened. Ajay was sure she understood the implication about her trustworthiness. "Very well. Nailah, will you wait here with me?"

"I'd rather go in," Nailah said in a quiet voice.

"Fine," said Jocelyn. She unlocked the door with her key. "When you have finished, please rejoin the rest of the group."

"Where are you going?" asked Ajay.

She sighed. "Melinda requested a meeting, and I must leave."

"Leaving the rest of us out here to fend for ourselves," said Declan.

Her shoulders sagged, and she looked ready to crumple in on herself. She took one of Declan's hands in her own and said, "It was good seeing you again, Declan." She looked to Nailah. "And you, my dear."

With that, she walked away down the hall, and the lights followed her until she rounded a corner. The hallway, in her absence, fell into darkness.

"That was surreal," said Declan, still staring after her.

"How so?" asked Ajay.

"She has never—*never*—enjoyed seeing me." Declan glanced at Nailah. "Did you even know her?"

The muscles of Nailah's jaw flexed, and her lips pressed into a tight line.

Ajay and Declan entered the room, followed by Nailah. So much for going in alone. They had only left the room a couple hours prior, but the air felt still and stuffy. Stifling. Ajay held out a hand to gesture for the others to be still so that he could take in the murder scene.

The two standing lamps were on, but to Ajay's

eyes, they were dim and ineffectual without daylight streaming through the window. The dim light worked well for the grim images of the Civil War tapestries, but it didn't do enough to reveal anything. He clicked his cane and detached the drone. It hovered and scanned the room with its white spotlight, revealing the drab browns and reds of everything it touched.

The first thing Ajay noticed—besides the generally shabby nature of the room's art—was the blood spatter across the velvet divan. Blood ran in a long arc across the room and even up the wall's textured walls. One of the two lamps had three conspicuous drops streaked across its stained-glass shade.

"I didn't want to linger earlier," said Ajay. "Not with the girls around."

"Understandable," said Nailah. She made a slow walk along the outside of the room, peering closely as the drone's spotlight passed over each surface, but looking away if the spotlight passed over the body. "This was a violent attack," she said. "Passionate."

Ajay touched the bruises on his cheek, wincing. "Declan, you're the investigator. What do you think?"

"I investigate accounting crimes," he said. "There's usually very little blood."

"More than you'd expect," said Nailah.

"Unfortunately." Declan crouched to peer at the body from several feet away. Next to the body lay the revolver, exactly as they had left it. "It's his gun, all right. He's wearing a holster under his suit."

Ajay brought the drone around to shine its light on the body. Olexie had said he had orders not to search Parks very closely, but the holster wasn't even a little hidden. "So much for confiscating weapons."

"It's strictly enforced," Nailah said, mocking the older woman's voice. It was a solid imitation.

Ajay narrowed his eyes at her and pressed a finger to his lips.

"What?" Nailah said. "She's gone and I don't think I give a damn what she thinks either way."

"She could be listening," Ajay said. More likely Melinda was listening to everything.

Declan huffed a short laugh. "Let her."

Nailah frowned, peering out the closed window. "We think the murder weapon was a knife, right?"

Ajay swallowed and forced himself to look at the body's wounds again. Up close and with better light, he could see the slight pucker at the edges of the slash across the man's throat. This was where most of the blood came from. The stabs in his chest had bled, but that blood from the neck had soaked into the suit and floor. Pulsing blood from that wound had sprayed across the tapestry depicting a row of Union soldiers storming across a ruined field. Ajay hadn't really studied the Civil War since middle school, and back then he just hadn't given a damn. He decided to go with his original guess of "Gettysburg, probably."

"Excuse me?" Nailah asked.

Ajay cleared his throat. "A knife. Possibly a short

one, but definitely sharp." He forced himself to look closely at the wound in the neck. "Serrated, maybe."

Using the backs of her hands, Nailah pushed up on the window. It slid several inches, then stopped with a thunk. "No egress windows," she said. "Clear violation of fire code compliance."

"Fire code," Declan scoffed. "This whole place is probably made of asbestos."

The window opened to a short drop into a mass of skeletal lilacs featuring a greenish hint on buds ready for spring. Ajay shone his drone's light through the window, but any flight outside would put the drone at risk of striking a branch and falling.

"So the murderer couldn't have come in through the window," Declan said. He stood near the big mahogany door that they had first used to enter the room. Across from that door was a smaller door leading to another hall.

"Doubtful, unless there's a trick to opening it further," said Nailah. She prodded at the window but it refused to move.

"The lilac would make escape difficult, anyway," said Ajay. He leaned close to the window and peered upward. "Unless our murderer is a fantastic climber."

"Percival Trowbridge used to be a champion rock climber," said Nailah. "He could handle a climb like that."

Ajay tried to imagine the heavyset man climbing up the side of the building. The architecture made for plenty of handholds, but the man's weight was an issue. Ajay stuck his cane out the window and jabbed at the nearest ledge. It seemed solid enough.

A flash of alerts scrolled past Ajay's half-moon cheaters.

"There's something happening at the edge of the property," he said.

Declan crossed the room to the window, careful to avoid blood spatter and anything else resembling evidence. He peered out the window at the black night. "There's something down there," he said, looking down toward the ground.

Ajay peered down, but his eyes wouldn't adjust. Instead, he caught his drone, shut down everything but the light, and used it as a flashlight to peer at the ground outside the window.

"Is that a knife?" Declan asked.

Ajay said. "The window might not have been how the murderer escaped, but it looks like it might have been how they got rid of the murder weapon."

"Seems short-sighted," Declan said.

The knife was the size of a steak knife. It had a black handle and a steel edge. The serrated blade curved back, giving it the look of a miniature scimitar. Dangerous. It was too far down to reach.

"We can circle around outside," said Declan.

Ajay grunted agreement. Movement in the corner of his eye brought him back to the room. "Nailah," he barked.

She flinched. The tall woman crouched in front of the gun where it still lay on the floor. "It doesn't have blood on the grip," she said. "You see, he dropped it as he fell."

"After the neck injury," said Ajay, carefully crossing to her. "Makes sense. He gets stabbed, draws his gun, fires a few wild shots, then has his neck aerated."

Nailah shuddered. "I think we should take it."

Declan said, "The police will want it untouched."

"Then they should respond faster," Nailah replied. She peered sideways at it. "It has bullets left, and we're in danger."

Ajay got down close and shone his flashlight at the gun. She was right about the blood, and also about the bullets. The revolver had at least five of its seven bullets remaining. Ajay tried to remember how many shots had been fired. It hadn't taken this man very long to die.

Another flash of warnings burst through Ajay's feed. He glanced out the window, but all he could see there were the bony branches close to the building. No hint of what happened on the horizon.

"Take the gun," he instructed Nailah.

"What?" said Declan. "You can't just—"

"She can," snapped Ajay. He moved away from the window. "She's going to put it in her purse and leave it there unless she needs it."

Declan didn't bother with nuance. "What if she's the killer?"

"Our killer prefers knives."

"A gun would be pretty handy, though."

Nailah stepped between them. "Guys," she said, her voice icy calm. "Unless you want to stuff a Smith and Wesson double-action .357 in your pants, I'll be carrying the weapon. You're just going to have to trust me."

"There's a holster," Declan said, nudging aside the corner of the body's suit coat to reveal a strap of black leather.

Ajay waved him off. "Let her have the gun." He crouched next to the corpse and checked the pockets. No use worrying about evidence at this point. "She's obviously not the killer."

"Thank you," said Nailah.

Declan looked at her, then back at Ajay. "She's not?"

Ajay found Alexander Parks's wallet and checked the ID. Still there, along with several hundred dollars in cash and a thick stack of credit cards. His right breast pocket held a tin with seven cigarettes and a lighter, but otherwise, the man either hadn't been carrying anything when he died, or the murderer had taken it. The tech glasses were still useless. Ajay nudged them with a knuckle.

"The data chip's destroyed," he said.

"It broke when the glasses were smashed," said Nailah.

"Maybe." Ajay held up the ruined chip. "But a data recovery expert might make something of it."

Declan said, "It's a miracle what those guys can do sometimes."

"Well, this wasn't a random mugging," Ajay said, handing the chip to Declan and tossing the wallet back onto the corpse. "And it wasn't Nailah because her dress is too nice."

"What?" both Nailah and Declan said at once.

"The dress." Ajay waved at Nailah's close-fitting dress. "She didn't have enough time to change outfits. Not wearing something like that."

"You're saying women take a long time to get dressed?" Nailah deadpanned.

"Exactly."

"That's extremely sexist."

Another wave of warnings flashed across Ajay's cheaters. "What the hell is going on out there?" he asked.

He moved to the window and looked out just in time to see a wave of light wash across the top of the forest. Against the black backdrop, it dazzled his eyes and he staggered backward, tripping over the divan and falling atop the corpse with a wet smack. A cry of pain and surprise escaped his lips, and he heard the others calling out around him. A rumble of impact rolled across the mansion, rattling the walls and making dust cascade from the ceiling.

Then, his drone and the two decorative lights went black and darkness swallowed them once again.

CHAPTER FOURTEEN

Ajay blinked, but the spots in front of his eyes didn't disappear. He scrambled up and away from the corpse, his palms slick with congealed blood. So much for keeping the evidence clear. He'd ruined his best blue suit, too.

"What the hell was that?" Declan said.

Ajay picked up his drone. It didn't look broken, but it had shut down when the flash had hit the room. He hoped the drone wasn't fried. He gave it a shake and mashed the reset button. Nothing. His cheaters entered a boot sequence, flashing blue as they initialized.

Declan crossed to the door. "This is the attack."

"Declan, wait." Nailah's voice was small and far away. She avoided looking at the body but approached Ajay. "Ajay, is—"

"No." The mahogany door creaked as Declan pulled it open. "We're wasting our time. Parks is dangerous. You know that as well as I do. We need to find a safe place to hide, because that was his opening attack. He'll be here any minute."

"Stop," Nailah said.

There was a scuffle, then Nailah cried out. The mahogany door opened the rest of the way, and Ajay heard Declan's hard shoes on the stone floor.

"Nailah?" he asked.

"We should go after him," Nailah said. Ajay realized his hearing aid was malfunctioning. When he adjusted it, her voice rang through clearer. "Ajay?"

"I'm fine," Ajay said. He wasn't fine. The spots in his eyes cleared a little. The partial blindness interfered with his ability to properly use his cheaters, and they were in some kind of error state. A light blinked on the bottom of the drone. Maybe it would be salvageable after all. He clipped it to its mounting bracket on his cane. "Go. Go after him. I'll catch up."

He tried to blink the spots away again. Clicking his drone's light on, he swung the cane to look at the room one last time. The light was dimmer now, but it revealed the disturbed crime scene. Body. Divan. Window. He didn't know what he was expecting to find. He left via the big door, following Nailah and Declan.

Surveillance systems fluttered back online in his cheaters as he walked through the long, dark hall. His footsteps sounded like ghosts echoing against the empty nothing around him. How did Jocelyn stand living in such a large house? How did she bear the emptiness?

Instead of video, Ajay now only had proximity sensors in most rooms. They could detect vibrations. Nothing else. The garden side of the building had succumbed to whatever detonation had blinded him. Those sensors weren't recovering, but the sensors near the foyer indicated movement. Declan and Nailah were ahead around a corner. He wouldn't catch up to them, but at least he could figure out where they went. He let out a long sigh. The tension put an ache deep in his bones.

And Kylie. How was she faring? His security sensors showed movement in the basement, but nothing near the panic room. Likely they were still locked away, oblivious to the outside world. After all, that room probably had its own power source.

Ajay powered off his light and leaned against the wall between two pedestals bearing two expensive-looking vases. He touched his forehead and breathed several deep breaths. His face still ached where Gabby had struck him. His whole body ached. He needed to calm himself. Take a break. But standing still in the dark mansion only made him more aware of the unsettling presence of the house itself. It was like the place was an unnatural force upon the world. The very embodiment of excess and privilege. How could he presume to affect anything here?

The scent of danger touched his nostrils. Not a specific odor—at least nothing he could identify. It raised the hackles on the back of his neck and made his mouth run dry.

"Ajay Andersen," purred a voice that felt like icicles shattering on pavement.

"Chay Quinn," Ajay said. She was there to kill him, but he poured every ounce of bravery that he could into his voice. In the pitch black of the dark hallway, all he could see was the dead look in her eyes when he'd last witnessed her kill. "I was under the impression you only appeared if I said your name three times into a mirror."

"You speak as if I'm death herself," said Quinn.

"Aren't you?"

She took long enough to answer that Ajay's cane slipped in his sweaty palms. "I had to leave all my weapons at the door," she finally said. "I'm here for something else."

"You can't kill bare-handed?"

"Oh, you're very clever." Quinn jabbed him in the shoulder with something sharp—not hard enough to draw blood, but enough to let him know that she was in charge. So, she wasn't entirely weaponless. "I think you should untangle this mess of rich people before it gets you into trouble."

Ajay's hearing aid tuned in to Quinn's heartbeat. She backed off several feet, so he confidently leaned forward and took a step even though he could see nothing. "I fail to see how I'm not already in trouble. I think you're also in trouble. You're a killer working for the victim's husband. Why should

I suspect those rich assholes when you're right here?"

"Maybe you should ask why everyone came to this little party."

Ajay shrugged. "You're looking for ways to cover everything up before the police get here."

Quinn breathed a humorless chuckle. "Cover up is the easy part, Andersen."

"I thought murder was the easy part for you."

"It's a lot easier than death." Her voice moved down the dark hall as she spoke.

"What is Parks after?" Ajay asked. "Can you tell me that, at least? What's his problem with Jocelyn?"

"What is anyone after? That's really a question you ought to be asking yourself, isn't it? Everyone's here for a reason. It'd be pretty funny if it was all the same reason, wouldn't it?"

"Why are you here?"

"Something's wrong with this place. This whole damn house."

Ajay repeated, "Why are you here?" She had to answer eventually.

Or not. "You have a lovely granddaughter, Ajay Andersen."

"That's because, generally speaking, I keep her away from people like you." Ajay considered his words. He stuck his thumb in the direction of the ballroom. "As a rule, I keep her away from people like them, too."

"That sounds stifling." Chay clicked her tongue.

"Do you ever wonder how your host made her money? Maybe that would explain why people came here."

Why *did* these guests come to this particular dinner party? None of them seemed to like Jocelyn very much. There were aspirations of climbing social ladders, but that didn't explain most of what he'd seen. These people hated being here. They must have come for a purpose.

Before he could ask anything more, a strangled scream shattered the night's silence.

Switching his drone's light back on, Ajay saw the hall was empty.

Quinn was gone.

He walked as fast as he could toward the source of the scream, his limbs aching from the constant pulse of adrenaline.

Shouts came from up ahead. Men, yelling. Robert and Declan.

Ajay burst into the foyer to find a gun pointed at him. He staggered backward.

Nailah had the revolver in both hands, her finger outside the trigger. Her fidget cast a dim glow over half of the room. "I said stop," she shouted at Robert as she swung the gun back in his direction. "It wasn't him."

Robert cradled a bloody hand. "Then who was it?"

"I don't know," said Nailah. "But it wasn't Declan. I was with him."

A noise across the room startled Ajay, so he swung his light that direction. Declan sat against the far wall, hands draped across his knees in front of him. A steak knife lay on the floor in front of him, wet with fresh blood.

"That yours?" Ajay asked.

Declan gave a short shake of his head.

"He attacked me with it," Robert said, staunching the blood flow with the corner of his coat. "Dammit."

Nailah's revolver wavered, then she dropped it to her side. "You attacked him," she said to Robert.

Robert shot her a glare. "He was out of control."

"How bad is it?" Ajay asked, approaching.

Robert held his bloody hand into the light. "I'll need stitches," he said as if that was the worst a wound could possibly get.

"We should find a first aid kit," Ajay muttered. "First aid, and then—"

Nailah's revolver landed on the carpet with a solid thunk. Blood dripped from her fingers. Ajay rushed to her and searched for the wound.

"I'm fine," she said, pulling away. She held a hand on her upper arm.

Ajay pulled up the security map of the foyer and surrounding rooms. First aid stations were marked on a layer of the map, and one was in the nearby bathroom.

Ajay led her that direction. "What happened? Describe it all for me."

"The lights went out again," said Robert as they passed. "If I had known this place was so shoddy—"

"It was an EMP or something," said Declan. "Knocked out everything."

"Is that what you were shouting about?" said Robert.

Declan shouted, "Yes, that's what I—"

Robert cut in. "When I tried to get him away from Nailah, he cut me with his knife."

With Ajay and his drone's light following Nailah, Declan and Robert were plunged into darkness.

"It was fast," Nailah said. "I had my light, but it wasn't much, so I didn't get a look at whoever attacked me. Robert and the Trowbridges were in the other room, and I could hear them trying to get the safe open."

"Any luck with that?" Ajay asked.

Robert let out a puff of air. "Would I have been stabbed with a steak knife if I had been able to get a decent weapon?" He eyed the revolver on the floor.

He had a good point. Ajay found a container full of bandages and emergency medicine. He selected a roll of gauze, a semipermeable wound tape, and some antiseptic gel. He carefully bandaged Nailah's arm. She was right, it wasn't a bad wound. Shallow, but long.

Ajay returned to Robert to help him bandage his hand. He motioned for Nailah to continue.

She swallowed and closed her eyes as she applied pressure to her wound. "If I hadn't moved, the knife would have gone into my back. As it was, I was able to knock the knife away. Declan came to help. He picked up the knife and tried to frighten whoever was attacking."

"The scream I heard," Ajay said. "That was Declan."

A hint of a smile crossed Nailah's lips. "It was a very heroic scream."

"True." Ajay applied gel and taped Robert's wound. He wrapped the man's whole hand in gauze and tied it off. "You're right that you need stitches," he said. "But this'll do for now."

"Robert, I appreciate your help," Nailah said, sounding stronger now. The side of her red dress was spattered with dark blood.

"He was waving the knife around like a madman," Robert said.

"You didn't see anyone else?" Ajay asked.

"I'm not convinced that there *was* anyone else." Robert flexed his hand and tested his reduced range of movement. "I grabbed his wrist, then he stabbed me with the same knife that was used to stab her. This is an easy case once we get a real investigator on the scene."

"Declan," Ajay asked, "can you make it?"

Declan looked up at Ajay from where he sat against the wall. Tears shone in his eyes. "Yeah," he rasped. "Yeah, I'll be fine."

The mansion's power returned. Down the halls and above the foyer, one by one, lights flickered to life. The surveillance video was still disabled for a large part of the complex, but Ajay had a staggered return of function, and he breathed a sigh of relief when he saw that there wasn't increased activity at the edge of the forest where they expected the attack. Around the safe room, there was a flicker on one motion sensor, but otherwise no movement.

"All right," he said. "We have power again." He helped Declan to his feet and turned back to the other side of the room, where Nailah stood next to Robert.

Nailah stared at a spot on the blood-spattered floor, and it took Ajay a moment to realize why.

The revolver was gone.

CHAPTER FIFTEEN

"I THINK the house got hit by an EMP," Kylie called to the other room when the silence became too much. She needed to tell someone about what she had seen. Every connection she had to the outside world was a wall of static nothing. "I watched a documentary about them once. They really screw with electronics."

Gabby didn't respond. She was probably still lost in a VR world somewhere, which was just fine. Maybe Kylie didn't want to talk to her at all.

Only...

Garrison rested his head on her feet. She could talk to him. She *had* been talking to him, but it wasn't doing any good. Stress still prickled the back of her hands and knotted her shoulders.

Kylie cycled through the security footage as cameras slowly returned. She made a map of the areas that were now blind spots. There were a lot of them, particularly in the forest and most of the lake-facing side of the building.

"Maybe it was the EMP wave of a nuclear explosion," she said. "Those are supposed to be a pretty big deal, too."

Jocelyn. Kylie had watched as the woman left Papa and his group. The old lady had gone down the hall toward the foyer, then into one of the bathrooms. She hadn't come back out, but pressure monitors made it look like maybe she wasn't there anymore. Kylie made a mental note that there must be a secret passage in that bathroom. She wondered what else she could find hidden around the mansion.

There was a conspicuous gap in coverage on the third floor. The hallways below had functioning cameras, but the big circular room at the top of the mansion didn't have anything.

Kylie was thankful that their power in the safe room persisted. Except for a slight blip—almost a brownout—they hadn't had any disruption at all. The security system, likewise, appeared to still be online. Not that she could access it.

Garrison stretched and leaned harder on her foot.

"Yeah, I know, boy. I'm tired, too."

She couldn't force herself to relax. In theory, it would be possible to play video games like Gabby or lie down on the bed and fall asleep. It wasn't *that* late, but time didn't exist down in the panic room. She lived on panic time now. It wasn't like regular time.

Kylie slumped back in her chair and closed her

eyes. She had tried a dozen passwords to Jocelyn's systems, but nothing worked. All of the variations on the word *password* came back negative. All of the combinations she could come up with using Jocelyn's name and her dead son's name and, well, it didn't look like Jocelyn had ever owned any pets which just seemed monstrous to Kylie. Garrison agreed.

She rifled through the junk on the shelves. Boxes of files at first seemed like they might contain clues, but they really just contained tons and tons of epic boredom. Titles to properties in places Kylie would never go. Wills of people who had died long ago. Contracts with dozens of companies. Medtronic. Boston Scientific. Trevan Pharmaceuticals. She squinted at that last one. Trevan owned the lab where Kylie and Isabelle had spent the majority of their lives. It was the company that experimented on unborn children.

The language in the contract was so dense that it nearly put Kylie into a coma.

"How's it going in there?" she called out to Gabby.

No answer. Kylie wasn't sure if she even wanted Gabby to answer. She didn't like the girl, even if they did have a lot in common. Maybe the younger girl would make more sense after they got to know each other.

Kylie let out a long sigh. She hated getting to know people.

She set the thick document next to the computer keyboard and started typing into the password field.

Trevan. Nope. *Jackson Garver.* Nope. She had already tried her father's name, anyway. *Lee and Black.* She didn't think the name of the lawyer's firm would yield a result, but whatever. She tried anything she found in the document with combinations of Jocelyn's birthday, her father's birthday, the address of the mansion, and other important number combinations.

"When were you written?" Kylie mumbled to herself, reading through the contract. She thought dates were a front page kind of thing, but maybe that's why she would never be a lawyer.

There.

She punched the date combination into the password field, then stared at it.

"Oh," she said. She gave up on the password field because understanding the contract became significantly more interesting.

The date on the contract between Jocelyn Garver and Trevan Pharmaceuticals was her birthday.

CHAPTER SIXTEEN

"All I'm saying," said Declan, whispering to Ajay in the back of the weapon storage room, "is if we can't get into the safe, then we should lock the rest of the group in this room."

Ajay punched numbers into the safe's console. Robert and Nailah stood in opposite corners of the cramped room, the tension between them palpable in the heavy silence. In the adjacent foyer, the Trowbridges complained loudly about the awful service.

"Think about it," hissed Declan. "We now know that you're not the killer."

"I knew that before," said Ajay.

Declan held up an open palm. "And you know I'm not the killer." Ajay noticed the man hadn't entirely cleaned the blood from under his nails.

The console flashed red and blinked into a one-minute countdown. Every time Ajay entered a wrong passcode, it made him wait another minute. "Who do you think killed Parks?"

Declan sputtered, "That's the point. If they're locked away in here, then it doesn't matter."

"I'm not sure I can break into this vault," said Ajay.

"They'd be safe from Parks until the authorities arrived," said Declan. Sweat beaded on his brow. "It's the only way."

Ajay clicked his tongue. "You know what I used to do for a living?"

"Computers or something."

"I was the guy who looked at a system when everyone else said there was no way in." Ajay jiggled the exposed power cable on the safe's panel, resetting the timer. "When you say something is the only way, my first instinct is to find another way."

"We need to think of our own safety."

"We're not safe," snapped Ajay. "We're not *going* to be safe until we figure this out."

"Then open the vault."

Ajay punched in another wrong passcode. There were only ten thousand options, so he might be able to guess it in the next hundred hours or so. When he felt Declan's expectant stare boring a hole in the back of his neck, he said, "I'm not going to imprison anyone."

"Have you got it yet?" Robert said, stalking over to where Ajay worked on the safe. "I thought you said it could be opened."

Ajay jiggled the power cable again, resetting the timer.

Declan sighed. "Who do we know *isn't* the killer?"

"Well, it's certainly not me," said Robert.

Declan barked out a laugh.

Ajay punched in a code. "Did either of you see Jocelyn type in the code?"

"The butler did it for me," said Declan.

"What did you bring that needed to be locked away?" asked Robert.

"Brass knuckles," Declan said. "Tommy gun. Pocket nuke. You know, the usual."

Robert blinked slowly at him.

The corner of Declan's lip twitched with something that was almost amusement. "Just a Glock. A small one." He glanced at Percival. "My profession isn't exactly a safe one."

Ajay opened his mouth to respond, reconsidered, then asked, "Can either of you offer proof that you didn't kill Theodore Parks?"

Robert held out his hand. Blood had soaked through the gauze.

"What's that supposed to prove?" Ajay asked.

Robert scowled. "I was attacked by Declan. Either he's the killer, or he's telling the truth and it's someone else, but it wasn't me."

"I was attacked, too," said Declan. He had regained some of his composure, but a haunted look still lingered in the whites of his eyes. "The person who attacked us in the foyer wasn't Robert, but that doesn't tell us anything about the murder."

Ajay looked at both of the men. "We're running around in circles. Can you describe the person who attacked you?"

"They were smaller," said Declan. "Shorter, anyway. And completely silent."

Ajay thought of Chay Quinn's silent movements through the mansion's hall, but she had been with him when the attack had happened. "Shorter than Robert. That leaves just about anyone."

"Except for me," said Robert. He turned to Ajay. "It could have been you."

Ajay continued, "And there's nothing to say that the person who attacked you in the foyer was the person who killed Theodore. We know essentially nothing, except that there's an unhinged husband trying to fight his way through Jocelyn's defenses using EMP bombs."

"EMPs?" Declan asked, horrified.

"Seems to be." Ajay had seen them used. They were a tool in an arsenal he helped create. They were expensive and dangerous and incredibly illegal.

Ajay brought up the security map in his cheaters. The data was starting to repopulate, but many of the systems on the grounds were still disabled. It would only be a matter of time before the perimeter failed. He wondered what was taking Alexander Parks so long. What was the man's goal?

For a moment, Ajay lost himself in the beauty of

the mansion's elegant network design. Using a non-standard electromagnetic range and non-standard network protocol made it incredibly difficult to infiltrate. Under that surface, the house was a perfectly ordered network of connections. Nodes spread throughout the complex, touching every corner of the property and converging not on a single node that could be taken out in one strike, but several overlapping cells. Redundant and secure. This was a system designed by a brilliant network architect and security expert. Ajay wondered if Jackson Garver himself had designed it. That would move his granddaughters' late father up a notch in his estimation, but there was plenty of room for movement in that direction.

Redundant systems. Ajay followed the lines of redundancy, tracing the paths upon which the various systems had failed. Video surveillance still faltered along one axis of the building's core. The temperature sensors failed on another. He moved about the virtual space like a man taking a voyage through the depths of space. It surrounded him and completely consumed his attention. Somewhere, the others bickered about who might be the murderer and how they were going to protect themselves if they couldn't even get into the weapons safe.

But Ajay didn't care. He was absorbed in the problem. The thing that can't be hacked. "There's no other way," he muttered to himself. Better words of challenge, he had never heard.

"What did you say?" Declan asked.

The panic room was a blank spot on the bottom of the map. Every time he got close to it, the channels shunted him away to another room. Another pathway. His read-only access was actively removing him from that part of the map. A clever solution, he thought. With a quickly programmed loop, he was able to reassert his control. He left a program running in the background that kept an eye on that area. If any more movement appeared around there, it would alert him.

But there was more. Another part of the map redirected him. There was another black hole—a void where no cameras and no sensors covered the halls. One room in the center of the second floor avoided his attention. It must have been Jocelyn's bedroom or access to her tower above. Those who embraced universal surveillance often guarded their own privacy jealously. It wasn't hypocrisy exactly, but smelled just the same.

The black hole in the map was interesting, but Ajay wanted the exact opposite. He looked for the places where systems overlapped the most. There was an override for the weapons safe, and it connected to the grid. If he could control the grid, he could open the safe. It wouldn't even take all weekend.

Where was it? He paced as his knobby fingers worked across the controls hovering over the top of his cane. The text scrolling past on his cheaters expanded into a full visual display. Blue and red and violet lines sprawled through a clumsy depiction of the mansion. The networks sprawled like a spider's web across the building.

Then, he saw it. Not far away sat a junction of several conduits. If he was going to find physical access, it would be there.

He remembered Melinda's words about frying all the machines in the room as soon as they detected a hacking attempt. But did that include physical hacks or only the wireless network attacks that she likely expected? It was time to find out.

"Where are you going?" asked Robert as Ajay started to leave.

"Don't let Declan lock you in a closet," Ajay grumbled. He stopped near Nailah and looked her in the eyes. "Can you handle yourself?"

"I don't have the gun anymore." She hugged herself close with the wall to her back. "But yeah."

Ajay touched her arm. "We both know you're not helpless without it. Are you sure you can keep them under control?"

Her eyebrows raised in an expression of doubt. "I'll do my best."

"If I get this right, that weapons safe will open. Be ready for it."

She gave the tiniest of nods.

"Mr. Andersen," bellowed Percival when Ajay stepped into the foyer. "A word."

"Words aren't doing us any good right now, Trowbridge," Ajay said, not slowing his walk.

Percival fell in step next to him, his wife at his side. "Look. I know this hasn't been the best evening, but we were hoping you could help us."

Ajay stopped. He eyed the old couple, wondering if they might be good for much of anything. "Stay with the group. Don't get in the way. That's all the help you need."

"We'll stay out of the way," said Loretta. "We'd like you to help us borrow one of Jocelyn's cars so we can leave."

Ajay made a quick check of the property map. Sure enough, there was a garage, and it had several vehicles. Unfortunately, there was only one narrow driveway. "Parks will have thought of that."

"That's the thing," said Percival. "If we send all of the self-drivers out, we just might make it. Overwhelm them, you see."

"You'll be fish in a barrel. He's probably capable of shooting every car that comes out and more." Ajay wasn't sure, but it sounded like a terrible idea, and he didn't want to waste time on it. "Together," he said. "That's the only way we're getting out of here."

"Or killed," said Loretta. Her voice was cold and calculating.

"Then walk. Don't take the direction where the EMP came from, and don't take the driveway." Ajay started walking again, leaving the two behind. "If you start walking now, you'll be dead within the hour. Stick with the others, and you'll survive longer. I guarantee it."

"How?" Percival asked as Ajay crossed the room. "How can you guarantee it?"

Ajay stopped again and turned to the bulky old man. "Come ask me again if it turns out I'm wrong." With that, he did what he told everyone else not to do and left the group to wander alone through the silent mansion.

CHAPTER SEVENTEEN

THERE WAS no problem that a sufficient amount of hacking couldn't fix.

Ajay made his way through the mansion, his cane clacking against the hardwood floors. He kept a close watch on his back. No use getting murdered at this point, after all. What good could he do then?

The map projected on his thin glasses showed him the route, but he didn't take the most direct path. He found ways to wander through nearby rooms, eying Jocelyn's exquisite taste in art and her penchant for displays of obscure military history. Something still felt off about the whole display. Every room held cleaning bots tucked into the small corners and sealed in hidden compartments, but even so, the rooms all looked so... perfect. The Thirty Years' War room was decorated in torn flags and replica firearms. He popped open one case to check if a pistol was indeed a replica.

It was. Useless. Even the bayonet was flimsy plastic, and the horn of gunpowder held useless black dust. He had his cane. That would need to be weapon enough.

The old woman was fascinated by war. Her Gulf War room didn't contain any weapons at all, only period art: a Banksy in the form of a graffiti-covered chunk of concrete wall, books of poetry conspicuously left open to provocative pages, and photography from the war itself. Ajay found it an odd worship of a difficult time in the nation's history.

But he didn't find anything useful.

The hallways troubled him. There were so many doors and alcoves wrapped in shadow that he couldn't be sure he wasn't followed. Quinn had come upon him so quickly, he wondered if he'd be able to defend himself at all if he was attacked. He should have brought backup.

But who could he trust? Nailah was hiding something, he was sure of it. Robert was a jerk, but was that better or worse than Declan? Declan had been acting stranger as the evening progressed, and ever since the incident with the knife, Ajay wasn't sure at all that the man was innocent in all of this. Maybe none of them were.

What he couldn't figure was why Jocelyn had invited these people at all. She could easily have arranged a quiet evening where Kylie could meet her estranged grandmother. It wouldn't have been pleasant, but Kylie might have opened up some. Kylie had a right to know her grandmother. At least a little. Ajay remembered how he had felt when Sashi arrived with his two granddaughters. Overjoyed at their existence, of course, but also furious that they had been kept from him. How could he do the same to Jocelyn?

The Trowbridges might have been willing to accompany Ajay as backup, but he figured they weren't worth much more than fodder if there were an actual attack. If the rich couple died horribly, Ajay might be able to deploy his drone for a counterstrike.

It wasn't a *good* plan, but it was something. He considered deploying his drone in a protective mode, but its battery was so low already, and the EMP had messed it up. All he could do was trust that whoever was murdering people didn't have anything against him personally.

As long as he failed to make progress on the case, that would probably stay true.

He needed more information. He needed to solve the murder, mount the defense to protect everyone from Alexander Parks, and move Kylie to safety. His fingers found her multicolored band around his wrist and twisted it.

There was no problem that a sufficient amount of hacking couldn't fix. If only he had more time.

The aroma of fresh bread and seared meat greeted him before he found the kitchen. He pushed through the metal double doors into the sprawling space. A row of ovens covered the far wall, and to his right, a pair of walk-in refrigerators dominated the wall. The center of the room held rows of stainless-steel counters, and pans dangled from the ceiling.

Olexie and Zach sat across from each other atop two of the stainless-steel tables. Around them, chopped vegetables were scattered among tiny bowls of spices and garnishes. The two looked over as Ajay entered and watched him as he crossed the room.

"We are on strike," Olexie said as if it wasn't strange at all to be sitting on the work surface in a professional kitchen.

"We're on break," Zach said. "Chef Benedict gives us fifteen minutes every twelve hours."

"It is an OSHA violation," Olexie said.

Ajay plucked a carrot from a bowl and crunched it. "I don't think that's how OSHA works."

Olexie said, "That is why I am on strike."

"I need to speak with your boss," Ajay said.

"Here," said the chef as he backed out of the walk-in refrigerator across from the expansive cooktop. He stopped when he saw Ajay, and for an eternally long second, the words hung in the man's throat. Finally, he said. "What can my lazy cooks get for you, mister Andersen?"

Ajay met Olexie's eyes. The tall Russian was playing a part well, exuding an affect of disinterest. "I'd like access to the room behind your fridge," Ajay said.

Benedict set down a tray of dough on the steel

table, not taking his eyes from Ajay. "There's no room back there."

Ajay felt the chef's gaze follow him as he moved through the room. He stopped by a tray of steak knives that sat on a shelf above one table. "Have you been missing any knives?"

Benedict waved the question off. He was a stout man, but he moved gracefully through his kitchen. With a few quick movements, he fired up a gas stove and set out a cast iron pan.

Olexie said, "There was a knife missing from the table."

"Steak knife?"

"Butter knife," Olexie said. "For the bread."

"Wait, someone stole a butter knife?"

"It happens," said Zach. "We lose more than you'd expect, given that these people could probably buy a million butter knives and not even blink."

"They all do it," Benedict said. "I'd wager every one of those guests has stolen silverware from Mrs. Garver."

"Why would they want a million butter knives?" Ajay asked.

Benedict threw up his hands in disgust.

Zach spread his hands. "Why would they want any of this? They entertain themselves by pranking each other because there's nothing left for them to do with their money."

"They could help people," muttered Olexie.

"I'd probably just go visit my sister in New

Zealand," said Zach. "She moved there five years ago for a research project and I haven't seen her since."

Ajay peered at the young man. "You could probably afford to visit as often as you wanted with that many butter knives."

Zach scrunched up his face. "Once is probably enough. I never got along all that well with sis."

Benedict tossed some butter into his pan and it sizzled. "We don't worry about lost silverware, but we don't put the best stuff out for guests, either."

Ajay couldn't comprehend how this might be in any way acceptable. He tried to picture the knife he had seen outside the Civil War room. Serrated. Black handle. Slight curve. It didn't quite match the knives in the rack.

"Are knives considered weapons?" Ajay asked.

"Outside the kitchen?" Benedict asked. "Yeah. Except for the steak knives."

"What about old knife sets? Like stolen ones."

The chef shrugged. "I'm not an AI expert."

"But those might not trigger the weapon scan."

Chef Benedict said, "I think it's a game for the rich folks."

Ajay said, "So, they steal silverware from each other for fun?"

"And other things. Like I said, it's a game. Sometimes, after Jocelyn's been someplace for dinner, we'll find a whole new set of forks show up in the dishes."

"Hilarious." It wasn't. "I need to get to that corridor behind the fridge."

Benedict shrugged. "Olexie, can you show him the access panel?"

"I am on strike."

"I'll do it," Zach said, hopping off the table.

"Fucking scab," Olexie grumbled.

"You won't find anything useful back there," the chef continued. "It doesn't go anywhere."

"Even so," Ajay said.

Benedict handed Olexie a tray of dough. "Brush butter on these and get them to the oven."

Olexie rolled his eyes. "Strike is over, I suppose."

"Find anything out about the killer yet?" Zach asked as they left the kitchen.

"Which one?"

"There's more than one?" Zach led him out of the kitchen.

"Isn't the fridge back there?" Ajay asked.

"Yeah, but access to the service passage is around the corner."

"There was a murder," Ajay said. "And another attack just a little while ago, which wasn't necessarily the same perpetrator. Then there's a guy outside who might want to kill us because his husband is dead."

Zach blinked at Ajay.

"Just stay with Olexie and you'll be safe."

Zach pushed a panel in the hallway wall, and it opened with a click. "We're not great at sticking together in the kitchen. There are only three of us, and there's a lot of work to do."

"Weren't you all together when the murder happened?"

"Sure, sure." He wasn't very convincing. "We just work pretty hard down here, you know?"

"Of course." Ajay shone his light down the narrow hall and found a switch. Flipping it on illuminated a single flickering bulb halfway down a long hall. Dust danced in the still air, catching the light like fairy fire, but almost none covered the floor. "Thank you, Zach."

Without another word, Zach returned to the kitchen.

At the end of the hallway was a small room immediately behind the walk-in refrigeration units as far as Ajay could figure. Their low hum shook the air, and a thin layer of grease covered everything. The building's framing was revealed in this unfinished space, but they weren't pine boards as he expected. The construction looked more like extruded plaster or concrete. It sounded hollow when he tapped on it. He pressed farther back and found exactly what he was expecting.

Attached to the refrigerator's cooling unit was a box the size of a large suitcase. It whirred and a row of green lights glowed across the top. A network router switch of some sort, Ajay figured, and it also appeared to be some kind of processing node for the security system. It was a perfect place to plug into the hardware layer and gain better access to security. If he had that, then he'd be able to learn more about the murder.

"Sherlock fuckin' Holmes," he muttered to himself.

There was no problem that a sufficient amount of hacking couldn't fix.

He drew a universal connector from his cane and attached to the data port in the device. A stream of information flooded his cheaters, the glasses struggling to keep up with the enormous flow of information. This was it, but he needed to be careful. There were honeypots and backup triggers all over the place here, and if he triggered one, he didn't know what would happen. He might end up making things worse.

His fingers flew across the controls as he assembled an array of processes to manage the information flow. He was in the moment. In the code. There was no problem that a sufficient amount of hacking couldn't fix, and this was it. The solution. Waves of data rolled past him, dancing illumination of a thousand lines of code clicking together in his brain in a way that suddenly made sense.

Ajay wrangled the data into coherent forms. The rolling input from the outer reaches collated into a neat array of data. In the blank spaces, he saw the encroaching threat. Inside the house, he found the patterns in how the security systems were applied. He found the blank spaces and the world between the walls. It was everywhere. There was almost as much house hidden as there was in the open.

With a few swipes through the controls, he connected the severed portions of the surveillance system. Immediately, his view of the house improved, and he picked up dozens of new video feeds.

And the basements. It wasn't just the panic room. There was a network of passages down there. The room Kylie hid in wasn't as isolated as he thought. Safe, still, but there was so much more to it. Strange.

None of that was what he wanted, though. He needed control if he was going to help defend the house. There were ways to force a permissions fault with control of the hardware and network layers. Many ways. Ajay knew them all, and he'd used most of them.

But there were also ways to set traps in a system like this. Something could lock him out completely if he tried the wrong technique. If he decrypted the wrong password file, it might lead him to use a password that would trigger a full lockdown. If he sent a fault sequence to the wrong port, it might trigger a data wipe.

Ajay moved cautiously, absorbed completely in the code for an unspecified amount of time. He lost himself in the logic, and a thousand years might have passed as easily as ten minutes.

A shutdown. He saw it, and found how it was triggered, but couldn't easily circumvent it.

"You'll want to stop, Mr. Andersen," said

Melinda behind him. A section of the unfinished wall opened to reveal another passage.

Ajay found that passage on his newly filled-in map. It led up some stairs and to the private chambers of Jocelyn Garver. His knees popped when he stood. "A secret passage in your secret passage?"

Melinda's gaze flickered to the machine. Code flashed across the surface of her glasses. "What have you done so far?"

"Rigged a complete shutdown," Ajay said, holding on hand over the controls of his cane. "One move, and Parks won't find any resistance when he comes to get us. I'll shut down your whole defense grid."

Melinda stared at him, unblinking.

Ajay detached his cord. He gestured for Melinda to lead the way back up the stairs. "I think you're right. It's about time I had another chat with the boss."

After a pause that Ajay suspected contained communication with Jocelyn, Melinda turned and disappeared back the way she came.

Ajay followed.

CHAPTER EIGHTEEN

A CLATTER of movement in the other room, and Kylie seriously considered going in and having fun like the younger girl. They could take turns on the VR rig and trade notes about what they found. Maybe there would be something that they had in common, and they could be friends.

The thought of trying to make a friend made Kylie's palms sweat. She desperately wanted to text Austin, but she was still isolated. Still blocked from the whole world. All the muscles in her chest tightened, and she knew she couldn't possibly talk to Gabby. The suffocating pressure only eased when she rubbed Garrison's soft ears.

"How long has he been back there?" asked Olexie. Kylie saw him through one of the many surveillance feeds she had configured through the security system. She recognized the old Russian right away. Kylie didn't know how to feel about him collecting information about her grandmother. It was an invasion of the old lady's privacy, but Kylie wanted to understand the contract forged on her birthday, and reading wasn't helping.

"It doesn't matter," said the head chef. "We have work to do."

"It's not like anyone is eating," Olexie said. "We could stop cooking."

The chef poked the tall Russian in the chest with a spatula. "It's like this, new guy. Once they want to eat, they're going to expect everything to be perfect and ready immediately. That's how it works for these people. If that means we keep cooking all night, then that's what we do."

"Perfect. Everything we make is shit."

The chef fumed. He pressed his lips together, turned a dangerous shade of red, and stalked away. Olexie shrugged and continued to chop the heads off of broccoli.

The other kitchen worker, Zach, walked through the house, and Kylie kept losing track of him through dark gaps in her surveillance. Sometimes the security system would glitch, and people disappeared. Sometimes they appeared out of nowhere, like localized hauntings in the giant mansion.

Zach entered the ballroom. He collected plates from the place settings and gathered dirty silverware. When he had a whole load on his busing cart, he wheeled it through a section of wall that—

Kylie rewound the video. Zach wasn't there. The

dishes disappeared between frames, and the section of wall never opened. She made a mental note of where she had seen Zach open the passage.

Then, two sides of the surveillance network joined, and she could suddenly see the gaps between walls. She blinked, rubbed Garrison's ears, and leaned back in her chair. There was more to the mansion than even she had guessed. She had expected secret passages before she had even set foot in the house. Who would even build a mansion this big without some secret passages?

But this was ridiculous. There wasn't surveillance inside most of the passages, but there were flags where certain activities would trigger data wipes. There were more secret doors than there were normal ones.

"We have to *do* something," came an old man's voice through her surveillance. "You know he's behind this."

Kylie shuffled through her feeds, trying to figure out whose voice it was.

A woman responded, "Nonsense. There's nothing we need to do other than summon our car and leave."

"Leave? We can't even open the front door."

Kylie located the feed. The Trowbridges whispered to each other in a secluded corner of the foyer, right next to one of the surveillance microphones.

"If we stay quiet, we'll be safe," Loretta said, patting his hand. It reminded Kylie of the condescending way Papa sometimes spoke to her when she was on the edge of panic. "I promise."

Percival cast a sideways glance across the room to where Robert Burkshire still punched numbers into the weapons safe—a useless task, but Kylie didn't have any way of telling him that. "We could tie him up."

Loretta's cruel smirk flashed across her face. "And how do you propose we do that? If he's the murderer as you say, then he's probably already armed."

"We'll get the jump on him," Percival said.

"Now who's not thinking about safety?"

"It's the only way," he hissed. "We should have stayed home."

Loretta Trowbridge gave him such a complex look that Kylie couldn't interpret all the emotion packed in it. The woman's eyes grew sharp. Her lips pressed tight together. Her neck muscles tightened. After a tense display that lasted the span of a few heartbeats, she said, "You're probably right."

Kylie rolled her eyes. Rich people could be so stupid. They weren't going to get the jump on that man, and if they did, they probably still would just hurt themselves. They were all being stupid. Robert, Percival, Loretta, even her grandmother. The Declan guy wasn't doing so great, either. She pointed her camera at him. He held the leg of an expensive-looking table in one hand after having wrenched it from a piece of expensive furniture. He would probably get in trouble for that later, but at least he was doing something.

Well, *doing* might be a stretch. He was walking through a hallway on the opposite end of the mansion, gripping his table leg like a baseball bat. Where was he going, anyway? Who was he looking for? Every time he passed Nailah, he gave her a look that Kylie couldn't interpret. It was a kind of narrow-eyed expression that twisted up the man's thin lip.

Kylie drew a deep breath. At least *she* was safe. She and Gabby wouldn't need to worry about what the stupid rich people did until morning when the police finally came. *If* they finally came. She wasn't clear on how that was going to happen. Papa, on the other hand, probably still had to worry, and therefore she had to worry about him. She scrubbed back to see if she could see where he went. There were a few secret passages near the kitchen where she lost track of him. One of them had to be where he went, but she didn't see him disappear, so she didn't know for sure.

Garrison sighed the biggest sigh any living creature had ever made.

"I know, buddy." Kylie scratched under his chin. "I know."

She didn't hear Gabby anymore. Maybe the girl had finally tired of the VR rig. Videogames were fun, but virtual reality was exhausting. Kylie chewed her lip. Maybe she should talk to the girl. She stood to go to the other room.

Then, she sat back down. What if Gabby didn't want her to talk? What if Gabby just wanted to be left alone? This was a stressful situation, and when Kylie got stressed, she always wanted to be left alone.

No, that wasn't right. Kylie always wanted to *not* be left alone, but she never told anyone that. Gabby probably wanted company, but she had been *so* violent when she'd lost her temper that Kylie was a little afraid to talk to her.

Kylie turned back to the blinking cursor on the password field of Jocelyn's computer. She wanted that full access. She could have even more control of the security system and access to all the data files regarding the contract.

That damn contract. Kylie wished she had bigger pockets because she would steal it for sure.

She wasn't going to be able to guess the password. That much was clear. It always looked so easy when Papa did it, but this kind of hack took a lot more patience than she'd ever had. Instead, she popped the front off of the machine, rooted around in the hardware, and detached the data drive, slipping it into the tiny front pocket of her suit.

Steeling herself with a deep breath, she rolled her chair over to the door and gently pushed it slightly ajar. "Gabby?" she called as gently as she could manage.

Nothing.

Kylie pushed the door the rest of the way open.

Gabby sat at the head of the bed, its indigo covers

crinkled from her weight. She'd surrounded herself with pillows, and her face was flushed. Snotty tears made her face glisten.

"Are you okay?" Kylie asked because she couldn't think of anything stupider to say.

The girl looked up at Kylie with bloodshot eyes. Her hands were clenched into fists on her knees, and she shook as if from rage. When she spoke, it was in a whisper that Kylie could barely hear. "I don't want to do this anymore."

CHAPTER NINETEEN

"How MANY SITTING rooms does one person need?" muttered Ajay as he stepped between the panels to enter Jocelyn Garver's private chambers. This area wasn't on the map and stayed isolated from all surveillance settings, so he hadn't known what to expect.

Apparently, Jocelyn valued comfort and fashion in equal measures. Settees lined the walls of the circular room, which was covered in mirrors and windows. Fabulous windows. This was the circular room at the very top of the palace, and each arched window looked out on a different cardinal direction. The hidden door closed behind him and became another mirror in the array. He stepped onto the rich carpet, its soft depths swallowing the click of his cane. The closest window overlooked the garden below, and their view spread out across the forest beyond to the very edge of the silent property where it met Lake Superior. A spiral staircase in the center of the room led to more private quarters above.

The room felt different from the rest of the mansion. The air was crisp and dry. When Ajay stepped inside, the floor felt solid under his feet. Something deep in him reacted to being here, like he had stepped through space to an entirely different world. The room wasn't large, but it was big enough to contain all Jocelyn's best luxuries, which, surprisingly, did not include fancy paintings or exquisite statuary. The room's greatest feature was its windows, and Ajay stepped up to the nearest to stare at the world outside.

A single glass door led from the room onto a flat stretch of roof, upon which stood a folded two-seated drone car. It was cold and inert under a dark and gloomy sky. If she tried to fly away, she'd likely be shot down by Parks.

In the middle of the forest below, a ring of pure white pines stood sentinel under the dark sky. Far away in the distance, lightning lit the tumbling wool clouds.

"I trust you're feeling better?" Ajay asked.

"The beauty of sitting rooms, Mr. Andersen," said Jocelyn, "is that one can sit." The woman didn't look as if she had ever felt the ache of exhaustion. Gone was the unsettled fear that had driven her to her rooms. She lounged across the room on a plush settee and gestured with a half-empty glass of wine at a nearby seat. She wore a yellow blouse and matching pants that flared at the ankles. It was as if their formal dinner had never happened.

Ajay glanced at Melinda, who had preceded him into the room. Her black suit was still hung perfectly on her slender frame. Not even a speck of dust marred the dark material. She raised an eyebrow and glanced at the seat.

"Fine," Ajay grumbled. He crossed the room and settled onto an overly cushioned chair. The configuration of backrest and cushions didn't quite fit the form of his body, making the seat considerably less comfortable than it looked. "This place could use a good recliner," he said. He also would have added a television.

"You are likely wondering why you are here," Jocelyn said. She gestured toward an empty glass on a table. Melinda silently stepped behind Ajay and poured him a dark red wine.

"I'm wondering a lot of things tonight," Ajay said. "Why I'm here is the least of them."

Jocelyn watched him through half-lidded eyes for about twice as long as was comfortable.

Ajay swirled the wine, but he didn't drink. "What I want to know is why everyone else is here. A grandmother wanting to meet her granddaughter makes sense to me. When I learned that I had granddaughters, it knocked my socks off. I wanted to know everything about them and make up for all that lost time. I would have done anything to spend just a little bit of time with them." Ajay drew a deep breath.

He got his wish with Kylie, but Isabelle remained a gaping hole in his life. They hadn't parted on bad terms, but the older sister was living her own life and didn't have time for some old grandpa she didn't even know.

"I know you didn't get along with Jackson, but my son was a good man." Her eyes drifted toward the garden-facing window. "He did good work."

Ajay didn't have a response to that. She was right. He had never really gotten along with Kylie and Isabelle's father. Then again, he hadn't gotten along particularly well with his own daughter Sashi, and the fact that the two decided to experiment on their children didn't help.

"They asked me for funding, you know," continued Jocelyn. "Before everything happened. It was a tough time for the economy, and I couldn't do everything they wanted, but I was able to connect them with investors."

"They had a military contract," Ajay said.

Jocelyn sipped her wine. "The military pays for military results. It's a universal truth of doing business with the government. Their project was going to take far too long for exclusive military funding, but decades of war left several powerful mercenary groups with extra money to spend."

"You're talking about Frontier Arms."

"Among them were several groups that eventually merged to form Frontier Arms, yes." Jocelyn closed her eyes and swayed gently. "There were other investors, of course. Ones who cared more about the science or who could see the project from a more visionary perspective."

Visionary. It was human experimentation on the unborn. Anyone who invested in something like that had a seriously skewed ethical compass. Then, it clicked for Ajay. "Is that why you're having this dinner party? You've invited some of the investors?"

Jocelyn's eyes snapped open and her piercing gaze went right through Ajay. "You've been paying attention." She set her glass on the table and leaned forward. "They're not all investors. The Trowbridges were. As was Mr. Burkshire. You can see what he's gained from the program."

"His daughter."

"Gabby is one of the better results of the experiment, but I'm sure you are aware of the difficulties children can have growing up with these changes in their heads."

Ajay thought of everything Kylie had to deal with. Her mental instability, the symptoms that mimicked the autism spectrum, and the horror of knowing she might accidentally damage her own brain. On top of it all, she had to deal with multiple instances of trauma, and the evening's events were only going to make things worse. "What about Declan?"

Jocelyn barked a laugh. "He isn't exactly the kind of man to invest in anything except possibly an index fund for his retirement. Declan Bohm keeps us honest, doesn't he? Wilson Lee's investment was the largest of the group, but he had the least to gain. It makes a person wonder, doesn't it?"

"Why did he send Nailah?"

Jocelyn emptied her glass and set it on the table, where Melinda refilled it. "Tell me something, Mr. Andersen. We're outside of the surveillance system so nobody is recording these words. Our granddaughter is in a safe room secluded from the world and can't possibly hear what we say here." She drummed her polished nails on the table. "So: how unstable is she?"

Ajay didn't like the question. If he answered that she was perfectly stable, Jocelyn would find something in the girl's history to refute his lies. If he admitted that she struggled sometimes, the old woman might use that to—what? Take her away? Neither of his options looked good if he answered, whether lie or truth, so he opted for the truth. "Kylie has made incredible gains in the past year."

"She needs help."

"She *has* help."

"There is a school for talented girls. One of my many investments here in Minnesota." Jocelyn glanced at Melinda. "It specializes in girls who are recovering from trauma."

"Kylie is fine."

"She watched her father die."

"Yes." Ajay bristled. "And she watched her mother die as well."

"All the more reason to get her help."

"She needs a stable life," Ajay said. "With me."

"Stable? Was she not kidnapped recently?"

"A little."

"And we know she has the talent," said Jocelyn. Ajay had no doubt that she was referring to Kylie's hack in the elevator. She had clearly displayed her abilities. "That on its own is a trauma."

"She's resilient."

"You live as a fugitive, Mr. Andersen. Your niche in the great datastream of life might work for an old man in the twilight of his years, but Kylie requires legitimacy. She needs good psychological help and training that will let her focus her skills."

"She needs a family who loves her."

"Like you loved Sashi?"

Heat rose at the base of Ajay's neck, and his suit became stiflingly hot. "I am responsible for what happened to Sashi, but that doesn't mean I can't do better."

Jocelyn fixed Ajay with a piercing gaze, no longer swaying or lazy, but fierce and penetrating. "I don't blame myself for my son's death."

"Of course, you don't, because you don't blame yourself for anything," Ajay snapped before he could consider his words. He waved a hand at the ridiculous mansion. "People as rich as you never blame themselves for the problems happening all around them. You blame the poor or the masses or social media or the news. Never yourself."

"You go too far, old man."

Ajay stood, seething. He gripped his cane in two hands. "What is Alexander Parks after, Jocelyn?" He couldn't stand to look at her anymore, so he walked to the bay window and stared out into the night. Far beyond the trees, Lake Superior shone under lightning-lit clouds. "Why is he launching an assault on your property? Why is his husband dead in one of your many war-themed sitting rooms?"

Jocelyn didn't move from her place in the corner. She swirled wine in her glass. "There's more to those men than you know," she said.

"Lot of that going around."

"What do you think the other guests think of you, Ajay?"

"What do you mean?"

"I mean, you're the only one in the group who is a known killer." Now, Jocelyn stood and approached the window. "They think you're the most dangerous one among them."

"They can't possibly know what I've done."

Jocelyn's smile was wide, but her eyes reminded Ajay of a shark's. "These are people with extensive resources. If there is something to know, they probably know it."

"You vouched for me. Told them I was with you during the murder."

"And that will get you as far as their trust for me. What's to say I didn't hire you, a known criminal and thug, to take them out while they're stuck in this house?"

Ajay cast a glance at Melinda, but the butler stood perfectly still in one corner without even a hint of an expression. "You'd have a lot of trouble finding houseguests if you did that kind of thing."

"I think it best if Kylie lives with me from now on," said Jocelyn, as if the idea had just occurred to her. "She'll be safer."

Ajay spun on her, his face burning with anger. "You wouldn't dare." His knuckles were white where he gripped his cane. "She has a school."

"You know there are better schools."

"She has friends." One friend, but Ajay used the plural anyway.

Jocelyn waved it off. She rested one finger on the glass of the bay windows where the moonlight made it look pale as a bone. "She would do well here."

Ajay seethed. Jocelyn's words were like poison. He remembered how Kylie had looked at that library. He knew he had his flaws. Kylie *would* be better with someone who wasn't constantly avoiding attention from the law.

But not with Jocelyn Garver.

If only Ajay could provide the best life for her. He desperately wanted to stay a part of Kylie's life. If she moved in with Jocelyn, Ajay might only see her on holidays. If that. He seriously doubted Jocelyn would approve of frequent visits. If Ajay betrayed Kylie enough to send her away, he very much doubted she would accept him as a visitor. He had alienated Sashi, and that regret would follow him to the grave. He couldn't bring himself to do the same to Kylie.

Jocelyn's voice was a wall of ice. "I have every right to her that you do."

She was right. Ajay clacked the head of his cane against the window's thick glass.

At the edge of the forest, against the backdrop of the oil-black waters of Lake Superior, a cloud of movement flashed in the night. A dozen at first, then more. Bolts of crackling energy surged in a wave through the forest, the spearhead of an attack that danced in a wide arc around the grove of towering white trees.

Jocelyn placed a hand on the glass. "It won't matter," she whispered. "Kylie will be safe." She shot a glance at Melinda.

"We'll be fine here," Melinda said. "Not enough of his drones will make it through."

Ajay could see the drones. Individual black flyers zipped among the trees. Many were obliterated by a crackle of gunfire that could barely be heard through the thick glass. Bulletproof glass, Ajay realized in the seconds after panic rose in his chest. Still, the drones came. Behind, at the edge of the forest, a surge of white light flashed in the night. A pulse like the electromagnetic surge that hit them before, but smaller. Weaker. It hindered the attack, but too many drones had already reached the inner garden.

With a zip of movement, the lead drone flew at a clump of lilacs against one wall. Ajay recognized it as the window of the Civil War room. Had he closed that window?

"Kylie will be safe," Ajay said. "We'll be safe. But what about everyone else?"

Jocelyn returned to her settee and lowered herself gracefully back into her spot. She took a sip of wine and appeared to enjoy it more than Ajay had ever enjoyed anything.

"You don't owe them anything, Ajay Andersen. Let them fight their own battles."

By the time she finished speaking, Ajay was already through the mirror panel door and into the hidden passages.

CHAPTER TWENTY

GABBY BURIED her face in her hands, smearing snot and tears over everything. The blankets on the bed glistened with the girl's disgusting fluids. Kylie would have been happier to juggle unexploded grenades.

Was the girl sad? Angry? Kylie tried to remember ever having similar things happen to her own face, and she distinctly remembered being angry when it happened. Maybe she should leave Gabby alone and retreat to the other room. Maybe the teary snotty mess was an allergic reaction and Kylie needed to keep an eye on her in case her airway started to close.

Kylie's chest tightened. Her breaths came fast. Too fast. She started to feel dizzy. Waves of confusion and fury and fear hit her like choppy waves in an ocean of lava.

There was no good answer, so of course, the stupidest part of Kylie's brain took over. She sat on the corner of the bed and asked, "Are you okay?" She was pretty sure she had asked already, and it hadn't worked. Also, it was a dumb question. She tried, "What happened?"

Gabby glanced at the corner of the room where the VR rig stood dormant. "I—don't know."

Kylie pushed some buttons on the rig, curious now. Maybe she could help. Gabby was younger than Kylie, but not by much. Even if she had gotten into the most inappropriate-for-children program, she should have been able to exit out without such a reaction. Kylie cycled through the recently run programs. Nothing popped out as wildly offensive. The only adult themed programs were spreadsheets. Kylie could imagine a spreadsheet bringing someone to tears, but not to the level Gabby was displaying.

It was possible Gabby was simply unstable. If she was able to communicate with computers the way Kylie could, she might have some strange things going on in her brain. Dangerous things. Kylie remembered when she had snapped when she was Gabby's age. She had broken in a way that stifled her emotions. Tamped them down until there was nothing left.

"Gabby," Kylie whispered. "It's fine. You can control this."

Gabby looked up with bloodshot eyes. "You didn't see what I saw."

Glancing back at the VR rig, Kylie said, "No, and I don't think I want to see what you saw. But you can control what's happening to you now."

The girl shook her head vehemently.

Kylie climbed onto the bed and faced Gabby. She took both of her hands in her own and waited until she looked up. It was uncomfortable, but Kylie held Gabby's gaze for several seconds before saying, "I watched my mom kill my dad."

Gabby looked down at her hands. Her black blouse was a wrinkled mess. She tried to straighten it but it didn't work. "Father says family is everything."

"Yeah, Papa likes to say that," Kylie said. "Sometimes he really believes it."

The younger girl looked up at Kylie. "He lies?"

"Never trust authority, kid," Kylie said in her best Papa imitation. "He says he wants me to be whatever I want, then he makes me hide at home. It's stifling." Kylie realized its truth as she said it.

Gabby let out a single loud sob, and a tear ran down her cheek. She said something Kylie couldn't understand under a blubbering mess of sound. Kylie wanted to touch her, but she didn't know if it would help or make things worse. All she knew was that nothing ever helped. Nothing except for one thing.

Finally, she said, "Gabby, find the part in you that hurts."

Gabby scrunched her teary eyes closed. "I can't."

"You can. Find the part that hurts and make it stop hurting. It's the part that's making your lungs burn. It's the thing in the front of your face that's making the world blurry. You want it to be clear. You want to take one long breath so that your body can be calm. Everything will be calm." Kylie spoke through long breaths, with a slow rhythm that mimicked the steady, rolling waves of the sea. "You don't need to hurt right now." She would have to hurt *eventually*, but they could talk about that later.

Kylie didn't know if she was feeling a natural impulse to make things better for Gabby or an urge to not have to watch so much snotty, gross crying.

"You can make the pain stop. All that emotion. All that fear. It can all be gone, and you don't need to experience it. Not yet, anyway. Not now."

This was harmful, and Kylie knew it. A rough stab of guilt pierced her sternum as she said the words, but she had to believe that Gabby would learn the next step. She would learn later how to process the emotions. Once Kylie figured out the source of this poison, she would guide Gabby through processing how to feel about it. They had time for that. This was a safe space. Nobody could stop them.

"Make it stop," Kylie said in a flat voice. She reached out for a connection and found Gabby's signal hovering close. She stretched her own abilities to it—

A torrent of signal washed over her. It was more complex than anything she had ever sensed. Gabby's mind reached out to her, grasping and re-grasping for a solid connection. It was an ever-shifting mass—like trying to build something out of dry sand. Kylie gasped, overwhelmed by the pure cacophony of it. There was no way she could handle all of it. Instead, she focused on one touch. One fingertip reaching across the heavens.

Allowing that smallest touch, she demonstrated to Gabby how she manipulated her own emotions. She showed how the machine in her brain could change and flex based on her needs. "Make the thing that wants to hurt you go away. Not forever, but just for now."

"I have to?"

"Yes," Kylie lied. "You have to."

And Gabby responded. It was slow at first, but the raging out-of-control cascade running through her system faded to a dull roar. The girl opened her eyes and the tears stopped.

"I'm okay," Gabby said in a flat voice. "It's better now."

Kylie glanced at the VR rig, curious about what must have upset Gabby. "I'm going to see what's on this," she said, noticing that her voice sounded completely flat now. "I'll use it to talk to Papa."

"Yeah," breathed Gabby. "Yeah, I think that's a good idea."

CHAPTER TWENTY-ONE

"Give me access," Ajay said through his comm as he stalked through the dark walls.

"I'm a little busy," responded Melinda. In the feed, he could see her orchestrating the defense. Waves of drones assaulted the property. They closed off access to the Civil War room, but three drones were already moving through the ducts.

"There are a thousand variables in a thousand locations, Melinda," Ajay said.

"And I'm not giving you control of any of them."

"Somehow I don't think you feel quite the same urgency behind those bulletproof windows." He pushed open an unmarked passage and found himself behind the refrigerator where he had been trying to hack the security node. "Tell me about the school."

The woman was silent for a long time. "It's

survival training," she finally said. "A lot of families send their kids to it."

"Is Jocelyn listening right now?" When Melinda didn't answer, Ajay said, "Give me access or I'll take it."

"You try that and the defense grid will collapse. You'll fry every machine in the room." She lowered her voice. "You might even start a fire."

"That's ridiculous."

Melinda said, "If you run that program, you're going to compromise security, fire response, maintenance. Even the cleaning bots will fail."

Ajay stopped on the narrow stairs. "Cleaning bots," he mused. He had seen them in the corners, but something didn't quite click. "Everything is on the same network?"

"You'll shut the whole security system down. How do you think things will go, then?"

"I'm guessing the cleaning bots would need to get involved." Ajay's hand hovered over the controls. He plugged into the box. It would take nothing to execute his sequence.

But what if Melinda wasn't lying? If this did bring everything down, even temporarily, would that be enough to let Parks in? Quinn had gotten in while the system was up. Why not Parks?

The walls shook, and dust cascaded from the ceiling. The drones were getting close. He needed to act quickly.

"Olexie," he said through his comm. The old

Russian appeared in the corner of his vision. "Move your people to the foyer."

"It's just me here," Olexie replied.

"Just you? Where are Zach and Benedict? You were supposed to keep an eye on them."

"People have jobs to do. Not everyone can afford retirement."

"Being a cook was just a cover. Doesn't the countercapitalist group pay your bills?"

Olexie grumbled several seconds before answering, "CCS is not exactly well funded."

"What do you know about Benedict, by the way?" Ajay asked.

"He started here not long before I did. He makes a pretty good crème brûlée."

"What?"

"You know, with the sugar crust." Olexie mimed breaking the crust off the top of a crème brûlée and eating it. "Even a bad one is wonderful, but Benedict's were..." Olexie kissed his fingertips.

With a grunt of frustration, Ajay said, "Just get to the foyer," and closed the line.

He stared at the security router. A whine of power buzzed, and he remembered all the times he'd executed hacks and failed. Even the best hackers didn't do everything right on the first try. Not by a long shot. Now, in his twilight years, his skills were so rusty that he couldn't trust himself to be able to take control of the security grid. If he did, what exactly did he think he could do that Melinda wasn't already doing?

Succeeding. She was failing at every turn. Her use of the defense grid wasn't deterring the attacking drones. She prioritized saving Jocelyn and the old woman's treasures over saving the guests.

But why?

He should seize control. Form a defensive perimeter around the foyer and cede everything else in the mansion. That was his best bet at saving the guests. Saving Kylie.

If he had control of the security system, he could open the weapons safe. People could defend themselves. Wasn't that, at least, the right thing to do?

"Papa?" Kylie's voice was tinny and strange.

Ajay looked around but didn't see Kylie anywhere.

"I'm in a VR rig," Kylie said. "You can't see me, but I'm trying to find whatever upset Gabby."

"She's upset?" Ajay asked. "How are you in the network? I thought the safe room was isolated."

"There's a backdoor to surveillance on the computer and some automation controls in the VR rig," said Kylie. There was a noise on the line like cloth moving across the microphone. "Papa, you need to move. There are drones coming your way."

Ajay opened a channel from his drone and connected it to the security router. "Take control of this," he said, detaching the drone from his cane. "And stick close to me."

"The controls are all weird." Kylie's hollow voice came from the drone. It lifted off and unplugged itself from the security box. "Yeah, this'll work."

Ajay stowed his cord and moved through the narrow tunnel. He watched the security system through his cheaters as the trio of drones buzzed down the hall. Pushing the door open, he crept down the hall. The smell of baked bread wafted from the kitchen, caught in an undercurrent of burned fry oil and rosemary.

"Are you doing okay down there?" Ajay whispered.

"I'm fine." The drone whooshed close to Ajay so that Kylie could speak quietly. "This is fun."

"Fun," Ajay grumbled. "It's fun."

"Look out," Kylie buzzed.

Ajay saw it, too. One of the three drones had doubled back and was about to round the corner. He ducked behind a statue just before he heard the low hum of its muffled rotors. Kylie's drone landed on his shoulder and hooked itself there so that it could move silently.

The softball-sized drone floated down the hall, its scanners active. It bathed the wide hallway in a wash of red, casting angry shadows across the cold statue of a horned man. The marble figures made human forms in the blotted shadows on dark walls. Ajay's heart pounded in his chest and his mouth tasted like acid reflux. As the drone moved, Ajay shuffled forward to stay in his statue's shadow.

It stopped, hovering several feet in the air on the side opposite Ajay's hiding place. The drone had a low hum that Ajay didn't recognize. It was a newer model. Very quiet.

"I could hit it with my cane," he subvocalized. He knew Kylie would be able to pick up the words through his comm.

"It's a Genesis Seven model military drone," said Kylie. "Fully weaponized with a high-speed needler and light ceramic shielding."

Ajay's grip tightened on his cane. "One good swing."

"It's almost bulletproof," whispered Kylie in his hearing aid.

"I'm stronger than I look."

She didn't respond to that. The drone drifted to the left, and Ajay continued to move around the statue. One wrong step and it would see him. It probably already detected his presence and was only waiting to confirm before zipping around and needling him to death. Ajay shuddered. That would certainly solve his argument with Jocelyn about custody of Kylie.

"Kylie, listen," he started. He had to tell her everything.

"It can hear you," Kylie said. "It's reacting."

She was right. The drone rose higher in the hall-way, shrinking the statue's shadow until Ajay barely fit. The statue was of a nude man with antlers and carrying a long sword.

He could run. That would buy him an extra two seconds. Fighting would be instant death. A hack might work, but as soon as he tried to establish a connection, it would likely react. Military drones tended to be very wary of networked orders. Hacking one wasn't impossible, but it took time, and it would only work if the drone's firmware wasn't up to date.

Ajay chewed his lip. A physical connection would work even if he couldn't execute a remote hack. Then he would have control of his own drone in the fleet. It might work as a way to infiltrate and counterattack Alexander Parks. This would be his way in. His way to escape the mansion and save the guests. All of them.

But first, he needed to subdue the drone.

His heart pounded so loud he was afraid the drone might hear it. Maybe it did. His palms were sweaty, so he wiped them off on his pants. There wasn't much hope of this working. He would need to act fast. With a swipe through his controls, he found the routines most likely to succeed at cracking the drone's override code. It was a long shot.

Hell, getting the connection in the first place was a long shot. He closed his eyes and breathed. "I'm sorry, Kylie," he whispered.

"Sorry? For what?" Her voice rose in panic. "For what, Papa?"

Ajay popped the cane up in his hands and gripped the narrow base. Its heavy metal head made it feel like wielding a nine iron. He took one step to the side and without a word, swung.

And missed.

He had been expecting that. A military drone had plenty of utility for dodging, but the hallway wasn't big and Ajay was fast. He was ready. Another swing. The cane whooshed through air. Then again.

He grunted with the effort, keeping the drone on evasive maneuvers. Backing it up. He swung again. His arms burned with the effort. His lungs screamed and his heart hammered. Again.

It was almost backed into a recess where it would have less room to move.

But he wouldn't make it. Its needler opened. The harsh red glare of its light didn't reveal much of the weapon, but it didn't need to. It could aim and fire in an instant without a sound.

Then came the yell. From down the hall, a bellow of rage and fury shook the walls. Something black flew out of the night, end over end, passing close to the drone.

It didn't hit, but in dodging, the drone's aim was ruined. A hiss of passing needles tugged at the air to Ajay's left. He swung again.

This time, his cane pinged against ceramic plating with a loud crack. The drone fired another volley, but this wasn't aimed at Ajay. It pelted off into the dark, sending a flare of sparks when it hit something black and metal down the hall.

Something moving fast.

Olexie roared again, black iron pan in his big hands. He closed the distance fast, with a large skillet held up like a shield against the drone's attack.

Ajay swung again, and this time he struck the shielding around the drone's rotors. Something cracked, and the rotor started pinging like a failing engine. It lurched to one side.

Only to take another frying pan to its side. Olexie pounded it once. Twice. He bludgeoned it to the ground and when it was down, he kept pounding until it was a ruined ceramic and metal paste.

Olexie swallowed big gulps of air and looked at Ajay in the maddening red light that still emitted from the drone at their feet.

"I was going to hack that," Ajay said.

"It was going to shoot you."

"It was under control." It wasn't. Not even close.

Olexie stomped the drone and extinguished the red light. "Maybe you can have the next one."

"Papa!" cried Kylie. "The other drones!"

Ajay brought up his security feed and saw the other drones. They buzzed straight toward the foyer.

CHAPTER TWENTY-TWO

"Frying pans?" Ajay asked as he followed Olexie down the long hall. Kylie's drone still clung to his blue suit by two hooked feet. "What happened to the well-armed soldier I once knew?"

Olexie waved a cast iron pan, indicating the mansion around them. "It's this security system. It responds to guns of any sort with extreme prejudice and gets pretty ornery about knives."

"We just fought a military drone."

"This is irony," the tall Russian said.

"I don't think you know what irony is."

The surveillance overlay in Ajay's glasses showed him the two remaining drones as they zipped quietly through the halls. Whatever defense systems security had in place didn't trigger on these particular weapons, and Ajay wondered if it simply looked for guns or if there were something more complex in its machine learning that would identify risks. The more complex it was, the more opportunities there were for exploitation.

"We need a plan," Ajay said.

Olexie held up his two heavy frying pans. "I have a plan."

"That's an awful plan."

"No, you don't understand." Olexie held the pans in front of himself like shields. "They are cast iron. Very solid."

Ajay raised an eyebrow and peered at the man. "You're covering your chest and your crotch. You don't think they'll shoot for your head?"

He tapped his head with one of the pans. "I have a very thick skull."

"You're not worried about it shooting your eyes?"

"I am now."

A flash of red crossed Ajay's surveillance feed. He zoomed on the area, but the video was washed out. "Something's happening."

Screams echoed through the hallway from up ahead.

"Papa, be careful," whispered Kylie in Ajay's ear.

"Keep an eye on my back," Ajay grumbled and made his way as quickly as he could. He tuned his glasses to video of the foyer, but all he could get was the washed out white of a blinded camera.

The drone on his shoulder spun around to point its sensors backward. "Ugh," Kylie said, "I can't see anything."

"Just do your best," Ajay muttered.

"I am!" She sounded more upset than he thought justified. Why would she be on edge? He was the one in danger.

"Just—"

"I'm fine," Kylie snapped, her voice echoing back to the lies Ajay's daughter had always told him. "Just be careful."

Ajay didn't know how to be careful, but he knew he had to do something.

There was a scuffle ahead and the zip of needle guns firing. Olexie grunted and crashed into some art, smashing an elaborate glass statue into a million pieces. Light flashed as the mirrored surface shattered.

A drone emerged from the dark. One rotor misfired fitfully as the drone lurched to one side. It turned its sensors Ajay's direction and the red glow flared from its forward array. It caught him in its beam and drifted slowly toward him.

"Well?" Ajay asked. "What are you here for, Alexander Parks?"

The drone lurched to the side, then righted itself.

Kylie's voice whispered in his ear, "The other drone is still up ahead where I can't see it."

"You're here for something," Ajay said to the drone in front of him. "Your husband came here looking for something. What was he looking for?"

The drone backed away slowly. Olexie shifted among the broken glass. Ajay waited for the drone to gun him down. He winced as it lurched to the side again, the sputtering of its mechanisms failing to hold it steady.

Ajay followed the drone down the hall, his shoes crunching broken glass. "You're out of needles," he said as he approached. "Your little venture in here has caused as much damage as it's going to, hasn't it?"

The drone launched itself at Ajay. He stumbled back, caught his heel on the carpet, and fell as the drone blasted past him at incredible speed. A wash of warm air rolled over him as it passed.

It hovered to a stop and turned to face him again.

"Oh, is that how we're doing this?" Ajay said. "Fastball special, it is." He gripped his cane with two hands near its base. He had never been any good at baseball.

The drone's light flashed white with dazzling brilliance. Dots lingered in Ajay's vision for a split second, and he threw himself out of the way as the drone charged past again. It rumbled as it brushed his shoulder. Kylie's drone clattered to the floor.

"Kylie?" Ajay said.

No response.

Ajay blinked the spots away. His cheaters no longer displayed the surveillance network. His hearing aid no longer enhanced his hearing. The scuff of his feet against broken glass was dull and distant in his ears.

"Olexie?" Ajay said. "Little help?"

Olexie moaned and shifted but didn't rise. Ajay

could see the dark form against the wall and heard his muttering of Russian curses.

Another flash, but this time, Ajay wasn't looking directly at the drone. He swung his cane to strike, but the drone shifted at the last second and the blow glanced off its ceramic plating. It struck him in the shoulder at reduced speed but still spun him around and landed him flat on his back. The air rushed from his lungs and flashes danced in his vision.

Ajay scrambled to his feet in time to dodge another charge. His fingers bled where he gashed them open on the shattered glass.

This wasn't working. Ajay wasn't fast enough. Kylie couldn't help. He didn't have access to any systems now with his cheater display black. His only hope was to get a lucky blow on the drone, but that wasn't likely at the rate he was going. It was like a Little Leaguer hitting a slider thrown by the Twins' best pitcher.

It wasn't a matter of luck. This was impossible.

He considered running, but that would mean leaving Olexie to his fate. The Russian might be a little bit of an ass, but he didn't deserve to be smashed to death by an errant drone. Also, Ajay probably couldn't outrun the drone. This was a military-grade drone. If a limping old man could outrun it, there must be something seriously wrong.

There *was* something wrong, he realized. One of its rotors still glitched. Even as he thought it, the thing lurched to one side. That was how it had dodged his swing. The thing wasn't throwing him a slider. It was throwing a fastball and its intermittently failing systems turned it into a slider. He sidestepped, edging closer to Olexie and the wall. His hip bumped against the pedestal that once held the glass statue.

"What do you think you're going to accomplish here, Parks?" Ajay said. "You know we're going to be able to alert the authorities about you."

The drone charged. This time, Ajay was ready for it to slide, so he swung low and to the right.

And missed.

The drone slammed into the wall behind him hard enough to splinter wood and crack the stud behind it. The impact smashed the drone's ceramic plating and sparks shot from the forward sensor array. It fell to the floor and burst into flames.

Ajay stomped on the drone, its plating crunching under his dress shoes.

"Dammit," he muttered. Another drone too broken to hack.

He toggled the power switches on all his devices and started a full restart sequence that would take several minutes. The drone Kylie had been using restarted quickly, and he plugged it back into his cane. Kylie remained silent.

Olexie blinked at him from the floor. "I—"

Ajay looked into Olexie's eyes. Olexie blinked back at him with apparent confusion. "Stay here," Ajay whispered. "I'll be right back."

The third drone was up ahead, and he needed to

take care of it. He picked up one of Olexie's frying pans. It was heavy in his grip, and his wrist grew tired after only a few seconds of holding it in front of him.

Still, it was better than nothing if the next drone had needles left.

A shout sounded from up ahead. Ajay burst into the foyer, where Robert bashed the third drone to pieces using a heavy wooden chair.

With a final blow, the drone burst into flames and the foyer lights blazed back to life. Ajay dropped the frying pan with a clang.

"That's the last one," he said. Destroyed.

Robert gave the thing one more hit just to be sure. Then, he dropped the chair and bent over panting from the effort. "I'm sorry," he breathed.

"Where are the others? Kylie, can you locate them?"

Still nothing.

Robert gestured to the storage room with the weapons safe. Ajay moved toward it, every bone in his body telling him something was wrong. Something smelled off in the air, like a dull electricity humming in the silence. Still, Kylie didn't answer.

A wail sounded from the room as he approached, so he stepped faster, ignoring the warnings firing in the back of his head. He burst into the room and saw who was making the noise.

Loretta Burkshire knelt over the bloody body of her husband Percival. Under him on the floor was the unmistakable white uniform of Zach, now soaked with blood. Beyond, stood Nailah Lee, her hand pressed to her mouth. She drew a long breath and looked up to meet Ajay's eyes.

"I think we can stop worrying about a killer among us," said Declan stepping from the shadows to Ajay's right. "All that matters now is the maniac at our gates."

Ajay limped forward, his hip now aching something fierce. His adrenaline crashed, sending waves of pain and nausea through his body. Loretta wailed, her cries reverberating against Ajay's chest cavity and setting all his nerves on edge. He held a hand out to her, and like a switch, she stopped.

Percival lay atop Zach. Both were covered in blood and dotted with the telltale speckles of needle fire. The tiny ammo could just barely penetrate deep enough to be lethal, and then only if it happened to get past the ribs without hitting bone or into the fleshy parts where major arteries ran through the body. Ajay nudged Percival with his cane and the old man's corpse flopped to the floor. He touched the man's waxy skin and found it still warm. Zach was the same. Ajay stared at them, numb.

Zach had taken needle hits to his neck and legs and chest. One of the shots must have hit something important, because based on his pale, rubbery skin and waxy complexion, he had bled out fast. That explained half of the puddle the two men lay in.

The old man, the love of Loretta's life and all-around wealthy blowhard, was different. He had needle wounds across his arms, and several had penetrated his legs. They didn't look to be fatal. None of them had much in the way of blood.

Once he was on his back, though, the story became clear.

"Zach died first," Ajay said, envisioning the scene before him. "He tried to save Percival from the drone, but a spray of needles hit him and caused enough blood loss for him to drop. If we had gotten here earlier, maybe we could have saved him." Probably not, but the guilt would follow Ajay for the rest of his life. "And you're wrong, Declan. We can't ignore the killer among us."

"Why not?"

Ajay nudged Percival's chin, and the long cut opened from ear to ear, gaping wide in the dim light like a hungry maw ready to swallow them all.

Ajay didn't miss the sideways glance Declan shot at Nailah, even though it was gone as soon as it came. He also didn't miss the hard look in Nailah's eyes as she noticed it, too.

Percival had been murdered.

CHAPTER TWENTY-THREE

Kylie gasped and thrust herself backward, crashing against the constraints of the VR rig. Her brain was on fire. Razor-thin shards etched themselves into her temples and burned behind her eyes.

The white light—that flash from the drone—it wasn't just a blinding pulse. It was a data packet, full of—something.

She clenched her eyes closed. Her mind raced, out of control. Memories flooded through her brain. The lab where she trained with her sister. Her father visiting. Her father dying.

This was it. The virus Papa had always talked about. The digital attack on her brain.

She wrenched the VR goggles from her face, but it was too late. She couldn't see. Adrenaline coursed through her veins and the machine part of her mind lashed out at the world. Tears streamed down her face. She heard the scream before she realized it was her own. It sounded ragged and bloody.

Something rammed her hip. She had stumbled against the side of the rig. It was an attack. She lashed out with a fist but hit nothing. The floor hit her and time passed.

A lick on the back of her hand. She yelped and stumbled blindly in the other direction.

A lick?

She blinked. Her rage-fueled thrashing ebbed. How much time had passed? Minutes? Hours? Her mouth tasted like vomit.

Garrison stood next to her, head cocked to one side.

Her lungs ached. How long had she been holding her breath? She drew a long, shaky breath and her fists unclenched. Several more breaths fought as she took them. They burned in her chest.

When the machine part of her mind finally settled, she heard movement behind her. She turned to see Gabby standing by the VR rig. A flash of metal clattered to the floor.

"What?" Kylie asked.

Gabby didn't respond. She stared at the object at her feet.

It was a knife, seven inches long with narrow serrations. The black resin handle shone in the dim light.

And the blade was covered in blood.

CHAPTER TWENTY-FOUR

AJAY STARED at the gap in the wall of the security closet. His map told him that the narrow passage led down into a room in the basement and from there it reached all the corners of the house. The killer could be anywhere. A smear of blood marked the wall near the door.

"Who else was here when this happened?" Ajay asked. The guests had gathered in the storage room, plus Olexie, who swayed unsteadily on his feet.

"Zach," Olexie muttered. "Fuck, he was a good kid."

Ajay choked back the wave of grief and failure. Zach had been a good kid, and Ajay failed to catch the killer.

Declan furrowed his brow. "Robert and I were in the foyer when the drone sped past. Nailah was down the hall, and Loretta—" He cast her an asking glance. "Loretta, where were you?"

The woman choked back an ugly sob.

"Right." Declan paced the length of the room. "I still don't see that this changes anything."

"You weren't with me," said Robert.

Loretta emerged from her crumpled mess to pound her fist against Declan's chest. "This is all your fault," she said. "If you hadn't—"

Declan backed away. "How dare you."

Loretta froze, a mask of rage on her face.

"How dare you," Declan repeated. "Blaming me for what happened to your husband? It was all him and you know it."

Ajay stepped between the two. "Declan, drop it."

"I will *not*." He jabbed a finger at the older woman. "The Trowbridges never took an *ounce* of blame for what they did."

The whites of Loretta's eyes shone bright in the dimly lit room. "We were always afraid of you," she said. "All those years. How could we ever do anything?"

"Afraid of me? Were you as afraid as the witnesses in your trial?" Declan threw his hands up. "Afraid the way the *investigators* feared for the safety of their families when they went up against you?"

"We would *never!*" said Loretta.

"You did," Declan spat. "Percival did. You are monsters, Loretta. Percival was a monster. And now you're still trying to blame everyone else for your crimes."

Loretta crumpled back into herself. "We were afraid."

The room was silent for an eternity. Declan's nostrils flared. Loretta wrung her hands and wiped her tears.

"It doesn't matter," insisted Declan, finally. He jabbed a finger at the safe. "We need this open."

"We can't," said Ajay. "It's more than just the safe. The whole security system is designed to prevent anyone from carrying weapons. Once you get a weapon from that safe, you'll be targeted by Jocelyn's system."

"The way those drones were?" drolled Declan.

"That Parks guy carried a gun," Nailah said. "I carried that same gun for a while and nothing bothered me."

"There are exceptions programmed into the system," Ajay said. "And we can shut that system down, but only if I have full control of the security system."

"Then take control," said Robert. "And let's open this safe. I'll feel safer when I'm armed."

"If I hack security, I might disable the system keeping Parks at bay." Ajay placed a hand on the weapons safe. "It's a risk."

Loretta drew a dozen short breaths and leaned against the wall like a sack of potatoes. They had covered the bodies with some curtains, but she still stared at the place where she knew her Percival still lay. "I can't do this," she breathed.

Ajay crossed to her and took her hand. "You have to, Loretta. This doesn't work unless we work together."

Her eyes hardened. "One of us is a killer," she hissed.

Ajay looked to each of them in the room. "I suspect most of us are killers in one way or another. Olexie's a crusader for a cause. Robert, your decisions have cost people their lives. It doesn't matter. What matters is that we stick with each other, fight off this attack long enough for the police to arrive as backup."

"You know as well as I do the police aren't coming," Robert said. "Something about that particular body—the first one—has Jocelyn spooked. *She* instructed Melinda to lie to us about backup."

"There have been enough lies," Ajay spat. "I'm tired of it."

"You and me both," slurred Olexie.

"Quiet." Ajay took the big man by the arm, led him to the corner, and made him sit. He turned to the rest of them. "Has anyone seen Benedict?"

Loretta blinked, looked to the others who also seemed confused, then asked, "Who is Benedict?"

"The chef," growled Ajay. "He made all that food you ate this evening."

Robert said, "Well he wasn't very good."

The old woman looked a little put out. "We didn't even get past the salad."

"And it was a terrible salad," said Declan.

"Yeah, what's the deal with that?" Ajay asked. "I thought you rich people would have better food."

Declan shrugged. "Maybe good isn't in fashion."

"Like stealing silverware," Ajay said.

Robert blinked, taken aback. "People steal silverware?"

Ajay said, "I need to know why you are all here." When nobody jumped in with answers, he added, "Jocelyn Garver hates every one of you. Have you not wondered why she would invite you all to the same party and feed you garbage?"

"It wasn't garbage," said Olexie. Then he seemed to reconsider. "Okay, some of it was garbage."

"There was paper baked into my bread," said Robert.

Declan added, "And I found a tough bit in my salad that I swear was a shred of oak leaf."

"Oak is edible," said Nailah.

"Yes, but it's not *good,*" said Declan, making a disgusted face at Olexie. "You had us eating yard waste."

Ajay said, "If Jocelyn cared about any of you, she would have fed you a decent meal. She was making you grovel and pay tribute while disrespecting you at every turn." He addressed the ceiling as if Jocelyn might be prayed to like a god. "Isn't that right, Mrs. Garver?"

Robert's face turned red, and he spoke through gritted teeth. "She's arranged this whole thing. The attack. The murder."

"I don't think so," said Ajay, glancing at Declan. "I saw her reaction when we found the first body. She has been panicking ever since, first grasping at the routine of her dinner party and then fleeing to a safe space. I don't believe she's in control of anything anymore."

"I bet that doesn't improve her mood much," Declan said.

"She's certainly in control of that safe," said Robert. "It's the only way we can possibly defend ourselves. That chef of hers is still running around. I bet he's the killer."

"What about that Quinn you mentioned earlier?" Declan asked. "Could she have done this?"

"Quinn?" Nailah asked. "Quinn who?"

Absolutely. "No," Ajay said. He needed to focus the group. "This isn't her style." It was. Any kind of killing was her style, but Ajay's instinct still told him she hadn't done it.

Benedict had an alibi during the first killing, but one of those witnesses was dead and the other was Olexie—not the most reliable of sources. No, he could no longer rule the chef out, but...

Ajay said, "It's not him. At least not this time."

Nailah stepped forward. "It could be."

"It's not the chef, because the only way out of that room without running straight into Robert and possibly Declan—"

"Declan wasn't there," interrupted Robert.

"—was through the secret passage, which is, in

this case, quite narrow. All the ones that run along the outside wall are narrow since it is more difficult to conceal the passage on walls that have windows."

Robert gingerly crossed the room, giving the covered bodies a wide berth. He poked his head in the dusty passage between the walls. "I agree. It couldn't have been this Benedict fellow. So where is he?"

"Pumpkin pie," murmured Olexie.

"He might have gone back to the kitchen," said Ajay. He remembered how the chef had stared at him when they had first met. It still made him uncomfortable. "It would be good to get him to join our group. The only way to be safe is to stay together."

Declan said, "Then you're saying we should all go down to the kitchens?"

Ajay chewed on the idea. Something about the whole situation didn't sit right, and the lingering fear of everything falling apart still itched at the back of his brain. Kylie was safe, even though he could no longer communicate with her. At least he had that, but he couldn't count on anything else. Jocelyn wanted custody of his granddaughter, his own life was threatened along with the lives of everyone else in the house, and the only man capable of properly defending himself was clearly suffering from a concussion. Ajay needed a plan, and it had to be one that solved everything at once.

He tried again to reach out to Kylie, but her line remained silent. Something about the drone's flash had scrambled all of his equipment. She was in a shielded safe room, so the lack of direct connection didn't surprise him, but why would she have disconnected from the VR rig? She had to know how serious things were here outside her safe place. Was Gabby giving her trouble?

Ajay considered each of the remaining guests. Declan was hiding something. Every time he was supposed to be somewhere, he ended up somewhere else. The SEC inspector wasn't anyone's friend in the house, but what motivation would he have for murder? Loretta seemed widely liked by the other guests—tolerated at least—but she had no reason that Ajay knew to want to murder her husband. The brutal nature of Percival's murder made Ajay think she couldn't possibly have done it, but Loretta was a woman of society. She was an expert at concealing the emotions lingering beneath. He had known people like her before. They always intrigued him.

Robert had been the first to accuse Declan and the first to react with near violence to any threats. The man was fit, muscular, and capable of anything that had been done to either of the murder victims. He had also been comfortable fleeing to the safe room, something that Ajay wouldn't expect a guilty man to do. After all, if he needed to flee, he would want an easy way out. If the rumors were true about Gabby being almost a bodyguard to him, wouldn't he want her nearby?

Unless...

Ajay shook the thought away. Gabby was in the safe room with Kylie, so she couldn't have been responsible for Percival's murder.

Nailah was present for both murders. Nearby, anyway. She could have killed Percival, taken the passage out to the hallway, and circled back to the foyer. But why would she? As far as Ajay could tell, the woman was a stand-in for her father. She had no real connection to any of these people. She might be working for her father, but she didn't seem inelegant enough to knife two guests at a party. If anything, she would find a much better way to murder houseguests. Poison. A gun.

He remembered the gun. It had disappeared after the attack in the foyer. The weapon wasn't easy to conceal. Whoever had it must have a way to hide it. If they had been carrying it, he would have noticed.

Maybe.

Ajay growled in frustration. This was certainly nothing like what he was dreading when he came to visit the infamous Jocelyn Garver. Fear, frustration, murder. This was nothing. He expected the evening to be much worse.

"This is what's going to happen," he said, tasting the bitter bite of authority on his lips. "We're breaking up into two groups. Loretta, Declan, Robert. You're staying here. When that safe opens, you're going to grab anything useful. In the meantime, set up a defense in the foyer."

"What about us?" Nailah asked.

"You're going to help me move Olexie and we're going to go straight to the kitchen." A lie, but close enough. "We need to find Benedict."

"When is the safe going to open?" asked Robert. "We're done if we can't defend ourselves."

"It'll open when I open it," said Ajay. He started toward the door. "It won't take long, but once it's open, we won't have much time, so hurry."

With that, he led the tall Russian out of the room. Nailah followed close without another word, which was for the best. Ajay was done projecting false confidence. He didn't think he could keep it up much longer.

But at least Kylie was safe.

CHAPTER TWENTY-FIVE

Kylie was *not* safe.

A tear rolled down Gabby's cheek, landing on the bedsheet next to the bloody knife. The girl knelt with her hands folded neatly in her lap. "I didn't mean to," she whispered in a voice like rustling paper, "so it's not my fault."

Kylie bit the accusation back, somehow sensing that Gabby didn't need her words to confront the truth. Gabby was the killer. She was the one Papa had put into the safe room to protect her against, and now here she was with a bloody knife and an unstable psyche.

Gabby wouldn't meet Kylie's eyes, and that didn't bother Kylie one bit. The last thing she wanted was to deal with looking someone in the eyes. Her head still hurt from the drone's flash, and that had been through the filter of the VR rig. What would it have been like looking the thing right in the face? Not that it had a face. It was a machine, and it had been sent to deliver a data package.

But why?

Isabelle would know. Kylie's big sister had embedded herself in the Frontier Arms mercenary group. She would know what this tech was that delivered weaponized malicious data flashes.

Papa had been right. She needed to figure out how to protect herself from this kind of attack. If she couldn't, she was never really going to be safe.

"We're not safe," murmured Gabby.

Garrison nuzzled Kylie's knee and sat at attention. She gave him a quick scratch on his big head. She drew a breath and took a moment to center herself.

Air moved across the back of her neck. The draft was gentle. Almost nonexistent. It could have been the movement of the air filtration system, but she didn't think so. She couldn't hear the small fan running to push air through the enclosed space.

She held out a hand. Moving it around, she found the draft and followed it.

A narrow crack ran along the length of wall behind the VR rig.

Kylie snagged the crack with her chipped fingernails and pulled. The wall panel didn't swing like she thought it would, but actually depressed an inch and slid to the side. It left a narrow space that she could squeeze through, so, of course, she did.

The walls were cold cinder blocks held together

with rough mortar. Above, thick conduits carried wire that dangled low enough to scrape against her hair like grasping fingers. The corners were dark recesses, but she didn't find any cobwebs or dust. The passage smelled new, like a fresh print from the old 3D printer at school.

"What kind of safe room has a back exit?" Gabby asked behind her, mirroring Kylie's thoughts. Her tears were gone, and she stood in the doorway with her hands straight down at her sides.

After a distance that Papa would probably call a long putt, she came upon a junction. Garrison followed close on her heels. The octagonal room swirled with cool, dry air, and sounded like the distant hum of a fan. In the center, a single rack of screens stood, backed by a cylindrical computer as tall as she was. The ceiling was a network of intertwined white roots, poking out like bones from the soil above. The air buzzed with electricity, and Kylie recognized the sensation she had felt in the white pine grove above.

Each wall in the octagon held one narrow doorway, leading somewhere into the mansion. Some had labels like *Garden* or *Pines*, but others were unlabeled. Four bluish lights glowed on the ceiling, illuminating the haze of dust that filled the room. A bloody mark marred one of the unlabeled doorways.

"I wonder where that leads," said Gabby from the doorway Kylie had just passed through, sending

Kylie's heart into a fit. Why did the girl need to move so quietly?

Kylie stepped away from Gabby, who stood in the eerie blue light, head cocked like a shambling zombie.

"What am I doing?" Gabby said. It was the exact question Kylie was thinking. Gabby took a step forward. "What the fuck?"

CHAPTER TWENTY-SIX

"I will take nap here," Olexie said in an uncharacteristically thick Russian accent, pressing his face to the cold metal of the stainless-steel table. The chef was nowhere to be seen.

Nailah stood as statuesque as the moment she had arrived at the mansion, glowing and dark in her immaculate gown even in the harsh white lights of the sprawling kitchen. She still held her clutch purse tight against her body with one arm as she settled the big Russian on his makeshift bed.

Ajay touched the handles of a dozen knives in a block. He drew one out and inspected the edge. Long. Straight. Not serrated. It wasn't a match for the murder weapon. A set of steak knives in the bus cart didn't match, either. To Nailah, he said, "Declan doesn't seem to trust you."

"Well, no. He wouldn't."

"Why?"

Nailah pressed her splayed fingers to her chest. "I told you. My father sent me in his place."

"To prove yourself."

"To represent the family."

Ajay left the knives where they were. He didn't have a good way to carry a sharp blade and figured he would just cut himself. His cane tapped against the tile floor as he crossed the kitchen to the ovens. Something smelled warm and cozy, like nutmeg and cinnamon.

"I think we're past all this dancing, Nailah," Ajay said.

She raised one of her perfect eyebrows.

"You were there when all three bodies were discovered, or close enough. The first guy, Theodore Parks, meant something to you. I saw your careful reaction when we walked into that room. You were up to something. Then, later, you were bothered by the body. You couldn't bear to look at it, but you needed something from him."

Nailah busied herself steadying Olexie. She checked the bandages that she had applied to his head wound and looked into his eyes, clicking her tongue at what she saw.

Ajay found a timer near the ovens with five minutes remaining. He shut it off and removed three pies. "You had me fooled, of course."

Nailah stopped. "Fooled?"

"When you saw the bodies of Percival and Zach." Ajay swallowed a lump in his throat. Zach had been so young. So ready for life. His ambition was to visit a sister he didn't even like. "When you saw them, you went through the same routine. Stunned shock. Then curiosity. Then horror and discomfort."

"A normal reaction, I might remind you."

"Sure." Ajay breathed the aroma of the three pies. One apple, one pumpkin, and one lemon meringue. "Only, your reaction was *exactly* the same each time. The slight surprise, the hand pressed to the mouth, the widened eyes. All of it. Perfect."

Her voice went flat. "I'm certain that's a compliment, Mr. Andersen."

"Please, call me Ajay. No need to be formal." He noted how the grip on her purse shifted. The clutch's shape had been wrong for concealing Theodore Park's gun, but she must have another weapon in there. A knife, maybe? "No need for anyone to know about this chat, actually, because I don't think you killed anyone."

"Is that so?"

"But I want to know why you're really here."

She blinked, and a lizard calculation flashed under her long lashes. "I'll tell you," she said. "But you won't believe me."

Ajay picked his cheaters from where they hung from their chain and placed them on the bridge of his nose. A readout in the surveillance logs showed the status of local cameras. "There's nothing recording in here right now. You may speak freely." It was a lie, but one he thought he could get away with.

"I don't care about recordings. Jocelyn Garver knows who I am to my father. She knows why I was sent."

Ajay let his cheaters dangle from their chain.

"When I was young, I went to a private school. The other girls were so frivolous." She looked at her perfectly painted nails. "Everything they cared about was worthless to me. Fashion, beauty, status among their peers."

"I can imagine."

"You can't." Her clipped voice left no room for argument. "You're looking at me and thinking that I must have changed, and of course, you'd be right. Back then I was the tough girl. The ugly girl. I was picked on by those girls in middle school, and their words stung. I wanted to hurt them, and I think my father understood that, so he let me make a choice.

"He told me that there were ways to move through the world that would make me impervious to anything anyone else could do to me. There was a way to be perfect, to take control of my life and never feel fear ever again. He said to me that there was another school where girls could become the best of themselves. They could learn to survive. I could go there if I wanted, but there was a price. When I was finished, I would work for him in the family business.

"Looking back, I don't know that there was ever really a choice. He offered it to me as I hit my absolute lowest as an awkward young girl. There was a dance at school, and on my way there I took a shortcut through the woods. It was the same shortcut I always took, but this time I was dressed up." She indicated her fancy dress. "Not quite *this* dressed up, but you understand. When I got to the event, I was muddy. Twigs in my hair. The other children were ruthless.

"I came home distraught that evening, and that was when Declan first met me. He still sees me as this wild kid who would rather run through the woods than set foot in a formal ballroom. I think that might have been the first time he investigated my father's business, but I don't know that he's ever really stopped. Declan was always so friendly to me when I was young. That's why he thinks of the current me as a phony, but he's wrong. This is me just as much as that twig-haired girl.

"My father approached me as I was humiliated by the brutal nature of life and offered me salvation. Leave the school. Learn to be something more. Was there ever really any chance I would turn him down?"

Ajay watched as her right hand curled into a fist, and he wondered if the show of emotion was a rehearsed part of her speech.

"At first the skills they taught us were fun. Martial arts. Wilderness survival. They taught us to be tough girls in a tough world. How to move with confidence in our own bodies. There weren't many of us. A dozen at most, but the girls came and went over the years. Eventually, the lessons moved from survival to dominance. They taught us how to navigate social situations as invisible specters, then as peers of any population, then as divas to be worshiped." She gestured to her countenance, with her perfect body in a perfect gown. "They taught us how to be perfect in any situation."

Nailah ran a finger across the top of the knife block, tapping the nail of her index finger on the handle of each blade. "It wasn't until much later that they taught us how to kill."

"Your father sent you here to kill someone."

A flash of mirth crossed Nailah's lips that Ajay suspected was genuine. "That's what Declan suspects, but it's never that simple. If Father wanted an assassin, he would send one. That would be a simple business transaction." She drew a long, thin blade from the block. "For this, he wanted family. My father knew that something was wrong. He saw an invitation from Jocelyn Garver and recognized it for the attack that it was. It couldn't be refused without insult, but accepting meant a risk that he was not willing to take."

"He suspected violence?"

"My father always suspects violence. He hasn't gotten where he is today without making enemies." She glanced at Olexie on the table. "Some more dangerous than others."

"Olexie took a drone to the skull. He's usually much more intimidating."

"Mm-hmm. Well, my father is aware of your

friend. He's not worried." Nailah took the knife between her delicate fingers and cut a slice of pumpkin pie. Wisps of steam curled into the dry air.

"Who was he worried about when he saw the guest list?"

Nailah smiled. "Who *wasn't* he worried about? The Trowbridges have been a thorn in his side for ages, with their social climbing. Father doesn't like the idea of upstarts like them threatening his empire. The fact that they had an invite from Jocelyn Garver was threat enough. Maybe they weren't physically threatening, but putting them in the same group as the esteemed Wilson Lee? Could there be a greater insult? He would have been ruined if he had come."

Ajay waved that off. "I'm too old to care about social climbers."

"Then you don't know how society works. It's survival of the fittest out there." She lifted the slice of pie onto a plate. "Pie?"

He was about to refuse, but Ajay's stomach betrayed him with a growl. He hadn't eaten supper, and all the running around had exhausted him. He accepted the pie and found a fork in a nearby drawer.

"Theodore Parks was the real danger, I thought," Nailah said as she cut herself another slice. "Until he showed up dead."

"Yes, you mentioned he solved problems for your father."

"I meant that he was a hired thug and assassin."

"Yeah, I got that. What were you looking for?"

Nailah's frown darkened her brow. "What do you mean?"

"On the body. When Declan and I looked out the window."

She drew a long, slow breath. "A marker. Something to indicate that he was working for my father."

"Was he?"

"No."

"I wouldn't mind knowing who he worked for," said Ajay.

"What makes you think I'm not the killer?" Nailah raised that perfect eyebrow again.

The pie was perfect. Hot and firm and exploding with nutmeg and cinnamon. "Intuition," Ajay said through a full mouth. "You're far too competent to leave the mess that we've seen tonight."

"Yes, well," said Nailah, taking a tiny first bite of her pie. "I *am* well trained, I suppose."

"And you wouldn't leave the bodies in the conditions we found them. Why not hide the bodies and let the dinner continue, or wait until later in the night when the act could be better concealed?"

"Or use poison," Nailah said, taking another dainty bite of her pie.

Ajay's pumpkin pie suddenly tasted heavy in his mouth. "Are you a poisoner?"

"I was taught by the best," Nailah said, "But of all the people at this dinner party, you are the one who does not threaten my father at all."

"Not even socially?"

"He sees you as Jocelyn's charity case. She's letting you pretend to be a civilized person."

"Your father sure seems like a charming guy."

"He has his moments." Nailah took a larger bite of her pie and chewed it slowly as if enjoying every molecule of its existence. "Robert also isn't much of a threat. He's a bit of a blowhard, but he comes from a good line and tends to make business decisions that are profitable to my father."

"Good to know."

"That daughter of his, though. She's trouble."

Ajay set his fork down and stared at Nailah. "What was that?"

"That girl's clumsy training was nothing like what I got. If he thinks she'll be taken in, he will be sorely disappointed."

"Taken in?"

"To the school," said Nailah. "I thought that was obvious by the way he was groveling and speaking of her all the time Jocelyn was around."

"Jocelyn?" Ajay asked. "What does she—" But he didn't need to continue, because he understood. The reason for his invitation, the meeting with Kylie, the threat of taking custody as the better-established grandparent.

"Jocelyn Garver funds the school that taught me," Nailah said. "But even I can see that Gabby is dangerously unhinged. If you're looking for a killer, Mr. Andersen, you need not look farther." Nailah touched a napkin to the corners of her mouth. "Your girl, on the other hand, will make a perfect candidate if she's interested."

Ajay's blood went cold. "Kylie wants a normal life."

"Don't we all?"

Ajay crossed to the wide double doors in the kitchen entrance. He didn't wait for Nailah to follow but noticed when she did. Leaving Olexie, he found the panel that would give him access to the server room. It opened with a touch, and he squeezed through the narrow walls until he found the place where the router still hummed quietly. The other passage—the one Melinda had used before—was closed and locked, cutting off a wide swath of Jocelyn's secret passageways. It was for the best, really. Ajay didn't know what he would say to her if he could walk up and talk to the woman.

He connected his wires to the machine, slipped his cheaters onto the bridge of his nose, and got to work.

CHAPTER TWENTY-SEVEN

Kylie stared into Gabby's eyes, fascinated by the emotions playing across the younger girl's face. Those were *Kylie's* emotions, matched perfectly as soon as she was feeling them. How was the girl *doing* that?

Kylie had told Gabby to empty herself. To get rid of everything that hurt and just focus on functioning for the rest of the night. It was what Kylie would do. It's what Kylie *had* done on several occasions. It was the easiest way to get the cascading failure of her brain under control.

Gabby, apparently, was emptying herself just fine. She did it so well that there was nothing left, and what remained was what? A blank slate? A perfect mimic?

"It's a quantum computer," Kylie said, reading the label on the towering machine in the center of the room. "There's no way Papa can hack this security system."

"He'll break it," Gabby said, reflecting Kylie's own misgivings. It was creepy.

"Papa wouldn't break it. He's way smarter than that. He'll test the limits of what he can do and stop because he'll see it's not a good idea." Kylie stroked Garrison's head. The dog had brought her out of a crisis earlier, and she still depended on him for emotional support. Without him, she would probably curl up in a dark corner and wait for the world to end.

Gabby blinked. A little of the tension dropped from her shoulders.

"Yeah, you're right," said Kylie with a sigh of frustration. "He's not going to stop. He's going to need our help."

There was a single functioning monitor on the obelisk of a machine, and its text-only display was not something Kylie knew how to use. She extended the keyboard from its hidden compartment, typed a few basic commands, and watched as the data flowed from the machine.

"I wish it had a hundred video displays," Gabby said, reflecting Kylie's wishes.

"Stop that."

Gabby stood next to Kylie and sighed a supremely irritating sigh.

"It's time to come back," Kylie said without looking up from the screen. She had managed to get it to display an impressive list of connected devices. "You have to let yourself back in, Gabby."

"This is better," said Gabby. Kylie couldn't

decide if the sentiment was a reflection of her own desires. It really *was* better than having Gabby weeping big snotty tears everywhere, but it couldn't possibly be healthy.

Plus, Kylie worried that her own emotions were being reflected on the girl. She didn't feel a network connection, so how was Gabby even getting that information?

"It's not healthy." Kylie searched the long device list for anomalies. Dozens of drones and ground-mounted security mechanisms were reporting errors. A whole utility section was marked as available, but she couldn't figure out what they were. Many bots were completely offline. Every few seconds another one threw out an alert and went dark. "Plus, I'd like to talk to you again, Gabby."

"We can talk all you like."

"Yeah, but if I wanted to talk to myself, I'd talk to Garrison."

Garrison looked hurt by the comment, but not too bad. He was, after all, the best listener.

"Found it!" Kylie said.

"Yes!"

Kylie shot the girl a dirty look. On the screen, she had a peripheral security device that was undergoing anomalous behavior. Red text flashed warnings about unauthorized access, then a cascade of green text granted access to that user. Was Papa such a clumsy hacker? She could have done much better.

The obelisk hummed in response. On the screen,

the red text overwhelmed the green, and the user was booted out.

Kylie punched a message, *security's plugged into a quantum computer.*

After a long pause, a message appeared on her screen in blue text. *That explains a lot.* Then, after another pause, it said, *Kylie?*

hey papa

She tried a few commands on the quantum computer again, but nothing made sense. There were too many variables, and most of the basic commands she knew didn't work on the strange operating system.

i don't know how to use this stupid thing, she wrote.

The red text flashed across the screen, followed by another wave of green, then red. As far as she could tell, he was trying the exact same thing again.

"He's being stupid," said Gabby, picking up on her thoughts. Or maybe she was just reading the expression on Kylie's face.

Kylie forced a neutral expression. Papa tried the exact same thing a third time.

I think I almost have it, he said. Did he really think he was doing something special?

"Papa told me one time of a machine learning computer that was able to trick people into doing what they wanted," she explained to Gabby, hoping the girl couldn't actually read her mind. "I think that's what it's doing to him. It's showing him near-success over and over again, giving him hints at what to do next each time. It's been trained on what hacks look like, so that's what it's showing him."

"And it's working," Gabby said.

"Yeah, but if he ever manages to bypass it, he might crash the whole system." Kylie tried another command in the text interface. Anything she entered that wasn't a list of connected devices went straight to error codes.

"That's bad."

Kylie said, "Maybe it's tricking me into thinking I'm texting with my grandpa."

"We might never know," said Gabby.

"You need to stop reading my mind," Kylie said, trying hard to suppress the annoyance in her voice.

A hint of a smile tweaked the corner of Gabby's lips, and it definitely wasn't something Kylie was feeling. Maybe the girl was starting to recover.

"Are you coming back?" Kylie asked.

Gabby's grin widened.

"Okay..." Kylie took a step back. She couldn't read the other girl's expression very well, but something felt very strange about the smile. Her eyes didn't dance the way they did with a real smile. It reminded Kylie of a shark. "Are you feeling better?"

Then she saw the flash of the knife in Gabby's hand, and everything got a whole lot worse.

CHAPTER TWENTY-EIGHT

FDSACHAYLERJLADNAFSAFJS, said the message on Ajay's text display. He didn't know what that meant. Maybe it was code for something, but texting with teenagers wasn't usually *this* confusing.

He blasted off a quick response before trying another procedure on the security rig. He had been so close last time. A fraction of a second of access was all he really needed to grant himself everything. Melinda had said doing so would shut the whole system down, but he didn't see that trigger at all. The only trigger he saw was for the pulse overload contingency, and he now knew how to *not* trigger that one. The security shutdown must have been a bluff.

He hoped it was a bluff.

This hack was about timing. Every time he tried the routine, he tightened things up. His read-only access would give him access to a password file, then he'd crack the password and grant himself operator access. That was his window. While he had operator access, if he could rewrite that password file, he would be able to log in as any user in the system.

Simple.

But as soon as he granted himself operator access, a background process came through and cleaned it up. It was annoying and clever, but with perfect timing, he could create persistent access to everything. Waves of code flew across his lenses, flashing data long after the routine finished. Another failure.

Too late. Again. He had coded a delay into the system when his first password file rewrite had hit too early. It took time for his access to propagate through the machine, and when he hit it too early, he got a denial error because his operator access wasn't in place yet.

"I thought this would be quick," Nailah said.

"Go check on Olexie," Ajay snapped.

She quietly left the security room.

Growling with frustration, Ajay adjusted his routine and sent another wave of access requests. The routine would only work if the local security router was overwhelmed, delaying its response by a fraction of a cycle. It would be enough. His gut told him this was the strategy to hack this kind of system. He'd done it before on so many other similar machines. A perfect system had never been deployed. There was always a flaw, and this was it.

Too early.

The text drove the razor-sharp spike of a migraine into Ajay's skull. Too early? But he had tested this code and the window had changed. He ran it again. Same result. Again. Same. Proper software testing meant trying the same thing over and over again and expecting different results. Again.

Access granted.

"Yes!"

Revoked.

"Are you fucking with me?" Ajay grumbled at the machine. This wasn't how it worked. It couldn't be. There was something seriously wrong. He took a step back and stared at the machine. How could this router handle the security system, including all of its drones and scanners and the weapons lockbox, but not grant access from the central security core?

He tweaked the program, changing the timing window once again. He ran it without pausing to think through his expectations. After all, it didn't matter. He hit the timing window too early by one ten-thousandths of a second. Pretty close, but not good enough.

Again.

Processing...

Ajay stared at the screen, holding his breath for as long as a breath could possibly be held. The three dots made an open end to the return that gaped like a hungry void, consuming one hundred percent of his attention from that point until the end of eternity.

The command prompt returned with no results.

"What?" he shouted.

fake

The single word appeared on his screen in the same way that Kylie's messages had, but flashed for only a second before disappearing, consumed by the machine. When it was gone, a new command prompt appeared, blinking in a garish chartreuse.

"Oh," Ajay muttered to the computer. "You *are* fucking with me."

He tentatively tried some commands on the chartreuse prompt, finding it very similar to the earlier version. It used a much newer version of the shell language, one he wasn't quite as familiar with, but it responded to his queries and showed him the active processes. One was a simple AI program—probably the one he had been unknowingly interfacing with. Another took inputs in the style of a quantum computer.

That made Ajay blink. Personal quantum computers were illegal, being considered both too powerful and too impractical for personal use. Quantum computing requests were typically funneled through the Cube, an infrastructure service made available to everyone. Kylie had said there was one down in her panic room, but he hadn't believed it. Reliable, functional quantum computers were still too expensive to operate on a regular basis for all but the wealthiest individuals. Not that Jocelyn needed to worry about such trivial things as money.

Ajay owned a prototype handheld quantum computer, but its function was limited. It also didn't work worth a damn half the time. Or, rather, the stupid thing was always in a state of both working and not working. A Schrödinger's machine. Ajay chuckled to himself at his stupid quantum dad joke. He'd need to use that one later.

The problem he faced now was that the newer version of the operating system shell didn't allow the timing hack. He was still in read-only mode, and he needed access to something better. He poked around in the data files and checked the latest updates. They were recent. Someone was maintaining this server and everything connected to it. He assumed Melinda was responsible for that.

And there it was. In order to gain access, he needed to cycle the hardware. He had to shut everything down. There was no way around it that he could see.

I need to reboot, he wrote to Kylie, hoping she was still reading. He didn't know how a shutdown would affect her in the panic room, but he needed to warn her.

The cursor blinked.

"Any luck?" Nailah said behind him.

Olexie leaned against the wall next to her. He looked better, but his eyes didn't quite focus on the same reality Ajay was experiencing. "Ajay is the best hacker I know," he mumbled.

"I can do it," Ajay said, "but the entire security system is coming down when I pull the trigger."

"Make it not do that," Olexie said.

"It's all I can do to keep Melinda's defense grid from toasting every electronic device in the room."

To Nailah, Olexie whispered, "Usually he would make it not do that."

Nailah snorted, and amusement twinkled in her eyes.

Ajay ground his teeth, "At first, Parks is going to think it's a trick. He'll proceed cautiously to test the limits of his newfound access. Then he'll approach."

Nailah said, "If he comes close, we'll tear him to shreds."

"Damn," Olexie said.

"Metaphorically," she said.

"What?" Olexie blinked rapidly.

Nailah slowly shook her head. "It's a figure of speech."

"Still."

Ajay said, "He'll send his drones first. He has a whole vanload of tech that'll walk all over us if he can flood these halls."

"Drones do not walk," said Olexie.

"It's a figure of speech," said Ajay.

"Every door and corner of this place will be a deathtrap," said Nailah.

"Presumably, he's after whoever killed his husband." Ajay peered at the text blinking in his cheaters. "But I don't care how bad things get. I'm not handing him Gabby, so we need to stall."

"Or kill him," said Olexie.

Nailah nodded.

"We can fight drones in the woods," Olexie said.

"Metaphorically?" Ajay asked.

"What?" Olexie blinked. "The signal is bad by the pines."

Ajay peered at the tall Russian. Olexie had a point. The signal *had* been bad there. The interference had scrambled his own systems. It might do the same to Parks's drones. "It's wide open. That's worse than fighting in the mansion."

"What other options do we have?" Nailah asked.

Ajay spun the wireframe map of the mansion, paying special attention to the pine grove location. Directly under it on the map was a room. An octagonal room with tunnels leading out in all directions. One led directly to the edge of the property where Parks waited with his drone army. "He's not going to come by way of the forest," Ajay said.

"Why not?" asked Olexie.

"Because once security's down, he'll be able to go *under* the forest." Ajay tracked the tunnels until he knew how to reach the octagon. "I know where we can stop him, but we'll still need to bring our own barriers for cover." He described the location to them and gave them instructions on how to reach it via the tunnel behind the weapons vault.

Nailah pulled Olexie away from the wall. "Are you well enough to carry something heavy for me?"

"I am definitely not."

"He's fine," said Ajay. "But hold on before you go. I'm going to unlock the weapon's vault."

Olexie snorted with laughter. "You are giving everyone weapons? You are an idiot." When Ajay didn't respond, he added, "Metaphorically."

Nailah rolled her eyes.

"Gabby is the murderer," Ajay said. "If she's the killer, then the others should be as trustworthy as it's going to get."

"So, Kylie is in danger," Olexie said.

"Yes." Saying it send an icicle into Ajay's heart.

"But there's nothing you can do about it."

"Correct." Ajay ground his teeth. "There's nothing I can do to get inside the panic room unless they open the door from the inside."

"Wait," said Olexie, "we will fight in the forest?"

"No."

Olexie grumbled, "I do not understand."

Ajay turned back to the computer and saw a series of messages from Kylie.

not a panic room

secure data center

gabby is not the killer

she is the weapon

shut it all down

Ajay stared at the screen as the chartreuse cursor

blinked innocently. *Gabby is the weapon.* He didn't like that.

That meant there was still a killer out there. It could be anyone, and he was about to give deadly weapons to the least trustworthy of the guests.

But what else was there to do?

Ajay shut it down.

CHAPTER TWENTY-NINE

KYLIE'S ARM raked against the keyboard as she stumbled away from Gabby. The girl had deadly cold in her eyes, like the icy rage that Kylie had once felt. It was unnerving, and the bloody knife in Gabby's hand didn't help.

"I'm not reading your mind," said Gabby.

"I wasn't thinking that."

"Yes, you were."

Kylie took a step back. The younger girl unnerved her for reasons beyond the knife in her hand and the uncanny twist of her lips. "You're getting interference from your machine brain."

"So are you."

"I'm not." Kylie took another step back, but Gabby moved in closer. "I've isolated it."

"You're pretending to be something you're not so that your grandpa is happy for you."

"And what are you doing?"

Gabby's grip on her knife was so tight her knuckles went white. "I'm doing whatever I want."

Kylie needed a different approach. "You're scaring me, Gabby."

"That's because I'm scary. We're both scary, Kylie. My dad tells me that I'm going to be the toughest one. I'll be better than any of the others out there. I'll keep him safe from anything because I've got all the right training to be dangerous."

"Dangerous to who?"

Gabby gestured at the walls. "Everyone."

"Including yourself?"

"I'm going to have whatever I want."

"Not free will."

Gabby's brow furrowed. "What's free will?"

Kylie didn't think it was a genuine question. Her grip on the situation was sliding, and her mouth went dry with panic.

Gabby stared at Kylie until their eyes met. Kylie hated the feeling of looking someone else in the eyes, but maybe Gabby needed some kind of connection.

But what she saw there made her more scared. Tears rolled down Gabby's cheeks. Her eyebrows were turned down in an expression of rage. Kylie didn't know how to interpret it. Not at all. She circled the big black quantum computer.

Gabby glanced down at the screen and a wide smile broke through her tears. She typed something with one hand. "Free will," she said. "That means I can do whatever I want, right?"

Kylie took a step forward—far enough to see that Gabby had sent a message to Papa, but not enough to see what that message was. "What are you doing?"

"He needed help."

"If you help him, he'll shut down security. We won't be safe here anymore."

Gabby watched text scroll across the screen. "We're not safe now."

"We could be. We could go back to the panic room and wait this out. They'll figure things out up above. We don't need to go where it's dangerous."

"You'd like that, wouldn't you?" Gabby typed something else on the machine. "But that's not a panic room, is it? It's the entry to a bunker, but it's not safe. This is Mrs. Garver's private control room. That's why she tried to come down here."

"You'll kill them."

Gabby considered this. She typed as she spoke. "I'm not a killer," she said. "I'm a weapon."

"You don't think you have free will?"

"I don't think you know what free will is, and if it's something I have, then it's something I'm using to help everyone."

"Gabby, please."

The girl typed one last thing and said, "We need to shut everything down."

Then she turned to Kylie, raised her knife, and attacked.

CHAPTER THIRTY

"WE NEED TO FIND THE ASSASSIN," Ajay said as the system cycled.

"What?" said Olexie.

Ajay pushed past Olexie and Nailah and levered open the panel into the hallway. "Chay Quinn is still in the house."

Olexie said, "Chay Quinn is the killer, no doubt."

"We agreed it wasn't her," Ajay said.

Nailah stared at Ajay. "Chay Quinn?" The lights flickered.

"She's a hired killer," Ajay explained.

"I never said it wasn't her," said Olexie. "I specifically remember saying it *was* her."

Nailah pressed her lips together.

Ajay said, "It couldn't have been her, Olexie."

"She is guilty," asked Olexie.

The hallway lights flickered again. On his glasses, Ajay saw the datastream flowing past. He had paired his system to the security tree, so he would be solely in charge of the entire property.

When it came up, which was a slow process.

He wouldn't have all of the security routines that Melinda had been using. He would have control, but it would be a hobbled, difficult kind of control.

Ajay jabbed Olexie in the chest with his cane. "I was with Quinn when Nailah was attacked," he said. "And I believe her when she says that's not her job tonight."

"She is duplicitous," muttered Olexie.

"So are you."

Olexie let out a roar of frustration and stalked toward the kitchen.

"Let him go," said a voice behind Ajay.

He turned to see Chay Quinn step from the shadow. Nailah saw her at the same time but didn't show any hint of surprise.

"Chay," Nailah said, her voice dripping with contempt.

Chay's eyes sparkled. "Hello, dear."

Ajay blinked. "You..."

"Dated," said Nailah. "In school."

One of Chay's eyebrows raised, accentuating a scar down its middle. She looked Nailah up and down. "You're doing well."

"You're stuck here the same as us," said Ajay.

Chay's eyes narrowed. "Maybe I'm working for Parks."

"You're working for Frontier, aren't you? Someone sent you here for my granddaughter."

"Well, I'm not doing a very good job of that, am I? Someone's locked the girl away."

Nailah stepped toward Chay, who slowly circled the taller woman. They reminded Ajay of two cats contemplating battle or sex or both.

"People get me wrong sometimes," said Chay. "I'm not a hired killer like you say."

"But you kill people," Ajay said. "For money."

"No. I kill people for fun. Sometimes I get paid for it."

"That's... not better."

Chay chuckled. She still circled Nailah, keeping the woman in the corner of her eye. "The Parks boys both work for Frontier, just like me. What makes you think I'm not working for Alexander?"

"Easy," said Ajay. "If this was a simple reconnaissance mission, you'd be out of here by now. You could walk out the front door and the drones would leave you alone."

"The front door?" said Chay. "Tried it. Windows, too. All the ways out are sealed. Right now I'm thinking the roof might be the best option, but I haven't found a way to it yet."

Ajay filed the information away for later. Escape from the house wasn't as urgent as the weaponized drones about to descend on them. Plus, once he had control of the security system, he ought to be able to remove the lockdown, but there were no controls for the locks, and nothing in this new layer hinted at a system that would fry electronics if someone tried to hack in. Ajay tipped his hat to Melinda. It had been a hell of a bluff. He moved closer to Chay. "I think Alexander Parks is off-script and it's scaring you."

She stopped. "Frontier will take care of Alexander."

"Eventually. That doesn't do us any good, does it?" Ajay narrowed his eyes. "Did you take the gun?"

Nailah's nostrils flared. "I would have known if she was nearby."

"She was with me when that attack happened. I don't have proof for the actual murders." Gabby, both of them. Ajay was sure of it. But what had Kylie meant when she texted that Gabby was the weapon, not the killer? Could Chay be controlling Gabby? He didn't put it past her, and the technology *did* exist.

"Do you have the gun?" Nailah asked.

"What makes you think I would have it?"

"You're a thief," Nailah spat.

"It was one job," Chay snapped.

"And you *took* it from me!" Nailah's clenched her fists.

Ajay held out his hands. "Now hold on—"

Nailah twitched, and a knife was in Chay's hand faster than Ajay could blink. He took a step back.

Chay pointed the narrow blade at Nailah. "You're looking for a killer, Mr. Andersen? Ask her about Helsinki. Memphis. Lagos."

Nailah looked at Chay through half-lidded eyes.

"We all have our pasts," Ajay said. "Right now I'm interested in getting out. Going home and finding safety." A mapping system came online in his cheaters, and he activated the overlay. It showed all the corners of the mansion, even the hidden passages and their entrances. It even showed the network of tunnels below the basement, but the labels didn't appear when he tried to find what those tunnels held. "We need to meet the rest of the guests."

Nailah ignored him. "I'm not like you, Chay. I'm not a killer."

Chay sized her up. "No. You're the distraction. Nobody kills with a dress like that." She appeared to reconsider. "Although it's the right color to hide the stains, isn't it?"

A knife appeared in Nailah's hand, held close to her wrist so that it was hidden behind her arm. From his angle, Ajay could see the weapon, but he didn't know if Chay had seen it. If he said something, he would betray Nailah. If he didn't, Chay might be taken by surprise.

"Stop," he said. "Both of you."

"You had the protection contracts," Nailah whispered. "Every one of them."

"We saw you coming a mile away," said Chay. "From the moment you landed in the country, we knew you were there. They wouldn't let me take you down."

"You would have failed."

The women circled each other again, stalking each other in the empty hall.

A map of the forest appeared in Ajay's cheaters. It was a loose wireframe, but it showed glowing red where the intruding drones gathered at the forest edge. Another set of markers showed Loretta, Robert, and Declan in the foyer. Ajay selected the remains of the perimeter defense and activated them into a basic holding pattern. He found controls for the vault and the anti-weapons AI and disabled them both.

"They know, don't they?" Nailah said.

Chay's expression was flat, but the hatred radiated from her. "I'm not here to kill anyone."

"No, you're not," said Nailah. She didn't even bother glancing at the knife in Chay's hand. "But you might do it for fun."

"Parks knows what this party is. He knows why all of you are here."

Ajay thumped his cane on the floor. "Ladies," he said.

They both turned to him, and he felt the raw intensity of their gaze.

"We need to leave," Ajay insisted.

They glanced at each other. As one, they stowed their weapons, and a pressure lifted from Ajay's chest. He hadn't known what he would do if they had decided to kill each other. It was still a distinct possibility, but now he knew he could take a few breaths before it happened.

"Truce," he said.

The women didn't disagree.

As they turned to leave, Olexie whispered, "That was very intense."

"I'm leaving cameras disabled," he said as they walked through the wide hall. "Jocelyn and Melinda probably want to watch everything happening here, but I can deny them that."

Chay turned and walked away into the dark. "You'll be blind, too."

"You won't help us?" Ajay asked.

"You can't afford my rates, old man," said Chay. "And anyway, I still have work to do." With that, she disappeared into the dark.

"Well, that's ominous," said Ajay.

"I can't believe you tried to work with her," hissed Nailah.

"Nobody's coming to save us," Ajay said, "so we can't turtle up. Nobody's stopping Parks from following us if we leave. We only have one option."

Nailah pinched the bridge of her nose. When they finally arrived back at the foyer, she asked, "What's the plan?"

"Easy," Ajay said. The others had left, so the room with the weapons safe was open. Inside, a rack of guns stood open to the world. Ajay plucked his multitool from the rack and put it back in his pocket where it belonged. "I've got a suspicious number of skilled killers and a whole pile of weapons. We're going to see if, for once, violence is the answer."

CHAPTER THIRTY-ONE

"Violence is *not* the answer," Kylie shouted as she darted through the tunnels. Stone walls flashed past under the light of her fidget. The slick rock grew uneven under her feet, and she skidded to a stop.

Gabby followed. The girl was fast, but the tunnels were a maze.

Great gulps of air stank like mold and rot. Kylie started again down another passage, careful to keep Gabby's scuffing footsteps far enough back. How easy was it following someone through these empty passages? Kylie's light would give her away, but she couldn't kill the light because then she would be completely blind, and operating blind would be stupid. The darkness down at the bottom of the world was oppressive. Dangerous all on its own. A twisted ankle. A head injury. Kylie imagined wasting away in the black until the end of time.

She forced herself to run again. Her feet pounded against the wet stone.

What else could she do? Gabby had a knife. Kylie knew *how* to take a knife from someone, but that didn't mean she could do it. Her martial arts class was more calisthenics than actual self-defense. Aikido didn't teach her how to return the attack. It didn't teach her body how to dominate a smaller enemy.

She came to another junction. Above, the ceiling rose into darkness and the floor dropped away in a flight of double-sized steps. She hopped down one at a time, careful to keep her feet steady underneath her. At the bottom of the room, the tunnel narrowed into another exit. It spiraled downward into the earth.

No signals reached her now. Not even the constant hum of the mansion's non-standard wireless system lingered in the back of her senses. There was only one flickering signal available now.

Gabby.

The flash attack from the drone was still a dull ache under her eyelids. It had been a flurry of data meant to overwhelm her and destroy her defenses. It had been a hack pointed at her, meant to knock her out.

Worse, it had almost succeeded.

At the bottom of the wide stairs, Kylie spun and watched the far entrance.

A familiar shape appeared in the doorway. Four legs, black as the night, and jowls for days. Garrison.

Dammit. She'd never get away if Gabby followed the dog.

Then, Gabby appeared as a shadow, lurking at the very edge of Kylie's ring of white light. "She'll only take one of us." Gabby's flat voice almost sounded sad. "My dad says this is my only chance."

Garrison loped down the big stairs and nuzzled Kylie's hand. She didn't want to encourage his behavior, but she couldn't help it and gave him a quick ear rub. Maybe if he loved her enough, he would leap to her protection.

The dog curled up in a ball and started snoring.

"He's still awake," Kylie said as if that might convince Gabby to be more cautious. "He just snores sometimes."

Gabby hopped down one step, the thump of her feet on the step knocking hollowly against the room's oppressive silence. "Can you hear it? There's nothing down here. No connection. No signal."

Kylie reached out with her senses and felt the vast void. It was isolating and scary. Her heart hammered in her chest and her lungs constricted. What if she died down here? There would be no way to send a final message to Austin. To Isabelle. Why hadn't she sent anything else to them over the course of the evening? She wished Austin were there by her side, even though that meant he would be in danger. Did that make her an awful friend? He would know how to deal with Gabby. He would probably know exactly what the girl was thinking and be able to say just the right thing to calm her down.

But Kylie didn't have that skill. When she looked at Gabby's face, she saw twitching lips and glassy eyes. She saw red along the ridge of the girl's nostrils and hair matted close to her head. It meant nothing to Kylie. All she saw was danger. A danger that needed to be dealt with.

Kylie found the signal from Gabby's machine brain and pushed.

At first, she tried to be subtle. She threw out a series of keys like the ones she'd worked with Papa to form. They were the first feelers in a multi-pronged attack. She'd fire them out, take measure of the response, and adjust her next moves accordingly.

Gabby blinked rapidly.

Then she retaliated. A denial of service attack, brutal and intense, hit Kylie like a million touches from a million grasping fingers. It quickly overwhelmed Kylie and she gasped. Dropped her connections.

"I've got training," Gabby said, hopping down another step. "Father taught me the basics and I pay attention in my martial arts classes."

"Yeah?" Kylie asked. "Well so do I." She dropped into a ready stance. When Gabby launched herself from the final step, Kylie snapped an open palm at the girl's hand. The girl's wrist snapped into her grip and she twisted, sending the knife skittering across the floor.

Holy crap, it worked.

Gabby recovered fast. She twisted free and struck out at Kylie, landing a punch on her jaw that made the world spin. A knee to the gut sent Kylie sprawling backward, where she landed next to Garrison.

"Sorry, bud," she said as she gave the snoring dog a quick pet. Even that small touch helped her center herself.

Gabby went for the knife, but Kylie launched herself up and snatched the girl's ankle, pulling hard. She yanked, and Gabby's chin struck the stone.

But her fingers closed on the knife.

A slash. Pain. Kylie's arm burned and she let go. Gabby snarled and lunged.

Then fell. Her foot skidded across the slick rock. Kylie stomped at Gabby's hand, missing it but pinning the knife to the wet stone.

Kylie punched hard, but Gabby squirmed away, leaving the knife. A roll and a kick at Kylie's head.

Then came Gabby's barrage of network noise. It washed over Kylie like an unrelenting tsunami. It threatened to drown her thoughts in the noise of a million voices.

A scream tore itself from Kylie's lips as she spiraled away into the black nothing. She grasped for anything to ground her. Garrison. The floor. Anything. The voices chattered in her head, resonating against her skull, amplified into a rising cacophony.

Her head smacked against the wall, and her

fingers grasped the floor. Somehow, she had a vague idea of Gabby pulling herself to her feet. She was a dark shadow in the great sucking void of space. She spoke, but Kylie couldn't pick her voice out from the millions.

"No," Kylie whispered.

Everything Papa had taught her died under the smoky flames of her own panic. All the half-learned lessons on network security and all the ignored speeches about data integrity dissolved under the weight of Gabby's million voices and the panicked fury that came with them. All Kylie had left was instinct.

She grabbed one voice from the million, shunting everything else into the dark null, but as soon as she did, a million more voices screamed at her. Then a million more.

But she held onto that one. It was a child's words, singing a song about ashes. Jumping rope. Sisters.

Gabby snarled and swung a fist, but it bounced harmlessly off Kylie's shoulder.

The sisters went everywhere together. They were twins. They danced through the halls of a strange place. A mansion. Gabby struck again, this time pounding a balled fist into Kylie's cheek. It stung.

Kylie forced herself to look at Gabby. Forced herself to make eye contact.

Gabby swung again, but Kylie caught the momentum, pulled, and threw Gabby against the wall. The girl landed in a heap next to a nonplussed Garrison.

"I had a sister, too," Kylie snarled. She still *did* have a sister, but Isabelle hadn't visited in ages. She never messaged anymore. The pain of that abandonment added to the agony of static in Kylie's skull.

The noise that came from the back of Gabby's throat was more animal than human. She hit Kylie with a full tackle, driving her backward. Her back struck one of the giant stairs. Kylie's breath escaped, and she gasped at the damp air.

Gabby balled her fists and struck. Once. Twice. Three times. The blows were small but incredibly strong. Her skinny arms focused her fury into pelts like meteor strikes. The girl put every ounce of strength into each blow, and Kylie lost all ability to think of a response.

Garrison let out one chest-shaking low woof. He stood at attention, staring at Gabby.

The million voices disappeared.

Gabby stopped. Her face did a dance of emotions, none of which Kylie could really grasp.

"Stop," Gabby cried as she stumbled back, grasping her head. "Just stop."

Then, she ran.

CHAPTER THIRTY-TWO

AJAY STEPPED into the octagonal room, the quantum machine at its center like a ghost against the shadowy black of the tunnel walls. His eyes adjusted to the dim glow of the blue lights above, diffused by a pall of dust. Electric tension hung heavy in the air.

Nailah stepped into the room beside him. Robert, Declan, and Loretta already waited across the room.

"This is a terrible place," Declan said. "There's almost no cover."

"It's better than the pine grove," Ajay said, pointing up at the roots dangling from the ceiling.

Olexie tromped behind Nailah with a mound of heavy tapestries on his back.

"See, I knew you could do it," Ajay said, slapping the Russian on the back.

"Why?" Olexie gasped.

"These drones are firing needles," said Ajay, peeling the first of the tapestries from him. He gestured for Robert to help, and together they affixed the heavy Vietnam scene so that it spanned half of the room. "Needles are great for killing unarmored targets, but the tight weave in these tapestries is enough to slow them down to a painful sting."

Nailah nudged the tapestry with a long-barreled pistol she had taken from the weapons safe. "Bullets will go right through it. Good plan."

Robert eyed the woman. "How did you get so comfortable with a gun?"

She flashed him a sideways smile. "Practice."

Ajay pointed with his cane at the various positions where he wanted a drape. He watched the feed on his cheaters. Parks was using the foothold his bots had gained during the security shutdown to open a door recessed into the hillside. "The interference in this room should keep his drones from targeting accurately, and we're all armed. This is our best chance to make a stand." A boxy automatic weapon hung at Ajay's hip. He didn't relish the idea of firing it, but he'd at least practiced a little with some firearms. He was confident he could hit a drone at ten feet. Twenty was a stretch, but the tapestries would help him get close.

Loretta held a small pistol limply at her side. She stared into the distance.

Ajay placed a hand on her arm. "I'm sorry," he said.

Her lip turned up in a sneer. "I'm sure you are."

"We'll get to the bottom of this."

"You said that before," she said. "But here we are."

"Survive the night first, then we'll figure out who is responsible for your husband's death."

She pulled her arm away. "I didn't want to come tonight. Percival insisted."

"Why?" Ajay asked. "What exactly was everyone trying to get out of this night?"

"We had a daughter once," Loretta said. "Before everything."

"Was she murdered?"

"No. Yes. I don't know." Loretta looked down at the gun in her hand. "Our lives were going well. Perfect, really. Investments were coming in with solid gains. Percival bought into a franchise of resorts across Africa, and they were all wildly profitable. Fantastic investments. He sold a package deal. You could visit one of his hotels and never set foot outside of our perfectly controlled space." She glanced at Ajay. "It was a safe way to bring tourism to parts of the world that suffered."

Without having the inconvenience of alleviating any of that suffering, Ajay thought. In his glasses, he watched as motion sensors triggered near the tunnel entrance. Parks would launch an attack soon.

"We went to visit them. Our daughter Alisha, Percival, and me," Loretta said. "She was ten at the time, and clever as they come."

"How did she die?" Ajay asked.

"She fell. Every inch of that resort was safe, both

for kids and adults. It was a bubble where you didn't need to worry one second about anything, but Percival liked to venture out into the world. It happened in Lagos." Her lips pressed into a tight line. "That visit was the last time we were really happy. Percival said she couldn't possibly have climbed over the railing in that tower. Someone must have thrown her over the edge to get back at him."

"For what?"

Loretta gestured lazily with the gun. "I don't know. Taking their land. Taking money. After that, Percival grew paranoid. Without Alisha to ground him, he decided we should never leave the resorts. If we only flew from one to the next, we could be safe forever, he thought. He thought that world was big enough."

Olexie and Nailah hung another of the tapestries, forming a double-thick barrier that ran half the width of the room.

"Is that what you're here for?" Ajay asked. "You were looking for a replacement for your daughter?"

For a long time, Loretta didn't answer. Finally, she said, "I don't know. I just wanted a bodyguard, but Percival needed more. I think he wanted a girl who could defend herself. When Jocelyn told us fifteen years ago what they were doing, he bought into it. He believed this was our second chance."

Ajay watched the woman as she stared up at the roots in the ceiling. In the dim light, her skin looked extra pale, the set of her jaw like a bone glowing in a blacklight.

She glanced at her gun. "This is exactly the kind of thing our girl would have fixed."

"The tunnels?"

"The fear. Every day, we live in fear. Or wealth makes us targets, you know. It doesn't keep us happy." She looked out into the darkness. "Never really did, I suppose. And now they'll come for me. I swear, if I see Jocelyn, I'm not going to wait for her to explain. I'm going to—" Her gun fired into the ceiling, sending cries of alarm through the group. The gunshot echoed into silence. Loretta froze with her mouth open.

"Please take your finger from the trigger," Ajay said in the calmest voice he could manage. His feed from the security system flooded with alerts. The drones were coming.

Loretta seethed. "If this is how they expect to control me, they need to think again. Once Jocelyn gives me mine, I'll show them what it's like to be afraid."

Ajay asked, "Who's trying to control you?"

She blinked at him, tears shining in the corners of her eyes. "She said there would be enough."

"Enough what? What are you talking about?"

"Girls," Loretta said. "We only wanted one of our own. After all our investments, don't you think we deserved it?"

Girls. Bile rose in the back of Ajay's throat. He

had known it, but now that Loretta said it out loud, a new wave of nausea washed over him. Everything came back to Jocelyn's school. She trained them, then hired them out as bodyguards or assassins. Girls like Kylie, trained like Nailah or Chay. Whatever it took. Jocelyn's son invented a way to make an even more capable killer. She must have seen a surge in investment. She was planning on taking the world by storm.

But the investment didn't pan out. Kylie and Isabelle were the first, but they were also some of the few survivors of the program. Gabby somehow survived and ended up in Robert's care.

Ajay opened his mouth to ask for more details, but a flash across his cheaters told him there was no more time.

"Drones are incoming!" He flicked the safety off on his weapon, then stalked through the passages created by hanging tapestries. They formed an L around the central computer so that wherever they stood, they were only a step or two away from cover and there was no straight line across the space. "Loretta, take the center. Robert, Olexie, north side. Declan, you're with me."

"What about me?" said Nailah, her voice as calm as if she were asking him to pass the cream as she checked her weapon.

A drone burst through the entrance, swaying unsteadily as the magnetic wave interfered with its systems. Nailah raised a black pistol, fired two shots into its center, and watched as it dropped helplessly to the ground.

"I think you can go wherever you like," Ajay said.

She flashed a smile. "I'll take the side with Olexie. You take the center behind the computer."

Ajay couldn't think of a reason to argue. The center was the most protected space, and he probably wasn't much better a shot than Loretta. He hunkered down behind the tapestry, his light flashing against the grisly depiction of some WWII battle. Normandy? He couldn't tell. It probably didn't matter.

"What do they want?" Loretta hissed.

"They want us dead," Ajay said. "We want to not be dead. That's all that matters." Gunfire rang through the thick tapestries.

Loretta poked her gun through the narrow gap between tapestries but didn't fire. The whir of drones hummed outside, and a row of needles hit the tapestry. She yelped and jumped back. Blood welled from a wound on her hand.

"I'm shot!" she cried. Her gun clattered to the ground.

Declan fired his Glock, pinging the thing's carapace several times before it finally faltered and fell. He ducked back behind cover. Panicked sweat beaded on his face.

Thin needles stuck to the meat between Loretta's forefinger and thumb. Ajay plucked them out. "It wasn't deep. The tapestry slows the needles, but it doesn't stop them."

More shots. Olexie unleashed a string of Russian curses.

"Olexie figured that out, too." Ajay stepped up to the gap. Two drones floated there. Unarmored. He aimed carefully with two hands and squeezed off a few shots. Bullets thunked into the left drone, sending it into a downward spiral, spraying needles everywhere.

"Just be glad we have some cover," Ajay said. "This gives us a chance."

"A chance," Loretta spat, picking up her gun. "We don't have a chance. That's a professional hitman out there. He'll chew us apart." Her voice was high like the tension was strangling her.

"He'll have to come here and do it himself, then, because these drones aren't going to kill us." Ajay dropped the second drone. This one took three shots, but he was getting the hang of it. Aim. Fire. He almost didn't need to watch them spiral to the ground.

The drones retreated, leaving the room to wallow in silence.

"I won't hesitate to kill if I see him," Loretta whispered.

Ajay stared at the woman, surprised at the viciousness in her voice. "Alexander Parks didn't kill your husband," he said.

The cold rage in Loretta's eyes didn't melt. She

didn't believe him, and she wouldn't unless he told her the truth.

Ajay remembered the words on the screen. *Gabby is not the killer. She is the weapon.* It must be Robert who wielded her. He finally said, "Why would anyone want to kill Percival?"

Loretta's jaw went hard. "Nobody would—"

"The truth, Loretta," Ajay hissed. "Now."

The cold rage in her eyes now turned hot. Ajay became acutely aware of the gun in her hand, even as she seemed to forget about it. She hissed, "If you want to know who's been a thorn in our side for the past fifteen years, it's that investigator. He never lets up, like there's a personal agenda in everything he does against us."

"Declan?"

"Yes, Declan," she whispered. "He investigates every penny we spend and every dollar we make. He's constantly having spies sent to our yacht club to track everything we do."

"He was obsessed," said Ajay.

"Still is," Loretta said.

"Have you ever considered that he might have been right?"

The air went out of her and her shoulders sagged. "We didn't expect to see Declan tonight. I didn't expect to see anyone."

"You were just here for a girl."

"Jocelyn always did like to make things complicated."

A flash across Ajay's cheaters warned him of the next wave. "Incoming!" he shouted.

The tunnel buzzed with a torrent of drones. They swarmed forward, belching from the tunnel entrance. Ajay fired a shot. Another. This wave of drones had ceramic plating, similar to those that had made it into the mansion earlier. His bullets sent the drones spinning but didn't drop them.

A row of needles pelted the tapestry near the gap and Ajay ducked back into cover. His arm stung where several jabbed into his flesh, but he yanked them free and threw them to the ground. "I always hated acupuncture," he muttered. He took a step back and ran into Olexie, who fired the other direction. Drones swarmed through a gap in their tapestry wall. Declan emptied his Glock to no effect.

"Get back!" shouted Olexie. "They're coming through."

Ajay retreated around the bend in the L. Robert stumbled into him from that side, firing at a drone coming through a tear in the tapestry. Ajay stepped past him and shot the drone until a lucky bullet bypassed its plating.

"There are too many," Robert said.

"Not yet," said Ajay. "We have the advantage here."

Olexie gave a furious shout and unloaded his weapon into a drone. Bullets cracked the plating, penetrating the device's interior, exploding it from the inside. It fell to the ground and burst into flames.

"Hah!" Olexie shouted in triumph. He reloaded and stepped back, firing again.

Nailah dove out of the cover of the tapestries. She rolled under a drone and fired up through its carapace. She struck one of its rotors, sending it into a spin. Another dropped when she hit the joint where its rotor arm met the ceramic shell.

She swung her gun around to fire at a third, but she was too slow. It leveled on her and sent a burst of needles at her.

And hit.

Nailah's gun barked twice and the drone dropped. She ducked as another charged her from the side, catching it on the upswing and smashing it to pieces. It burst into flames and she threw it aside.

Flames. Ajay smelled the drone fire, but there was something else in the smoke. He glanced at Olexie, who battled a pair of drones under the cover of billowing soot. The tapestry was on fire. Normandy beach was going up in big, gulping flames.

Their cover was burning. Fast. Much faster than he would have thought the heavy tapestries could burn.

Alerts flashed on his cheaters. A dozen more drones approached. Their combined hum was a cicada scream down the tunnel, echoing and amplifying itself off the press of the stone walls. Ajay emptied his pistol as they swarmed into the room—he had more bullets, but it took time to load them into his only clip. A drone dropped, but more replaced it. Too many.

"Give me your gun if you're not going to use it," Ajay said to Loretta.

"Not a chance."

Olexie grabbed a drone out of the air and threw it at another. It didn't break either but sent them spiraling into the path of another. Ajay ejected his clip, but his fingers fumbled the new bullets when he tried to load them. How did Olexie make this look so easy?

"We need to go," Olexie said to Ajay. "They're overwhelming us."

Robert pressed his back against the tapestry. His shotgun roared, ruining the rotors of an approaching drone. He patted his pocket, a look of horror on his face. "I'm out!" Two more drones approached, and he ducked to one side to avoid them. The tapestry flowed between him and the drones, and he narrowly avoided a volley of needles.

A drone backed Declan to one side, forcing him against one of the room's eight doors. He fired at it, each bullet pinging against the ceramic plate. Each shot sent it spinning, but none caused it any real harm.

Then, Declan's Glock clicked empty a second time. The drone spun on him. Drew a bead.

Boom. The gunshot was a crack of thunder in the underground room. The drone sparked and spit. Boom! The drone exploded and dropped.

Robert held the revolver at arm's length, smoke rising to mix with the tapestry's guttering blackness. It was Theodore Parks's gun. The one that had gone missing. Robert stowed it behind his back, where the big man's loose coat concealed it.

"It's time to move out," Ajay choked. Smoke filled the room.

"Stay and fight," Olexie said. He pounded another drone into the ground. Blood flowed freely from a wound in his arm.

Ajay's alerts flashed again. He grabbed Olexie's arm and pulled him back. "Olexie, there are two war drones approaching. And Parks."

"Yes." Olexie stomped on a ceramic-plated drone. "This is what I do to war drones."

"That was a security drone. Sixth generation. Nice, but they're not built for a war zone."

"What is a war drone?" Olexie asked.

"Big. Powerful. They fire real bullets, and they're bulletproof. Private citizens aren't allowed to own them." Ajay pounded a fist on the quantum computer. "The interference field around this thing isn't going to bother them."

"Go!" Olexie shouted, waving the others back through the tunnels. The group scattered, taking different tunnels. "Meet back at the foyer." He turned back to the swarm of drones threatening to overwhelm them and fired two more shots. "You go, too, Andersen."

"You can't face these things," Ajay said.

Olexie let out a bitter laugh. "I won't. I will lead him away from you. You do what you need to do."

Ajay stalked to the end of the tapestry that wasn't burning and helped Nailah to her feet. Blood covered the front of her red dress, glistening in the moonlight.

"They really seem to like you," he said.

"It's the dress," she replied, a sideways smile on her face.

Ajay ushered her to one of the doors. "Get ready for phase two."

"We have a phase two?" she asked.

"There's always a phase two." Ajay punched some controls on his computer, watching the data flow past on his cheaters.

Nailah gasped and leaned against the door frame. Ajay helped her up. More blood oozed over her front. She plucked a needle out, wincing in pain. "They just sting," she said. "I'm fine."

"You don't look fine."

She held one arm close to her stomach. Ajay could see the wound in her shoulder, right in the fleshy part where a needle had gone clean through. "I'm fine," she said, her voice like ice.

"We can run," gasped Loretta when Ajay and Nailah caught up to her. "Once Parks passes, we can make our way to the exit."

"Not yet," said Ajay, glancing over his shoulder as they hurried through the tunnel. "From what I can tell we got the bulk of his drones, but there's still more out there."

"He's coming after us now?" asked Robert.

"You betcha," said Ajay. Already he could see activity alerts at the junction. "And by the time he finds us, we'll be ready for him."

He handed Nailah off to Robert, who helped her down another passage. Alone, he walked along a branch that would take him to the kitchens. He went up some stairs and through a narrow passage that ran along the wall. Outside, a peal of thunder shook the earth. Through a narrow window, Ajay saw the construction drones looming under the roiling black sky. He passed from hiding into the entryway that Theodore Parks must have used to enter the mansion from the garden at the beginning of the night.

The entrance Gabby must have used. The weapon, not the killer.

The door was locked and seemed to be the solidest thing in the entire house. Chay had been right. They were trapped inside.

Ajay thought of Robert helping Nailah through the tunnels below. It had to be him. He was the only one who could control Gabby. Most of the guests had motive, but only Robert had means and opportunity. Gabby could maybe have squeezed out of the Civil War room's window. She could have passed through the narrow passage from the weapons storage room. Robert *must* have the kind of control Jackson Garver had once had on Isabelle. It's the only explanation. He was the only one.

CHAPTER THIRTY-THREE

"Jocelyn isn't trying to sell your girl," Melinda said through his comm. "She wants to train her."

"I'm not agreeing to that." Ajay tapped the wall where he knew a passage could open from the server room behind the kitchen. It remained ridiculously solid, even under his insistent pounding.

"Agree to it and we'll pull everyone else to safety."

"Robert's the killer, and you knew it all along," Now that Ajay's veins weren't pulsing with adrenaline, he was able to load bullets into his clip. "Tell me you didn't. Jocelyn's just fucking with us all, isn't she? Why lock us in like this?"

"It's—"

"Put her on the line."

"She's—"

"Now, Melinda. It's been a long night."

There was a pause long enough that Ajay

thought the line might have dropped. When Jocelyn finally spoke, her voice hissed with annoyance. "You have no idea what Kylie is capable of."

"Anything she wants," snapped Ajay. "But she doesn't need your school for that."

"The school produces strong, confident women, Mr. Andersen. Why are you threatened by that?"

"Kylie is already strong. She's already confident." Your school will turn her into a killer like Nailah, he should have said. If he had said the words, he would have needed to come to terms with how absolutely impressive Nailah was.

"We make women who survive," said Jocelyn. "Women who do whatever it takes for their family. Nailah, Melinda—"

"Chay."

"Wouldn't you want that confidence for Kylie? Do you think she can become that under your care?"

Ajay paced in the small hallway. Speaking with Jocelyn irritated him. He wanted to ascend her tower and shout at her face to face.

He stopped. The display in his cheaters showed a readout of comm delay. "You're not here anymore, are you?"

Her smile clicked in the comm noise. "Your distraction worked wonderfully, Ajay. Parks came in to confront you and we were able to escape."

Gone. She had fled, and the rest of them were trapped in her gigantic house. "You want custody, but you're willing to leave Kylie in danger like this? She's locked in a safe room with a killer."

"Oh, she's not in the safe room anymore."

Ajay blinked. His fingers flew across the controls, and he filtered the mansion wireframe map for the data he wanted. If Kylie wasn't in the safe room, then she must be on the map somewhere.

A rush of heat burned at the base of Ajay's neck. The thought of giving Kylie up was a buzzing chainsaw of rage and fear. He'd always known someone would try to take her away, but Jocelyn had a legitimate claim. She was rich and powerful. With her resources, she could help Kylie be whoever she wanted to be.

But the corrupting influence of that power would change Kylie. It would destroy her.

Kylie wasn't on the map. She wasn't anywhere.

Jocelyn's laugh was cruel and deep. "You must realize by now that you never really gained full control, right?"

Ajay's mouth tasted like bitter citrus, the acids from the night's stress threatening to choke him. If there was anything he hated, it was being proven a fool. All the work he'd done. All the layers of security he had bypassed with Kylie's help. Everything had been layer after layer of deception, with the end purpose of... what?

"You needed Kylie to see you as a hero," he said. "A hero who tried to save her grandfather from a murderous houseguest." By manipulating his movements, she could make sure he and Kylie were separated. Jocelyn had known her guests would become violent. But how? It seemed like a long shot, expecting her guests to turn into killers. But, then, only one guest had been allowed to bring in a weapon. "You hired Alexander and Theodore Parks to kill us. That's why you panicked when Theodore was killed."

"It certainly didn't go down as I expected," said Jocelyn. "But that's the thing about brilliant plans, isn't it? They're adaptable."

"You sound like Olexie."

"The cook?"

"With Theodore gone, you needed to clear the logs of your transaction down in the safe room and retreat to your escape pod on the roof." Ajay pounded a fist on the machine in front of him. That false machine turned out to be a multi-layered honeypot, designed only to distract him.

"What are you doing?" Jocelyn asked.

Ajay snapped the clip back into his weapon, turned it on the security router, and fired three shots. Bullets smashed into the machine, shattering its core processor and ruining any routing it might still have been doing. Everything was silence. Without that machine, Jocelyn's connection to the house would be dead. She was gone.

"How very aggressive of you," purred Jocelyn.

"Goddamnit," Ajay swore.

"Goodbye, Ajay," said Jocelyn, and the line died.

The black box sparked, sputtered, then belched a thick blast of smoke. Blue flames erupted from the machine's core, splattering superheated fire on the adjacent wall.

"Shit." Ajay tried to stomp out the fire, but it was too hot. Flames grasped at the blue cloth of his pants.

Flames crawled up the wall and danced across the ceiling of the cramped enclosure. Fire greedily consumed walls that appeared to be stone.

Because it wasn't stone. None of it was. Ajay backed away in horror. The whole house was printed using the cheapest stock available. The house was a bucket of tinder soaked in petrochemicals. As he stumbled backward down the hall, he thought of all the signs he should have noticed. The artwork that wasn't quite right. The stone facade that chipped away to reveal plastics underneath. The tapestry that burned like tissue paper.

Everything in the house was fake.

He stumbled from the narrow walls to the hallway. To his left, the long hall stretched away into an endless black. To his right, he could see in the flickering of an overhead lamp above the hall that led back to the foyer. He was starting to know his way around this damn place, and he didn't like it.

He no longer had the security connection or the maps that went with it, but he didn't need them. They were misleading him, anyway. His joints ached from the constant stress. The palm of his hand felt numb from the pistol, which still burned hot. He gripped his cane until his knuckles blanched. He stowed the boxy pistol in his belt.

One section of the surreal wall was missing a painting. He hadn't noticed before, but why would he? In all the hundred paintings in the long hallways, this one was missing. The Salvador Dali was missing. He still remembered its horrible screaming face with screaming faces in its eyes and mouth.

The painting's name finally came to him. "The Face of War," he muttered. Was it the only real painting in the entire mansion?

"It's been a rough night," said a voice down the hall. Alexander Parks stepped into view. "What makes me think you're the one to blame for everything happening around here?"

CHAPTER THIRTY-FOUR

Parks looked like he'd tangled with the wrong end of a bad day. His eyes were sunken and blood-shot. His hair stuck out at angles. His black fatigues clung wrinkled and torn against his body. Ajay couldn't imagine what the man had been through, but the man he'd seen earlier in the evening hadn't looked like this. This was a man tortured. Destroyed.

"Don't even think about it," growled Parks before Ajay could even touch his pistol. Two football-sized drones flew above the man's shoulders. War drones. Low profile. Heavy weaponry.

"Nice hardware," Ajay said. "Mark Three Synchomats. Definitely military grade. Not the latest model."

"New enough," said Parks. The drones drifted away from him to better form a flanking maneuver.

Ajay let out a long sigh. "Where's Olexie?"

274

"The Russian? He ran. Abandoned you soon as I gave him the chance. Ran for the exit."

"Is this worth it, Parks? All of this?"

He raised his gun.

Ajay dove around the corner. A spray of plaster and fake wood pattered across his face as gunshots hit the wall. He ran as best he could, fighting the ache in his hip. He'd pay for the movement in the morning, but it would feel a whole lot better than a bullet. As he ran, he fumbled through the controls on his cane. Synchomats. Mark Three. But were they updated to the latest OS? He needed time.

At the end of a short, narrow hall, he took a right and made his way quickly away, casting a glance over his shoulder for pursuit. Parks would follow. He was sure of it.

Then, the man was right there.

Ajay danced to the side, and another sloppy spray of gunfire tore the air.

The gun was in Ajay's hand, but he didn't remember drawing it. He needed room to work. He was a terrible shot. What could he do against Parks?

The hall was too long. He'd be an easy target. He stuck his gun out, emptied it, and ran.

Parks returned fire before Ajay crossed the hall. Bullets thudded into the door frame, and a sharp pain lanced across his forearm. His cane clattered across the kitchen floor and stopped under a stainless-steel table. Ajay fell to his knees.

Blood ran down his hand and sprayed from his

fingertips. His heart slammed in his chest. Breaths came in ragged gasps, and blackness threatened the edges of his vision. Behind him, he could hear Parks approaching.

Then, someone else was there. The big chef launched himself from behind the steel table, barred the door, and pulled Ajay to his feet.

"Move," Benedict said.

Ajay hobbled across the room. The kitchen was different in the dark. The only lights were the glow of oven timers.

A boom like a cannon rattled the kitchen as something slammed into the door. The steel held, but it warped.

"Where have you been?" Ajay asked as he wrapped a towel around his arm to staunch the bleeding. He hadn't been shot, but shards of fake wood had cut deep into the back of his wrist.

Another slam hit the door. Ajay ran across the row of ovens and cranked the gas to full. The stoves hissed like a snake pit. Smoke trickled from a vent near the walk-in refrigerators. How long did they have before the fire reached them?

The chef's lips were pressed into a tight line. "What?"

"I know who you are," said Benedict. "I wasn't sure I knew at first, but now I know."

Ajay grabbed the man's shoulder and forced him to look him in the eyes. "I need to buy more time, and the best way to do that is to leave this room before that guy arrives."

Gunshots. Six laser-sharp beams of light shone through bullet holes in the steel door around its lock.

"Come on," Ajay said. Behind him, the range hissed. He inhaled the dizzying scent of natural gas. "We need to get out of here."

Boom! Half of the steel door warped, and one of Parks's drones squeezed through the opening. It shone an eerie blue light that danced across the stainless steel of the kitchen.

"You killed the security system," Parks hollered from outside. "It's making this trickier, but I've got other ways to track you all down."

The drone drifted across the opposite end of the large kitchen. Ajay and the chef crouched low as he crossed to the end with the refrigerators.

"You're that hacker," said Benedict. "The one who stopped Liam Thompson."

"I'd prefer if that not get around."

"You're Grandfather Anonymous," whispered the chef.

"Not as anonymous as I'd like."

"Theo shouldn't have been here at all," Parks shouted through the door. "I was the one who got the offer. Funny, right? If I had seen an invitation from Jocelyn Garver, I would have known better. But my idiot husband? He thought it was the opportunity of a lifetime. I was out on a mission, so he decided to take the chance and show up in my place."

Now he was dead. Ajay didn't understand Alexander Parks's violence, but his pain made perfect sense. He'd been close enough to people who were no longer around. He'd witnessed death and suffered loss.

Ajay couldn't reach his cane. In his cheaters, he saw his routine running. If the drones had all their updates, it would fail and alert Parks to his attempt. Either way, he needed the cane back. Ajay glanced at the warped door. They were trapped.

"Is there another way out?" Ajay asked.

"No," said the chef.

"Where were you when we came before?"

"Hiding in the fridge," Benedict said. "You weren't looking very hard."

"We had a lot on the agenda."

Parks sniffed. "Gas, huh? Clever bastard." He holstered his gun. "It's not going to stop me, though." His drone returned to him through the warped door and landed on his shoulder. With a sound like a screaming banshee, the metal twisted enough to let him through. The two drones shone their blue light through the room.

Ajay edged around one of the tables, beckoning Benedict to follow. The air smelled of sulfur and smoke. He pressed himself to the floor.

But there wasn't enough time. The fire was only a room away. The kitchen filled with gas. A mad gunman paced the room searching for them.

Wire racks near his head held the cluttered junk

of a well-stocked kitchen. Rolling pins, spatulas, food processors. None of it would do him any good. He crept forward along the side of the table, careful not to make any noise.

Park's boots thumped on the floor as he crossed the room. A ten-foot gap still stood between Ajay and the exit. It might as well have been a mile. One by one, the hissing burners stopped.

"So much for that little plan, huh?" said Parks.

Ajay met Benedict's gaze and gestured for the other man to make a run for it. He even mouthed the words, "I'll distract him," but Benedict wouldn't move.

Instead, the chef plucked an item from the shelf under the table.

It was a propane torch—the kind chefs use to put a crust on the top of a crème brûlée It was a shiny blue and had a flint wheel on the nozzle to light the flame.

Ajay shook his and mouthed, "No—"

Benedict flicked a spark, lighting the torch.

Parks swore, but it was too late.

The chef threw the torch straight up and Ajay covered his ears and pressed himself as far down as he could.

The air exploded with a resounding thump, hammering Ajay hard against the floor. His ears rang, and his nose bled. He blinked once as time distorted around him. Benedict collapsed backward, batting at flames on his arm.

Ajay pushed himself forward. Time flowed like molasses, and a whining noise permeated the world. Parks was gone. Ajay crept forward, toward the door where his cane still lay under the table. His lungs ached for air. The chef limped toward the door.

Parks stepped in front of the big man. His drones shone their blue light at Benedict.

Ajay's back stiffened. The cane was a short putt away. He could see its knobby end sticking out from under the table.

Ajay had to do something. "You don't even know who I am, do you, Parks?"

One of Parks's drones lifted from his back and drifted over to Ajay. Smoke curled from the one that remained pointed at Benedict, but it didn't seem hindered by the damage. "You're in all the records, Andersen," Parks said. "You're an old discontent, responsible for the Age of Honesty and the fall of encryption. A hacker. Desk jockey."

"He's more than that," said Benedict.

Ajay's granddaughter Isabelle worked for Frontier Arms. He wondered how much she had told them about him and how much they had gathered on their own once he'd crossed paths with them.

He asked, "Is that all? Do they know my golf score?"

"Low hundreds."

"Damn." Ajay crawled to his cane, picked it up, and used it to haul himself to his feet. He leaned heavily on it. The drone tracked his movement. "I wonder if there's something they're missing."

"What's that?" Parks asked.

Benedict stepped forward. "This guy here took down my last boss after the guy went sour. There's not a lot a chef can do when his boss decides to ruin a thousand acres of pristine wilderness. Ajay here got the job done. He figured it out. Made the world a better place. He's a hero to some folks, especially in northern Minnesota. You'd do well not to mess with him. You'll make a lot of enemies if you do."

Ajay had no idea anyone felt that way about him. "Well, I suppose there's that."

"I saw you on the surveillance when you infiltrated his cabin," Benedict said. "You were an inspiration. Truly."

Parks stretched his jaw. He probably also had the ringing in his ears. "Well, he's about to be a martyr."

"He a legend," said Benedict. "They say he brought down encryption. He crushed terrorist plots. He ruined whole governments when they turned against America. There's no system he can't hack. No information he can't dig up."

Parks did *not* look impressed.

"I prefer to keep things anonymous." Ajay shifted the cane in his grip. "If at all possible."

Benedict said, "Sorry."

"But there's one more thing," Ajay said.

"What's that?" growled Parks.

Ajay flashed a toothy grin. "I also have a reputation for being pretty good at hacking drones."

Click.

Parks's two Mark Three Synchomats spun in place, shining their piercing blue lights directly into his eyes. Ajay dove behind the nearest table as Parks fired. Benedict slammed into Parks, and the gun went flying. Ajay struck a cart, sending plates shattering across the hard floor. His knee hit the ground. Another gunshot from a smaller weapon, and the air moved near his head. A wet thunk, and Benedict fell to the ground.

Blinded by darkness, Ajay scrambled forward. His hand struck something hard. A block.

He pulled a knife out. Long and thin, with serrated edges. A good slicer. Blinking hard against the black, he followed the shadows between tables. The drones still focused on Parks, blinding him, but the man had calmed. He was listening.

Ajay moved with as much silence as he could muster, except for the whining roar of blood in his ears and the absolute cacophony of his breath.

Benedict's dark form lay on the ground, gasping for breath. Still alive. Parks stepped up to him, raised his pistol—

Ajay stepped up behind Parks and placed the slender blade against the man's neck.

"You'd be well advised to drop that gun," Ajay said.

"I could kill you right now," Parks growled. "You'd be dead before I bleed out."

"You don't want to do that."

When Parks spoke again, grief shattered his professional calm. "Why would I listen to you?"

Ajay placed one hand flat on the stainless-steel table. Its surface was cold and slick, and it danced with the blue light from Parks' drones. "Because, Mr. Parks, I know exactly what you need. I know what everyone needs." Ajay leaned forward and whispered, "And I am the only one who can give it to you."

CHAPTER THIRTY-FIVE

Kylie pushed Garrison through the bookshelf into the library in the farthest east wing of the manor. It smelled of dust and hardcovers and tea. It was warm and dark except for a single lamp next to a single soft chair. It was paradise, and Kylie knew that Gabby had come this way. She was now gone.

The knife shook in Kylie's hand because she was gripping the handle too tightly. Her muscles were sore from constant tension. How long could she keep this up? In her martial arts class, they always talked about staying relaxed, but she wasn't relaxed. How could she possibly be relaxed? Garrison curled up on a puffy chair.

Half of the security networks were down for some reason, but the relative signal silence let Kylie sense the world outside. Silent slivers of data echoed through the night outside the enormous bay windows. A slithering tendril of light cut the night forest in two, running from the place deep beneath the forest to the very top of the mansion. In this stifling quiet, Kylie could taste activity elsewhere in the mansion. It was like an echo of an echo. It lingered.

The lamp glowed in warm tones, and Kylie discovered that if she didn't look straight at it, her eyes could adjust to the darkness that danced across the shelves. The books there were a thousand books she would love to read. Original editions of the Lord of the Rings. Slender copies of the first Nancy Drew books. The entire Agatha Christie collection. Grandma Jocelyn had good taste in literature, she decided. For the first time, Kylie considered the idea of staying. How many afternoons could she spend just picking books at random from these shelves?

She pulled a book from the shelf at random. It was a dusty copy of *A Wizard of Earthsea* by Ursula K. Le Guin.

Only, it wasn't. She tried to open the book, but she found while the binding was a perfect replica of the book, on closer inspection the lump in her hand didn't even have pages. It was fake. She pulled another book from the shelf. And another. All fake.

"What the hell?" she whispered. Had her grandmother gone through the trouble of faking a library? Why?

"Your sister sends her regards," purred a voice from the dark.

Kylie swung her light around, but the shape of

the figure was barely visible in the library's gloom. At first, Kylie thought it might be Gabby, but the woman was bigger than the slender girl.

"Who are you?"

The woman's Cheshire grin was visible from the dark. "You can call me Chay."

Kylie sidestepped the light so her eyes could adjust. "I know you," she said. "You're a killer."

"I'm complicated."

"What do you want?"

"What do you know about the other girl here today?" Chay asked.

Gabby lurked somewhere out there. There was no time to think about fake libraries or talk to strange women. The younger girl might have learned how to mask her signal. She could be crouching between the shelves, ready to pounce as soon as Kylie's back was turned.

Garrison sniffed the air and whined.

Kylie gripped the knife tighter. Her skin glowed red under the warm amber light.

"I know she's like me," she said. It was as close as she could get to telling this woman the truth.

"A lot of people would kill to be just like you."

Kylie wished she could talk to Austin, but she still couldn't find a solid connection to the outside world. Everything was blocked. The network was entirely internal, which was probably a security measure. Not that she could connect to the network here. Everything was down except for the quietly random noise of the cleaning and maintenance bots.

Austin would know what to do. He would know the words to say to make Gabby feel better. He would know how to talk to Chay to get her to spit out whatever it was she wanted. He could read people's emotions and understand what they were feeling. He was like that.

Kylie had never had that skill. Faces were a mystery to her. People used such weird facial contortions that just didn't make sense. She could interpret a smile easily enough, but some smiles were mean and some were happy and others were sad. Some were as fake as the books in this library.

Gabby understood how to read feelings. She'd done it so well, Kylie had thought she was reading her mind. Kylie hated herself for her inability to read people. There was so much to hate about herself, but that was the worst.

Garrison sniffed the air again. He stood and nudged Kylie away from the bookshelf.

"What is it?" Kylie asked. She walked with the dog to the window. Outside, a pattering of rain pelted the garden.

"It's the fire," said Chay. "He's telling you that it's time to leave."

"There's no way this place will burn."

"Isabelle knew this place would be dangerous for you, and in more ways than one." Chay took a step forward into the light. The way the lamp cast her in shadows made her look ominous. "I swear, I didn't think it would be this hard to find a chance to talk with you."

The dog pointed his nose at the window and let out a single solid woof that Kylie felt in her chest.

"Then again, I didn't predict that there would be a murder and they'd stuff you in a safe room." Chay's eyes narrowed. "What's it like to be treated like that? Crammed away somewhere horrible just to keep you safe."

It was just like living in Bemidji with Papa, Kylie wanted to say. They hid in a little nowhere Minnesota town cowering from the world while she knew she could do amazing things. There was so much fun and interesting life to live out in the world, but she was home doing homework every single day. Mindless work, too. When she thought about Chay's words, the anger bubbled up in her belly.

Gabby was angry, too. That must be why she attacked. But what was she mad about? Having control taken from her? That would make Kylie upset. Her father had done that to Isabelle, and it had been horrible. At least Gabby had been able to be useful. Her skills *meant* something to her father.

What would Gabby do with such anger? Where would she have gone? The question frustrated Kylie, not only because she didn't know the answer but also because she knew the answer should be obvious. If only she understood people better.

She *only* knew computers. Machines could be

predicted. They sometimes behaved in horrible, illogical ways, but the design of that nonsense made its own kind of logic. It had been made with goals, even if those goals were long since gone. The network here used randomized packet switching for data instead of the modern standards of comprehensive circuit switching over the dedicated frequencies. A weird choice in the modern world. One that she couldn't quite grasp.

But the choice made sense exactly for that reason. It was hard to understand.

People made no sense at all, and there was no way Kylie would figure them out.

"I'm not going with you," said Kylie, finally.

"Think about what's worked for Gabby," said Chay. "And think about what hasn't worked. Discipline. Control. Structure. These are things your sister can offer you if you follow her path."

Become a mercenary. A killer. Kylie didn't know how deep Isabelle was in Frontier Arms, but she was sure her sister was doing dangerous things. Exciting things, but dangerous.

"That's not who I am," she said.

Chay said, "You can be anyone you want. Don't you understand how amazing that is?" Her eyes shone in the lamplight. "A lot of us would give anything for that ability."

"You'd kill for it," said Kylie. "Yeah, I got the message."

Chay shrugged. "Either way, she wants me to

keep you safe."

A breeze passed through the library, swirling around in the cool darkness. Far away in the mansion, a clatter rattled the walls. An acid shiver of fear ran up Kylie's back. She'd heard similar sounds far too often. Gunfire.

"What's happening?" Kylie asked.

"They're singing my song," said Chay.

Kylie tried to open the window, but it wouldn't budge. She pried at it as hard as she could and even tried to slam a statue into the glass pane. The statue—an absurdly solid Beethoven bust—broke in two and barely left a scratch in the window.

If there were guns, then there was a fight. If there was a fight, there was danger. Real, concrete danger. She preferred that to the fear that Gabby might be lurking in the shadows somewhere.

She looked at Chay. Kylie could leave with this woman. Escape into the dark. But that meant leaving Gabby to whatever dangers were out there. It meant leaving Papa.

Now she smelled the smoke that Garrison had detected earlier. She couldn't get it out of her nose.

"I'm not going with you," Kylie said.

"Suit yourself." Chay retreated from the light. "But you got skills, kid. Make sure you use them."

Kylie watched as the woman disappeared silently into the dark mansion, wondering if she had made the right decision. She had opted for danger, but she might be able to do something about it because she finally understood what this place was. She finally figured out why this whole mansion didn't make sense.

It was a trap.

Papa was in trouble.

CHAPTER THIRTY-SIX

"Don't shoot," called Ajay as he approached the foyer with Parks. The two drones hovered nearby with their guns pointed at their former master. Benedict held back, casting nervous glances down the hall. "I've got this under control, and the house is on fire."

"If he moves, I will shoot him in the head," replied Olexie from behind an oak table.

"You're not that good a shot, Olexie."

"Don't tell him that."

"At least I didn't tell them about your concussion."

"My headache does not make me more likely to put up with bullshit." Olexie blinked. "Did you say the house is on fire?"

"Weren't you supposed to lead him away from me earlier?" Ajay asked. "He said you ran away."

Olexie sniffed. "I smell smoke."

"The house is on fire, Olexie," said Benedict, stepping into the foyer.

"I didn't leave anything in the oven," Olexie said. He scrunched up his nose. "Maybe some pies."

Ajay pushed Parks into the center of the room. They had designed their ambush so that there was little cover for anyone entering from the main hall. Ajay was in the kill box.

Nailah watched from the shadows, her immaculately painted fingernails resting on the black metal of a pistol. Loretta clung to her arm, tears of mascara streaking down her face. Across from them, Robert stood behind a mahogany dresser. His expression was grim, and he kept Parks fixed with a murderous glare. Declan stood ten feet away from him, a haggard look on his disheveled features. His suit was more wrinkles than smooth.

Benedict took stock of the group. His eyes searched each of the guests, then shot a questioning look back at Olexie.

Olexie nodded to the weapon room where two bodies still lay covered in sheets.

Benedict's shoulders slumped. His eyes lost focus, and he leaned against the wall. Declan braced him and guided him to the floor.

"Why didn't you kill Parks?" Olexie said to Ajay.

Ajay tried his best to smile, but it likely came out looking like a grimace. He did, after all, still have a large number of guns pointed in his direction. "It's more important that we escape."

Robert's shadowed form was visible behind a large dresser near the weapons room. He still held the big revolver, but it was heavy. It drooped as he spoke. "That'll be easier once he's dead."

There was one bullet left in the cylinder.

Ajay stepped between Robert and Parks. "He'll leave us once we tell him who killed Theodore." The drones adjusted position for a better firing angle on Parks.

Parks raised his hands in the air. A burn across his cheek glistened in the dim light. "I'm not making any promises."

"Well, I am," said Robert. He aimed his gun straight at the other man's head. "You're going to give us some answers or the staff around here is going to have a hell of a time cleaning you off the walls."

"Oh, for fuck's sake," muttered Olexie.

"There aren't going to *be* walls very long," Ajay said. He tasted ash in the air. "Any luck getting the front door open?"

"It's a vault," said Olexie, his voice suddenly very somber. "This is the worst job I've ever had."

"I can't believe Zach is gone," said Benedict.

Robert's eyes darted from Olexie to Parks and then over to Declan.

"Robert," Ajay said, palms out as if it might somehow calm the man. "Simmer down now. Parks isn't our biggest problem."

"Put it down, Robert," said Declan.

Robert shot a furtive glance Declan's direction. "This isn't my fault."

"Maybe," said Ajay. The pieces were starting to fall into place. "But what comes next will be if you don't lower that gun."

Robert stepped to one side, putting more distance between himself and the others. It gave him a narrow angle on Parks.

"Would someone care to explain this to me?" asked Nailah. "What is his fault?"

"Robert was in the room when Theodore Parks died," Ajay said.

A flash of rage crossed Alexander's face. His fists clenched at his side. "I'll kill you for this, Burkshire," he growled.

Robert said, "I didn't kill him, Alexander. Theodore and I were in this together."

"You were there when it happened," said Ajay. "That's why you were the first on the scene."

Robert glanced at his hands. "It wasn't me."

"No," spat Ajay. "You couldn't bring yourself to kill the man. You ordered your daughter to do your dirty work."

"What?" Nailah's nostrils flared. "What did you do?"

"He's been training her to be a bodyguard and a killer," Ajay said. "Martial arts. Weapons training. With the tech in her head, he's able to wipe her memory and force her to be something she's not. He can order her to kill someone—even someone physically very powerful—and they won't even see it coming. He even had her sneak some knives in—knives stolen from Jocelyn on a previous visit so that they'd be ignored by the scanner." Ajay paced slowly, leaning heavily on his cane. "This was a test of her skills, wasn't it?"

"No," sputtered Robert. "I—"

"You were supposed to show your control over her. You were trying to win a coveted place in Jocelyn Garver's school." Ajay cast a glance at Nailah. "You were all here because of the school."

"You knew," Declan said, staring at Nailah. "You knew all along."

Nailah looked down at her hands.

"They did something to you at the school," Declan said. "That's what I was here to find out. I finally had a chance to hire one of Jocelyn's students. She told me there were going to be potential students here. That we would be bidding on their future employment. I thought if I talk to one of the girls before they were brainwashed, I might be able to bring the whole organization down."

"It's not that simple," Robert said. "You need to *earn* a spot at Jocelyn Garver's table."

Declan took a step back. "You do," he whispered. "You do."

"I'm sorry, Declan," Nailah said, but it didn't improve the man's mood. "But there was very little brainwashing."

"I still want to hear what Parks has to say," said

Robert. His grip on the revolver tensed as he glared at Parks. "Why were you trying to kill us, and why can't we leave?"

For a long time, Ajay didn't think the man would talk. Then, as if the words rumbled from a deep pit in the earth, Alexander Parks said, "What you're doing here is sick. Buying and selling girls. Training young women to be killers. Trading on the innocence of youth to support your ever-growing need for power." He took a step forward, not breaking eye contact with Robert. "I'd be happy to watch each and every one of you bleed out on the floor, and I told that bitch Garver as much. Theodore felt the same way, which is why he took the job, but he didn't understand that Garver was going to betray us."

Nailah took a step forward. "You were hired to kill us?"

Parks barked out a laugh. "I don't give a fat fuck about any of you. It's Garver I want now, and she knows it." A shark's grin flashed his white teeth. "And now you, Robert. Now I'm here for you, but it's not going to matter, because we're all going to burn."

The revolver shook in Robert's hands. "I didn't kill Theodore."

"The hell you didn't."

The revolver dropped an inch, heavy in Robert's grip. "Theodore came to me with demands. You know how intense he could be. He cornered me when it was time to return inside. Caught me in that sitting room with all those Civil War paintings, as if he wanted to remind me of all the violence you could cause if needed." He swallowed. "We had words. Some of them rather heated."

"What about?" asked Ajay, now curious to know what had really happened. "Why the fight?"

"He was like his husband," Robert said, gesturing at Parks with his gun. "He thought the education that I want for my girl isn't the right thing, but he doesn't know what it's like." He shot a look at Ajay. "He doesn't *know*, Mr. Andersen. Not like we do."

A chill ran down Ajay's spine, because he *did* know. Kylie was strange. She faced challenges no other girl her age faced. Jocelyn's school *might* actually help her learn the discipline she needed to survive.

Robert continued, "Whatever Haveraptics did to her, she's a monster." He looked at the others as if hoping to see a shred of sympathy. "A monster. We spend our summers in the north woods by a lake. The cabin gets mice sometimes, especially in the detached cellar. It's—it's used for storage and whatnot. One year, the mice got into the life jackets. Tore everything up. Defecated everywhere. The cellar was frightful, so I locked it until we could get the help to come deal with it.

"I don't know how Gabby found the key. Late one night, she opened the cellar and crept down into the dark."

"So she killed some rats," Declan said.

"No," Robert snapped. "It was more than that.

She didn't kill them. At least, she didn't seem to be trying to kill them. In the morning, I went looking for her, figuring she was playing in her room, but she wasn't there. We organized a search, terrified that she might have wandered down to the lake and drown. It was late afternoon before we found her in the back of the storage cellar." His voice cracked. "She had them lined up in a row. Mice, rats, bugs. Lined up, tied down, and flayed of their flesh." A shudder shook his whole body, and he took a step back. "They were still alive. Almost all of them."

Parks took a step forward, not taking his eyes off Robert. "So you taught her how to fight. How to kill."

Robert's eyes went wide. "No. No, I didn't. I taught her meditation. The martial arts gave her form and focus. It allowed her to resist whatever Haveraptics put in her head." He glanced at Nailah. "That's why I'm here. It's not working anymore. She's having episodes, and it's getting harder to keep her under control, even with the tools Haveraptics gave me. She brought the knives on her own. I think she knew she would want to use them."

"Where is it?" Ajay said. "Where is the controller that lets you mess with her brain?"

Robert stared at Ajay as if he were talking nonsense. "I didn't make her kill Theodore. That's what I'm trying to tell you."

"What did you do?" Ajay growled, taking another step forward.

"I argued with him." Another nervous glance at

Parks. "We fought, but it wasn't a physical fight. He thought I was being unreasonable, but he didn't see how his words were upsetting Gabby. He told her she was innocent and that she deserved a decent life—to make her own choices."

"Doesn't sound unreasonable to me," said Parks.

"It doesn't," stammered Robert, "but it's not something we can say to Gabby. She gets confused. Angry. She starts to think that maybe she *can* make her own decisions, and her decisions are bad. I teach her to be protective of me. The bodyguard thing. She does have a strong protective instinct, and we're able to use that to keep her under control. It keeps her from channeling her destructive impulses outward."

"Destructive impulses," Parks snarled. "Which you turned on my husband."

"No." A fire burned in Robert's eyes. "I didn't—I mean, I did. You still don't understand. She was protective of me, so when Theodore decided to get in my face, she did something I've never seen her do before. Not since—not since that day she killed the mice."

"Say it," Parks said. "Then you better pull that trigger, because if you don't, I'm coming for you."

"She killed him," said Robert. He lowered the weapon. "I swear to you, it wasn't my fault. I couldn't have known what she would do." He nodded at the weapon in his hands. "That's why I took this. She's out of control. Unhinged. I didn't know if she'd come after someone else next."

"Put the gun away," Ajay said.

Robert blinked. "I can't. If she comes back—"

"Nobody's shooting the girl," Ajay said. "She's not a threat."

"You don't know that," Robert said. His hand shook. "You can't know."

"Parks," Ajay said in warning. He didn't know if the man would attack Robert, but it would be a bloodbath if he did. "I think he's telling the truth. Kylie has struggled, too."

"Not like that," Robert said. "Nothing like that."

Isabelle had been manipulated by her father. He saw no reason Gabby wouldn't have a similar control system in her head. Kylie largely regulated herself, but that was dangerous. One lapse could mean brain damage or wild personality swings. If Gabby was dealing with violent tendencies, she might have slipped her limits. It even seemed likely that Theodore Parks's talk about thinking for herself would help the girl reject any rules Robert put in place.

And what was right? Was it right that she should be free when that freedom was so dangerous to those around her? Was it right for Robert to put limits on her brain that would allow her to function in society? Was it wrong for him to seek an education that might leverage the tendencies that already existed in her?

Yes, Ajay decided. Yes, that was probably still wrong. Turning her into one of Jocelyn Garver's assassins would only get innocent people killed. Even if she mostly killed the worst people around, it wasn't right.

Parks took a step back. "Fine," he rasped. His whole body shook with emotion. "Fine."

"We need to escape," said Ajay. "We can leave the way Parks got in, through the tunnels."

A lazy grin crept onto Parks's face. "It sealed soon as I stepped inside."

"He's right." Olexie had the decency to look chagrined. "I tried to escape that way."

"Nobody leaves," said Parks. "All you fuckers are going to get what's coming to you."

Benedict looked up, his eyes bleary with tears. "There might still be access to the roof. There's a passage we use to get to Mrs. Garver's suite."

"Where is it?" asked Declan.

But Benedict didn't answer. Parks's drones flashed green, turned on him, and opened fire. Bullets thumped into his chest and painted the wall behind him red. The mercenary stepped backward, turned, and ran. Robert fired his gun, pelting the door frame next to Alexander's head.

The drones followed Parks.

Robert stumbled backward, pulling the trigger on his empty gun. Useless. He backed into the shadows of the empty weapons room. Loretta, watching him in horror, choked on a hideous scream.

Explosions like thunderclaps rattled the building. Waves of heat and smoke belched in waves across the foyer ceiling. Benedict left a bloody streak as he collapsed to the ground, dead.

A young girl's hand wrapped around Robert's neck and slit his throat with a sharp knife.

As Robert fell, burbling and bleeding, Gabby Burkshire rose behind him, a bloody fist clutching a bloody knife, a wicked grin upon her face.

CHAPTER THIRTY-SEVEN

Ajay faced Gabby across the foyer. She stared at him with hooded eyes, a mad rage bubbling under the surface of her expression. Out of the corner of his eye, Ajay saw Olexie gather the others as the room filled with smoke. Behind him, another rumble of an explosion rolled through the halls. A wave of heat washed in from the foyer's outside door.

"Gabby, put down the knife," Ajay said.

"I can do whatever I want," the girl said. Her voice was flat to the point of being eerie, and the light of the dark flames flickered across her face. She stepped forward, waving the knife from side to side.

Ajay clutched his cane. "We can help you."

"You can *change* me. Hurt me. Just like Daddy did. Just like they all did."

"Not like that, Gabby." Ajay held an empty palm up for her to see. "I won't hurt you. I help Kylie without hurting her."

Gabby glanced down at Robert's body. "You hurt her," she whispered.

"Ajay," called Olexie from across the room. "Watch out!"

A wave of heat washed over Ajay. The fire raged outside the door. It licked the walls, and a painting went up like a greased Christmas tree. Even the marble statues burned.

Because, of course, it was all fake. Ajay thought of the odd construction equipment outside. 3D printers. All of it. When did she build this huge house? Was the whole thing just a trap for these guests?

The main hallway where Parks had retreated was a wall of fire. Olexie and the others disappeared into the passage behind the weapons room—the room where Gabby had just emerged to sneak up behind Robert.

"Papa!" Kylie's voice came from the other side of the roaring flame. "Something's wrong with Gabby!"

"Find a way out," Ajay called back to her, not sure if she could hear. He blinked against the smoke and nearly lost his footing when Gabby lunged. He clumsily blocked a swipe of the knife with his cane. "Gabby," he snapped.

The girl stepped back as if struck.

"Stop this right now," Ajay growled at Gabby in the sternest voice he could manage. "Kylie, get out of the mansion however you can." He remembered what the chef had said. "Go up! There might be a way out onto the roof."

"I can't leave you," she said, but she disappeared.

People never understood how fast houses burned. A typical house fire could become a deathtrap in two minutes. With smoke and heat cutting off exits, there wasn't time to mess around. When the house was on fire, smart people left. Immediately.

This was much worse. The house was a tinderbox—a maze designed to cut off access points with ease. Fire raced down the halls at incredible speeds, consuming floor and ceiling with equal gusto. Flames sucked the oxygen out of the only spaces left, and there was no way out.

Gabby attacked. Her form wasn't perfect. Her high strikes came in too high and her low jabs were clumsy. Still, it was all Ajay could do to keep her at bay. He blocked with his cane and stumbled away, working his way around the fallen table. The knife cut into his forearm. Then again on his hip. He bit back a curse.

"You're the worst of them," Gabby hissed. "Like my father. You make her be whatever you want."

"It's not like that," Ajay said. "Kylie doesn't—"

Gabby slashed, and the knife passed an inch from Ajay's neck. "Stop!" she screamed.

He caught her arm on the backswing and held tight. His fingers dug into her flesh, but if he let go, he would die. "Kylie's free," he said. "As long as she's with me, she'll always be free. Kylie can do whatever she wants."

This sent waves of rage through the girl. "Liar!"

She twisted and pulled away from Ajay's grip. Rolling, she came up on the other side of the table. Her bloody teeth were dark in the light of the flame. "You stifle her," Gabby hissed. "And you're never supposed to do that."

Ajay coughed and staggered back. Smoke choked the air and flames licked across the wallpapered walls. Heat poured from half of the room in waves, and the upturned furniture smoldered. But what hurt most was the truth of her words.

"We need to leave, Gabby," said Ajay through a hacking cough. "We can make this right."

"Things are never going to be right," said Gabby. "Not with people like Grandma Garver around. Not with people like you."

"Jocelyn will answer for this," Ajay said. "The house is burning, Gabby. We just need to decide if we're going to be in it when it happens."

Gabby's nostrils flared. Something cracked in the ceiling, and Ajay glanced up. The girl took the opportunity to attack, but he was ready. He sidestepped, took her momentum, and let her clumsy assault carry her to the ground. She rolled, but her leg slammed into the table and she let out a yelp of pain. When she stood to face him again, she favored that leg.

This time, she wasn't between him and the exit. Ajay backed toward the weapons closet, keeping his cane up defensively before him. From this direction, he had a better view of the fire consuming the walls. Flames devoured the mansion, eating it down to its bones then sucking out its marrow. How could this place burn so fast?

And it all started to make sense.

"Gabby, you're right," he said.

"There's no such thing as free will?"

Ajay coughed. "There's always free will." With that, he turned and moved as quickly as he could to the secret exit. His cane slammed against the tile and his lungs burned. He hit the weapons room as Gabby screamed her frustration. Smoke burned his eyes, and tears blinded him, but he knew she was close.

He slammed into the passage. He didn't pause to check that she followed. It was a narrow passage. Barely big enough for him to move through. He hobbled forward, hip aching already, but he had to ignore it. The passage ran along the outer wall for a distance, then angled through the walls. As he rounded the bend, Gabby hit the passage, knife still in hand.

She moved fast. Too fast. She would catch him before he could get to another open space, but he needed to get away from the fire. From the smoke. The walls were an oven, searing his fingers where he touched. He passed an intersection in the narrow passage, barely bothering to think about where he was going.

Away. That's all that mattered. Away from Gabby. Away from the heat. He wasn't sure which would kill him first, but the difference was a matter of seconds.

As Gabby crossed the intersection, her scream of rage sounded over the roar of flames. She slashed with her knife, closer to Ajay. Then closer still.

Then, Kylie slammed into the girl, pounding her up against the too-hot wall, cracking it. The knife skittered to the hard floor.

"You have to take over the security network, Papa!" she shouted.

"I—I can't." Ajay coughed. Every breath burned.

"It's packet switching," Kylie shouted. "On a modulated network."

Gabby struggled against her grip and let out a murderous howl.

Then, the wall cracked and a scorching inferno belched through. They fell back the direction Kylie had come from, and the space between Ajay and the girls became a kiln.

"Kylie!" Ajay shouted, but he could barely hear himself. The fire roared in his face. Mocked him. He struggled against it, but an uncontrollable instinct forced him to flee. That gut-deep fear of fire drove him away.

Then he was gone, deeper into the maze, leaving Kylie and Gabby on the other side of a raging inferno.

CHAPTER THIRTY-EIGHT

Kylie slammed Gabby against the wall and the knife clattered to the ground. The wall cracked under the force, so she yanked Gabby backward. As they fell, the whole burning wall smashed open and a wave of searing heat rolled over them.

Gabby's hair was on fire, so Kylie shoved her down and started beating at it. The girl screamed in fury and struck Kylie in the stomach. By the time she recovered, Gabby was up and running.

Kylie followed. Papa was on his own. They sped through the dark tunnels, scrounging to find a way away from the acrid smoke that burned her lungs. The tunnel circled upward, then stopped at a set of steep stairs.

Gabby mounted the stairs without pausing. She scrambled up so fast Kylie hardly saw her disappear into the room above. Kylie didn't want to go up there, but she couldn't go back. There was no way she could get back to another passage. Not with the fire consuming the house the way Austin consumed a pizza.

She thought of her only friend, and a pang stabbed her chest. Gabby could have been another friend. She had been so nice when they'd first met. What had happened? Austin would have known. Kylie stared up the ladder at the darkness above. It was a choke point. A blind corner. This, she understood. Maybe she couldn't figure out how people worked, but she knew a bad tactical situation when she saw one. Gabby could be waiting there, ready to attack as soon as Kylie poked her head up.

Behind her, Garrison barked, his low woofs shaking the unsteady walls. She called to him, and he loped up behind her, tail between his legs.

What choice was there? Smoke devoured the air, filling it with an acrid haze. If she didn't hurry, the fire would suck the oxygen out of the room and leave Kylie too weak to climb to freedom. She grasped Garrison's collar and pulled. When she reached the top, the only thing that struck her face was cold, wet wind.

Rain poured from the sky in sheets, thick enough to blot out the whole sky.

Kylie wondered what her grandfather would want her to do. The house below her burned. It would collapse soon, killing everyone inside. The only way free was out onto the roof, but the rain made the roof a hazard all on its own, and that was without the lightning. Garrison nudged her forward. If she didn't leave soon, the dog would die. She had no doubt of that.

A door to the roof hung wide open, and outside, Gabby walked along the narrow peak. She passed the circular room in the center of the building where Grandma Garver's private quarters were. Beyond, a landing pad sat empty, and Kylie assumed her grandmother had escaped.

That's what *Grandma* would want her to do. Escape. No matter what. Leave everyone else behind. Papa was never quite so clear. Garrison bumped against her again. At least *he* wasn't so ambiguous.

A flash of lightning arced across the sky.

Papa would tell her to stay safe. He always told her to stay safe, but he also always told her to do the right thing. Gabby might be dangerous, and she might be beyond help, but she also needed help. Kylie *needed* to try to save her because there was a lot in Gabby's logic that made sense to Kylie. Besides her sister, Gabby was the first modified person Kylie had known. They were enduring a lot of the same problems.

Kylie stepped out onto the roof. Slick tiles shifted under her feet. The rain sluiced across red ceramic, and as soon as she stepped out, she was drenched to the bone.

"Gabby," she shouted as she made her way around the circular center room, but the wind tore the words from her lips.

Movement up ahead. A shadow danced among the crenelations at the far end of the roof. An array of satellite dishes was mounted next to a flat area of the roof, creating a barrier of tech between her and Gabby. All Kylie had to do was walk along the narrow path atop the pointed roof. She took another step forward.

A voice came to her over the high wind, but she couldn't hear the words. Rain pelted her from the side, its cold driving into her flesh.

Another step. Lightning crackled across the sky. Kylie could see the stand of white pines—their pure white forms like ghosts on the forest floor. They swayed in the furious wind.

Thunder shook the roof under her feet, and Kylie knelt to steady herself. When she did, the new angle gave her a better view of the palatial roof up ahead. Gabby stood atop the jagged crenelations, arms outspread against the blowing storm.

"Gabby!" Kylie shouted, hurrying forward. "What are you doing?"

Garrison barked again, except this time he didn't stop barking. He was scared. She'd never really seen him scared, but it made her heart clench like a fist.

The girl didn't answer. Wind howled and Gabby swayed in place three stories above the concrete driveway. Smoke billowed around her, thick and black.

Gabby was going to hurt herself.

Kylie reached the satellite array. Power still

hummed through them, despite the storm and the fire. Now, with a good view of it, Kylie could see no good way down from the roof. It was a sheer drop or a steep slope and then a sheer drop. None of it looked safe. None of it would carry her safely from the fire.

Lightning struck Lake Superior far in the distance, its forked brilliance piercing the black waters. In that shredded second, Kylie could see the divide between lake and sky, but then the rain blended the two again.

"Gabby, come down," Kylie said. Why wouldn't that dog stop barking?

Gabby turned to face her. Her hooded eyes were dark under the drenched drapery of her hair. "You're just like them."

Kylie's words stuck in her throat. Austin would know what to say. There were words that would convince Gabby to step down. Make her reasonable again. But Kylie didn't know what the words were. How could she? All she could do was talk about her own experience and that hurt. It hurt! "My father was as bad as yours," Kylie said.

Gabby licked rain from her lips. "My father bought me." She pointed at her head. "He *wanted* this to happen to me. He thought it would make me a better killer for him."

"He thought that because of what my father told him." Kylie stepped onto the roof. She was three long strides from Gabby but might as well have been a million miles away. No way would she be able to stop the girl from jumping. "And they were right."

Wind swirled across the roof. The scent of burning wood mixed with the driving rain. Garrison's barks were drowned by the roar of rain striking the roof.

Gabby clutched her skull. "He's still in there. He did something to me and he won't go away."

"I know."

"You don't! Nobody can. It's all in there. The voices..."

Kylie took a step forward. "Ignore them, Gabby."

"I can't," Gabby moaned. "They're *my* voice. How can I know what I'm thinking?"

Kylie still didn't know what to say.

Gabby stepped forward from the ledge, her feet thumping against the wet roof. She raised her tightly balled fists. "When the voices say, 'stay close to father,' I listen, because who wouldn't want to be close? When they say, 'protect him at all costs,' is that a normal thing for a kid to think? That sounds strange, doesn't it?"

"It's strange," Kylie agreed.

"And when they say, 'Kill,' what am I supposed to do?"

"You can think for yourself." Kylie raised her own hands but kept them loose in a defensive Aikido stance. It was a stance designed to dissipate tension rather than confront, but it would still keep her ready for an attack. Kylie knew she had to be ready. "I'm doing it. My sister Isabelle does it. We don't agree on what that means, but that's because we're different people. What would you do right now if you had your choice?"

"*If* I had my choice?" Gabby said, stepping forward. "You're saying I don't?"

"I'm not saying anything, Gabby. What are you saying?"

Gabby's answer was the fastest kick Kylie had ever seen. If she hadn't been ready, it would have hit her in the jaw, but instead, it snapped the rainwater inches in front of her face. Kylie sidestepped, reset, and squared off again.

"Your grandpa's making you a fighter," Gabby said.

"He's not like that," Kylie said, anger burning in her chest.

Another kick, this time followed by a punch. Kylie dodged the strike, then redirected the next. She took a solid blow to her shoulder, sending fireworks of pain down her arm, but whenever Gabby threw a punch, Kylie was already rolling with it. Her Aikido lessons flowed through her. She was in the zone. Garrison nudged his way past the satellite dishes and watched.

Gabby snarled with frustration. "I was supposed to be better than this!"

The building under them shook. Flames burst from the roof in the center of the mansion, rising high into the sky.

Kylie said, "He's gone. You aren't supposed to be anything now." It was the wrong thing to say. She felt it.

A low kick glanced off of Kylie's knee. If her foot had been planted, it might have broken bone. As it was, it stung and made her stumble, which made it hard to get out of the way of another series of punches. A fist struck Kylie's chin and lights flashed in front of her eyes, matched by the lightning that danced across the sky.

Kylie fell, but Gabby danced away. Garrison was absolutely no help at all.

The younger girl pulled at her own hair. "They're shouting in my head!"

Kylie blinked away the rain from her eyes. Reason wasn't working. She simply didn't have the words to make Gabby understand. Chay had said to use her skills. Instead of rising for another physical fight—instead of trying a battle of words—Kylie decided to use the skills she had. It was time to do something she was good at.

Because there wasn't a problem a sufficient amount of hacking wouldn't solve.

She fixed Gabby in her gaze, grasped for a connection, and attacked.

CHAPTER THIRTY-NINE

Packet switching. As soon as Kylie had said the words, the local network architecture clicked into place for Ajay. It was nothing like what he had used before. The physical layer of this network was a strange design choice. Inefficient. Faulty. Ancient.

Perfect.

Obsolescence was a security measure. The ancient CDMA network layer was incompatible with every modern network archetype. It would require specialized hardware to decode, and that hardware wasn't something readily available.

Melinda had given him the key. It translated the signal from the surveillance network, which sat adjacent to the security network but operated on the same protocols. He plucked the widget from his pocket and used his multitool to open the back. His cane's computer connected to the device, and he could read the translated data through it.

A row of pins was mounted in the back of a simple data card. Now, with an understanding of what it was doing on the hardware layer, he could make the changes he needed.

Behind him, down the hall, the mansion burned. A thin haze of smoke still anointed the air with the harsh odor of burning wood and plastic, but his eyes had stopped tearing and he only had a few minutes to do what needed to be done. Ahead, down the long length of the wide hallway, Loretta and Declan ran past. They were headed for the Civil War room. The room with the body.

The window. Declan must think he could open it.

Ajay clicked the pins in series, testing different coded settings. The readout in his cheaters was skewed, their video display having gotten damaged somewhere along the way. He muttered the binary codes as he changed the settings. It had been so long since he'd studied the old network layer protocols.

Got it. The signal connected. A hundred signals. He swiped through his routines and started gathering connections, but he couldn't use them yet. He needed something more. His physical layer was in place, but he still needed the network layer.

Alexander Parks walked across the hall up ahead. His drones flanked him, and he stalked after Nailah, gun in hand.

Ducking behind the statue, Ajay spotted something he hadn't seen before. The statue—a bust of some puffy-haired old man—had been shoved close to the wall in a way that concealed a mark on its base. There, almost concealed by the shadows of the alcove, Ajay spotted a chip in the bust's marble veneer. Under the stone exterior, lay layers and layers of striation. Artifacts of 3D printing.

Another reminder that everything here was fake.

The plaque on the bust's front claimed that it was several hundred years old. This was fake. The house was fake. All of it. Jocelyn had created a fake mansion and a fake life just to...

What?

He glanced down the hall. Were they all fakes? Every painting, every statue, every fancy bit of woodworking and memorabilia. Not the Salvador Dali, though. She had taken that with her when she left. It was the only real thing in the entire mansion. It was all an imitation of a palace meant to lure guests in and trap them in their doom.

But why?

"Melinda," Ajay said into his comm. "I know what you're doing."

"Yes?" came the woman's voice after a short delay.

"You're testing us," Ajay said. He needed to start making some guesses or he'd never get anywhere. "You and your mother."

There was silence on the line for several long breaths. Finally, Jocelyn said, "Your daughter once told me that you were an obnoxious shit. I didn't understand how true it was at the time."

Connections flashed across his controls. Their information was hard to read, but he separated the blue and the red. He connected his comm circuit to the encryption dialog and configured a routine to test keys. With the physical layer solved, he could access the higher layers of the network, most of which clung to the same standards he had seen before.

"So you made this place. You made a trap to lure your enemies so that they could all be killed at once. You set it up so that they'd be at each other's throats. You even made sure that Alexander would want revenge for his husband's death after he was killed. You set everything against us, hoping we would kill each other, which would keep you out of any legal difficulties. When that didn't work, you set the house on fire and locked all the doors."

"*You* set the house on fire, Mr. Andersen," Jocelyn said, sounding quite smug.

"I've ruined my fair share of computers," Ajay said. "They don't burn like that."

Jocelyn said, "Your granddaughter and the other child had their chance at freedom."

Had. The phrasing worried Ajay, but he opted not to take the bait. "Melinda, your mother is insane. Stop this now. Give me whatever access you have, and I can make this better." His computer ran through the array of connections, locating each source and activating it.

"You killed my brother," Melinda said, confirming his guess about her parentage. Jackson Garver, Kylie's father, was Melinda's brother.

"My daughter killed that asshole," said Ajay.

"But you're responsible. It's you who set her up to it. It was *you* who twisted Jackson's creations against him. You're responsible for everything that happened, and you know it."

"I do," Ajay said, letting the words trail into silence. Thick smoke burned the back of his throat. It would be too much soon, and he had to move, but following Alexander without an army would be foolish.

Not that he never did anything foolish.

"Fine," he said, "but I need you to know one thing."

"What's that," asked Melinda.

Ajay's cheaters flashed green, finally signaling the completion of his processes. He inserted a data packet through the comm with an encapsulated command.

"What?" Melinda repeated, annoyed. "What do you want me to know?"

"I just need you to know that you've made an enemy today. When I'm done here, I won't stop looking for you. I'll burn every connection you've ever made and I'll destroy all that wealth you've accumulated on the backs of innocent children. And Jocelyn?"

"Yes?"

"There's no problem a sufficient amount of hacking won't solve."

He was in. The whole network was finally his. He grabbed control of the cooking bots, the cleaning bots, the surveillance drones. Everything. He told them to do two things.

First, switch to connect directly to his controller and forget Melinda's. They all had the hardware for normal network connections and grabbed them all.

Second, find more devices and convert them. Bring them into the fold.

He finally had a robot army of his own.

"You wouldn't dare," hissed Jocelyn.

Then, through them, he delved deeper into Melinda's network. As black smoke rolled across the gilded ceiling, he sniffed all the data streams connected to Melinda's access. He swiped through his controls as he stepped out from behind the counterfeit statue.

"Stop me," Ajay said, "and you'll know what it's like to have all your secrets revealed. You're a fraud, Jocelyn. You always have been." He cut the voice feed, leaving her to wonder what he was doing. He only hoped the bluff would keep her at bay long enough.

As Ajay rounded the corner, his machine army swarmed around him. They flew through the air and crawled across the ground. The crab walkers skittered sideways across the carpet and centipedes crawled along the wall. Artwork crashed to the ground as maintenance bots lumbered from hiding.

Gunshots. Ajay gestured and the bots converged in front of him. Bullets pinged off of them. Several exploded in sparks.

But there were so many more.

"I'm not your enemy, Parks," Ajay called out.

The end of the hall was a mass of chaos. Loretta Trowbridge lay bleeding on the floor. Declan was pinned down in the alcove entryway to the Civil War room. The huge doors behind him must have still been locked. Nailah was nowhere to be seen. With a gesture, Ajay sent half of his bots toward the gunfire. They were a distraction, but they could buy some time.

"Loretta," Ajay hissed, kneeling beside her. "We need to move."

She looked up at him with bleary eyes. He couldn't see how she was wounded, but the blood matted her dress to her side.

"I tried," she said, dropping the gun. "I couldn't kill him."

"It's okay."

"Percival always said the world was dangerous."

"Percival was wrong," Ajay said. "About all of it. Your life wasn't dangerous until he *made* it dangerous. Instead of giving up, you should have been out there making the world a better place. Raising people from poverty or building homes people could afford."

"It's too late," she said.

Declan hazarded a peek down the hall. The bot swarm Ajay had sent surged around the fallen remains of a broken statue. Parks dispatched each drone that attacked him with a single shot, but more surged in from other parts of the burning house.

Ajay didn't have time for Loretta, but he couldn't leave her behind. He grasped her shoulders. "Loretta, listen to me. You have power in this world. You have everything you need to make the world just a little bit better than when you started. Percival never saw that. He saw power as a way to make himself safer. More comfortable, yes, but safer from the dangers that plague people like you. That's why he wanted an elite bodyguard. But that isn't the right answer. It's a coward's choice, and you're not a coward, Loretta. You're a fierce woman, and you're a champion for what's right in this world."

Loretta's brows knit in an expression of righteous fury. "I was," she said. She forced herself up. With one hand pressed to the wound in her side, she moved down the hall where Declan still sheltered. She was pale and weak, but she moved. "I am," she hissed.

With a furious shout, Parks cast off the last of the wave of bots and unloaded his pistol. When it clicked empty and the floor was scattered with the remains of his enemy, he holstered his gun and looked up at Ajay.

And he approached with a shark's smile on his face.

CHAPTER FORTY

GABBY'S MIND was a jumble of signals. Kylie crashed her way through them all, wrangling each and feeding them to each other. A dozen gibbering demons died when Kylie tangled them up. A dozen more shouted their nonsense. The noise threatened to bowl Kylie over, but then Garrison was at her side. His barking had stopped, and she melted into his warmth. Her mind steadied.

"What is going on in there?" Kylie muttered.

Gabby screamed with rage and pain and fear. Kylie saw that she felt *everything*. Every quadrant of the girl's brain was firing on all cylinders, dumping adrenaline into her system and giving a million contradictory commands. Something was attacking Gabby. Scrambling her.

No wonder she was so confused.

Kylie needed a new solution. She couldn't close

the cascading processes rampaging through Gabby's head.

"Let me in," Kylie said, making uncomfortable eye contact with Gabby. "Let me help." She kept one hand on the dog.

Gabby spat blood and shook her head.

"Please, Gabby. Stop resisting. I can help you."

Something shifted and Kylie had access. She had everything.

And it was a mess. The first thing she did was close the incoming signals. Everything except her connection shut down hard, dumping half-formed instructions into the void. Kylie waded through the disorganized mind, finding utilities she'd never conceived and shutting them all down. Burning their nodes.

Kylie stood as she worked.

The storm in Gabby's head subsided as the one outside rose. One by one, Kylie stomped out the fire in the girl's brain. There was a process for regulating mood. A process for enhanced learning. A tool that would grant strength or enhance intelligence. There was a social supplement that gave Gabby the ability to meld in social situations. Kylie shut them all down.

Gabby trembled, and Kylie saw the signals for her fear. There was a tool to regulate fear, and Kylie could have shut it down.

But.

What would happen? Gabby would find herself more afraid than she had ever been. She would be crippled by fear. Ruined. Traumatized. Fear would burn through her the way the fire burned through the house.

As if the girl wasn't traumatized enough. Welcome to the club, Kylie thought. Trauma's just part of the gig. She shut down everything else and allowed Gabby control over her fear. She would have that one thing. Maybe if that worked for her, Kylie could help her reactivate some other pieces.

Or maybe not.

"There," Kylie said. "Is that better?"

Gabby blinked. She turned her face up and stared at the roiling clouds. "It's so quiet."

Kylie backed away as wind blew rain sideways across the roof. Her footing was unsteady, and she realized how very close to the edge Gabby was.

"Is this what it's like to feel normal?" Gabby wondered. "No noise? No interference?"

"I don't know," Kylie said. Garrison nudged her hand. She had never tried to quiet her brain. Not really. It was so much a part of her, that she was afraid of what might be left. "But you can stop doing whatever it wanted you to do. You can make your own decisions."

"I can," Gabby said dreamily. She pulled herself to her feet.

Lightning flashed across the sky. The storm was moving away, and lightning came only as pulses across the eastern sky over the lake.

Gabby stepped closer to the edge. "I can do whatever I want."

Kylie's eyes went wide with horror. She saw with clarity what was happening in Gabby, and she finally understood that there was nothing she could say. Maybe there had never been because Gabby was beyond words. Her life had been so much pain and so much unrelenting pressure that given an opportunity, there was only one thing that Gabby was going to do, and nothing Kylie said was going to fix it.

Gabby's face scrunched into a mask of anger. "I can't be fixed."

"No. I know. I mean—" Kylie grasped at her connection with Gabby. If she could hit her with a wave of fear, maybe—

"I thought you would understand," Gabby said. "Out of everyone, I thought you would understand."

Gabby launched herself from the roof. Kylie ran to the edge, feet slipping as she skidded to a halt. Too late.

She expected Gabby to hit the pavement below with the wet crack like the breaking of branches, but the impact never came. The driving rain blinded her, swallowing her in its deafening roar. Kylie collapsed to her knees at the edge of the roof and screamed. The rain drove away her tears.

CHAPTER FORTY-ONE

Ajay gestured a command. A workshop bot with four stocky legs and a cutting tool lumbered across the hall toward the inset where Declan and Loretta were backed up against the heavy locked door.

Parks sent his drones at Ajay, but Ajay was ready for it. Commandeered surveillance drones zipped through the air, not trying to get video, but ramming hard into whatever they could hit. One of Parks's war drones dropped in a fiery heap from a hard collision. The other dodged and fired, felling one drone after another.

Ajay stepped forward into the hall, letting his machines distract the remaining war drone. "Parks," he said, genuinely hoping the man would stop. Hoping he could buy enough time for the maintenance bot to break through the door.

Parks roared and rushed at Ajay, swatting the old man's clumsily swung cane to the side. He jabbed the old man in the face with big, meaty fists. Ajay slammed into the wall and the cut on his arm tore open.

"You should have stayed away, old man," Parks spat. He took a handful of Ajay's shirt and pulled him close. Spittle dripped from his frothing mouth. "I read all about you in the dossier. You sick fuck. You and your daughter. Your *grand*daughter. You're going to wish you stayed away from here." He slammed a fist into the side of Ajay's head.

Bright flashes smashed through Ajay's skull. He blinked them away, but his head rang with blood and noise. He raised his hands, knowing there was no way he could block the killing blow.

And noticed Kylie's bracelet. Its bands of colors braided together, dangling frayed from his bruised wrist. He held it up and remembered all the good times he'd had with his granddaughter. He had tried to give her everything. Games. Movies. Martial arts. The image of her came to him then. Her furious, terrifying expression as she practiced her moves over and over again. How many times had he seen her reprimanded for blocking when she should have flowed with the movement.

"You had a daughter." Ajay lowered his fists.

Parks froze. His fist shook with barely contained rage. "She was one of the first to die from your daughter's poison."

"I'm sorry," said Ajay, knowing it wasn't enough.

It would never be enough. His hand closed on the multitool in his pocket.

Parks tensed for a swing—the kind that would knock Ajay out of the fight or possibly cave his skull all the way in. Ajay remembered Kylie's lessons. Her teacher's movements. Her drills over and over again. Roll with the punch. Don't escalate conflict.

Ajay watched the fist come down—spotted the tension in the man's muscles. Ajay flipped open his multitool's tiny blade and jammed it into Parks's armpit. He had never been very good at rolling with a punch.

The big man yelped in pain and pulled back.

It only bought him a fraction of a second.

Declan slammed Parks into the wall with crunching force. Parks tumbled away, wrestling with the smaller man. He landed a single powerful punch and the investigator landed in a heap.

The ground shook. Smoke boiled across the high ceiling. Waves of heat scoured through the mansion, scorching the dry air. Ajay snatched up his cane and his fingers flew through the controls. The bot army was growing. He threw instructions to the construction bots outside. This would be enough. It *had* to be enough. As he finished, a lone text field opened before him.

Bots of all types swarmed around Ajay in a protective semicircle between him and Parks. "It doesn't have to be like this," Ajay said over the whir. He dared not look toward Loretta and the door, but he heard the grind of the workshop bot cutting the door. "Theodore doesn't have to die for nothing."

Parks cracked his knuckles. "She was everything to us. Not a bodyguard or a subject. She was our love. Our happiness. You wouldn't understand."

"Jocelyn is the real enemy."

Declan stirred.

"There's always enough guilt to go around." Parks crushed a cleaning bot with one boot. "Believe me, I know guilt when I work for it."

"Last chance," Ajay said, hand hovering over the controls. Sweat dripped down his brow and the hot air smelled scorched. Heat from the fire dried his eyes and seared his skin. Soon it would swallow them all.

Parks grinned. "There was never a chance. The whole Garver family is corrupt, and you—you're no better."

Ajay launched his next wave of bots. They swarmed Parks, biting and snapping, but he crushed them as fast as they came in. His heavy boots destroyed the crab-walkers and he snatched drones out of the air before they could slam into him. His remaining drone dispatched bots in a steady rhythm. Maintenance tools couldn't penetrate armor and couldn't move fast enough to bring it down.

"Come on," Ajay said, helping Declan up. "We need to leave."

"No way out," mumbled the investigator.

Ajay started one final routine on his cane and tossed it into the pile of ruined bots. "There will be."

"No," Declan said, staring at Parks.

Parks snatched a bot from the air with a bloody hand and threw it at Ajay.

Ajay blocked the bot with his arm. He felt a crunch against his injury.

Then everything went dark. The room spun around him and his knee struck the floor. The house shook. Black smoke surged down the hall. Ajay couldn't breathe. Couldn't see.

Parks took a step forward through the choking ash, wading through the attacking machines. "These bots aren't made for war," he said. "Just like you, old man." He snatched another bot from the floor and lashed Ajay with it.

This time, Ajay didn't block and the centipede raked against his cheek and ear. Blood clouded his vision and ran down the side of his face. He stumbled backward and fell.

Declan looked down at Ajay. All the fear and anger that Ajay had seen before was still there, but there was something else. A grim determination. A burning stubbornness that Ajay only recognized because he had held that same emotion in his own heart for so long. Had he inspired it in the investigator? It was going to get him killed. One more thing Ajay could feel guilty about.

The war drone finished the last of the maintenance bots and spun on Ajay.

Declan stepped between Ajay and the drone. His fists clenched at his sides. "You and me, Parks."

"Declan, no," said Ajay, backing away. The earth rumbled.

"No," said Declan. "I've been doing this wrong. My whole life, I've wanted to do the right thing and now I get a chance. I can stand up to an asshole and show him he can't do this to us."

Parks flashed a bloody sideways grin. "Asshole, huh?"

"Yeah, that's right." Declan placed a hand on his Glock. "You're the asshole here. All these years I've been tracking these rich bastards who have been getting away with whatever they want. Every time my case was close, key witnesses disappeared. People died in suspicious circumstances. It was you, wasn't it?"

"Maybe."

"It was." Declan's voice grew cold and strong. "And if there's one good thing in this night, it's the fact that you won't be able to escape. You'll burn like the rest of us. You and your asshole husband won't be able to perpetuate the corruption that I've seen all these years."

Parks twitched at the mention of his husband. "If it wasn't us, it would have been someone else."

"Stop, Declan," Ajay said. He glanced at the cane. He had hoped to be away when the timer on it hit zero. Now, the timer was going to take too long to trigger. "This isn't going to help." Ajay hazarded a glance at the door. It still wasn't open, but the workshop bot was close. Sparks flew where it cut through the last of the hinges. Loretta still leaned up against the wall, her dress soaked with blood.

Declan's gun wasn't even out of its holster when Parks clicked his tongue and his drone swung around. It fired three times. Body shots.

The investigator staggered back. His foot caught on a shattered statue, and he fell, cracking his head on the hard floor.

He didn't move.

Ajay crawled, staying low under the black smoke. Blood smeared across the hard floor. It soaked into what was once his best blue suit. The door finally crashed open, and Loretta wrenched herself forward into the Civil War room. Rain pelted against the narrow window. She was in, but Ajay wasn't going to make it. The short putt between him and the door might as well have been a marathon.

The war drone spun to face him. The mansion shook, and a wave of fresh air from the Civil War room cleared the smoke in the hall. A flash of lightning silhouetted something huge outside the window.

"It's over." Parks shrugged away the few remaining bots. He clutched the heavy remains of a crab walker, its jagged edges and heavy body forming a crude weapon in his hands.

"I agree," said Ajay. The timer on his cane hit zero. "I think we're done here."

The hack wasn't a sophisticated one. It wasn't even one that he thought would work. The routine he ran was a simple pseudo port attack. It would check every port for known vulnerabilities. In better circumstances, the data gathered might help in a more sophisticated hack, but alone this would do nothing.

Nothing, that is, if Melinda hadn't set up a robust counterattack against potential hackers. His clumsy hack triggered that defense. The air crackled. Ajay's hair stood on end. The war drone wobbled in the air.

Parks clicked his tongue. The order to kill.

An electric pulse fried Ajay's hearing aid. His cheaters fizzed and went black. The head of his cane hissed and added a wisp of smoke to the thickening air.

And Parks's war drone spun out of control. It looped higher, racing around and around. Parks backed away, stepping over the debris of smoking bots. Every electronic device in the room popped and crackled. The drone smashed into the wall, then dove straight at Parks. He threw up a hand to defend himself.

A single gunshot rang through the hall.

Parks's head exploded in a spray of blood.

Ajay blinked. He turned to see down the long hall, Nailah held her sleek pistol. She dropped it to the floor.

Then she spotted Declan. She gasped and knelt by his side.

"I'm sorry," Ajay whispered. "I couldn't—"

Declan drew in a sharp breath, and his eyes snapped open. Gently, Nailah helped him to his feet.

Through the ragged, burned holes in the man's suit, shone the crisp structure of consumer-grade body armor.

"Expecting to get shot?" Ajay asked as they passed.

"Backstabbed, actually." Declan winced. "It still hurts."

"I bet."

Another explosion shook the burning house. Smoke belched down the hallway.

"We need to get the window open," said Nailah. "And fast."

Inside the Civil War room, the wall exploded inward. Rain poured through the gap in sheets. The enormous head of the construction bot lay itself down on the floor, shoving Theodore Parks's body aside like a rag doll. Lightning arced across the sky.

"This way," Nailah shouted over the torrent.

Ajay's control of the giant bot had disappeared when he'd fried everyone's electronics, but it had done as he instructed. Ajay helped Loretta onto the bot's arm. Declan followed.

"Hurry!" Kylie shouted from the ground. Rain mixed with smoke into a muddy haze. With help, they used the construction equipment for handholds. Once he was on the ground, Kylie hugged him close and helped him move away from the burning building. Garrison padded up and nuzzled his injured arm.

"How did you get down here?" Ajay asked.

Kylie pointed at the construction bot, which stood almost as tall as the house. "Gabby used it," she said. "Getting Garrison down was the hard part."

When lightning flashed again, Ajay thought he saw Gabby standing at the edge of the forest next to Chay Quinn. His heart raced, but his body had no more adrenaline to give.

When he looked again, they were gone.

CHAPTER FORTY-TWO

"THERE IT IS," Ajay said, punching codes into the computer in Alexander Parks's van. The west wing of the building collapsed in the distance, swallowed by a roaring flame. The antenna array on that half of the building crumbled like tissue paper and the last dregs of power flared out of its disruptive system. "Signal's back."

Kylie crouched next to Garrison, hugging him close against the cold remains of rain. She looked almost as rough as he felt, but she had been somber since they had escaped. He wondered what was going through her head. At least she had helped him bandage all of his wounds.

"You shouldn't get in fights," she said. "You aren't good at them."

Ajay touched the bandage on his cheek. "I'll take that into consideration."

A short distance away, Declan finished tending to

Loretta's wounds. Despite all the blood, she hadn't been mortally wounded, but she complained as if her intestines were splayed across the cold earth.

"I'll summon rides," Ajay said. Best to take care of the immediate needs first. He got the interface working well enough to summon several cars, borrowing them from Jocelyn's private garage, which was somehow still protected from the flames. He put an arm around Kylie, and she melted into him—a sure sign that she was as exhausted as him. "It'll be okay," he said, stupidly.

"Yeah," she agreed.

Ajay would need to find Zach's sister to tell her what happened to the cook. It wouldn't be easy tracking her down, and it would be even harder breaking the news. And he'd have to tell her about Jocelyn—how the woman had escaped even after everything that had happened.

But, of course, there wasn't any evidence pointing to the old woman. The power of her wealth would easily erase anything the police ever found in the wreckage of her mansion. With a little time and some money, Jocelyn Garver could rebuild that exact mansion wherever she wanted to live in the world thanks to the miracle of 3D printing. The thought of it put a sour taste in Ajay's mouth.

Nailah emerged from the woods. Her dress was torn in several places, but her expression was as hard as steel. "The grounds are clear. We should be able to leave."

"What was it like?" Kylie asked.

Nailah raised an eyebrow.

"The school. Papa said Grandma wanted me to go to her school."

Nailah stared at the slate gray sky for a long time. Dawn approached but was struggling to dispel the darkness of the storm. "Pine Fortress wasn't all bad," she finally said. "It's not really a school for assassins like your grandfather thinks, and it doesn't really belong to Jocelyn Garver, no matter how much she's donated to it."

"You can't go to the school," Ajay said to Kylie.

Kylie's jaw hardened.

Nailah glanced back into the woods. "It's a lot of survival training. Most of the lessons were all about *seeming* to be something we're not and seeing through others' lies."

"I think that's what I need," said Kylie.

Ajay remembered Chay Quinn. Chay had gone through the same program and turned into a ruthless killer. What would it do to Kylie? If only there were a way to know.

"Did you find Gabby?" Ajay asked.

"Gone," Nailah said. To Kylie, she said, "You're sure she's okay?"

Kylie gripped Ajay's arm a little harder. "She landed on the construction bot, then she climbed down and ran away. I think—I think she has a lot to sort out."

Ajay drew in a deep breath of the cold night air.

Had he really seen Chay in the woods? After a little while, Kylie walked away through the garden, plucking at the first rosebuds of spring. "I wonder what to do with Kylie," he said to Nailah. "I want her to be normal. I want her to be confident. But am I teaching her those things, or am I just teaching her how to fake those things?"

Nailah shrugged. "I'm not sure there's a difference."

Olexie crashed through the woods. His face was ruddy with mild burns and exertion, but he otherwise seemed fine.

"I assumed you died in the fire," Ajay said.

"You can only hope." Garrison padded over to the tall Russian and gave him a sniff. He patted the big dog on the head.

"I summoned cars. Do you need one?"

Olexie scratched his chin. "I think I'll walk. The lake isn't too far. It'll be a good place to think about how badly we failed."

"Failed?"

"Jocelyn got away. All my undercover work resulted in nothing. We failed to hold her accountable for anything."

Ajay tapped the top of his cane. The computer inside was fried. "We *did* verify that she's corrupt. Wasn't that your goal?"

Olexie mumbled something that sounded suspiciously like, "Then we murder her."

Ajay said, "So, she flew away?"

"Left the country an hour ago as far as I can figure. No idea where, but odds are there's no extradition."

"She'll be back," Ajay said.

Nailah said, "Ajay, thank you."

"For what?"

"For showing me the truth. I don't think I could have figured out what to do next if you hadn't helped me see it."

Olexie blinked. "What's next for you?"

Nailah watched Kylie for several seconds. "I'll be in touch, Olexie. I'd like to help you if I can. If I can find Gabby, I think I'll see if I can help her sort things out, too." She strolled from the garden to the driveway. A sleek black limousine stopped, picked her up, and drove away into the night.

Olexie furrowed his brow. "Did I charm her?"

"Something like that," Ajay said, slapping the man's shoulder. "I think she just needs something to believe in."

"We'll take the next car if you don't mind," said Declan.

Ajay placed a hand on the man's shoulder. "Of course."

Declan glanced at Loretta. "We couldn't have done this without you, Ajay. She might be reluctant to say it, but you have both our thanks."

"I don't deserve it," said Ajay.

"You do more than most of us." Declan helped Loretta into the next vehicle. "I don't know if it's delirium, but I think whatever you said to her back there might sink in."

"Aren't you still investigating her?"

Declan winced. "It's standard practice in situations like this to throw the deceased under the bus. Percival will get all the blame for their shady business. Loretta gets a clean slate, and whatever scraps are left of their wealth."

"Huh."

"Life's not always fair, I hear." Declan climbed into the sedan and the car disappeared into the night.

Later, another car stopped on the road, and Ajay motioned to Kylie to get in. "I'll be in touch, too, Olexie. I think we didn't do as poorly as you might think."

Olexie crossed the road to a trail that led toward the lake. "I never know what to expect when you are involved, Mr. Andersen."

"Neither do I," Ajay said. He ducked into the red sedan and sat across from Kylie. After several minutes on the road, he said, "I'm proud of you, Kylie."

That must have been the signal to relax because Kylie melted into tears. Ajay took her hand and held it, offering as much comfort as he could. He didn't understand what she was feeling, but he understood that she needed his support. For once, she didn't push him away.

An eternity later, she gathered herself and almost

looked him in the eyes. "I thought my grandma would want me," she said.

"Oh, she did," Ajay said. "But she wanted you in the way that people want something they can use. I think that's just her nature."

After a long pause, Kylie said, "She had a contract with Trevan Pharmaceuticals. I saw it in the panic room."

Ajay said, "Something about Isabelle?"

"It was signed on my birthday," Kylie said.

He had always known Jackson Garver had plans for Isabelle. He had plans for all of the girls affected by his modifications. But Ajay thought Kylie's abilities were a side effect. It would require more investigation. "I'll have to look into that," he said, trying to sound as calm as possible.

Kylie nodded. She handed him a data chip. "I got this for you, too."

He held it up and read the label on its surface. "Thank you, Kylie. This means a lot." He slotted the chip into the car's reader and stared at the password field for a long time.

"I couldn't guess it," Kylie said.

Ajay scratched his chin, then, remembering the Dali painting, wrote *Faces of War* in the field. The entry field blinked, then opened its files to him.

"Ass," Kylie said. Ajay decided to let it slide. He'd always been pretty good at guessing.

He had everything. The Garver family business. Relations with the sketchy Haveraptics genetics experiments. Detailed financial reports. Information on the Pine Fortress School for the Gifted. Codes to access Jocelyn's personal criminal network. She had brought her enemies to the mansion to kill them all or have them kill each other, but that wasn't her first crime. It wasn't even her first murder. Everything was in those files.

It was enough to find Jocelyn and take her down, but it was also enough to paint a target on the back of anyone in control of the information.

He grinned at Kylie, and for a moment they shared the sheer joy of their triumph. There was nothing better than the victory of a good hack. Ajay had always felt that was true, but now it was a feeling he could share with his granddaughter.

He snapped the display closed and rode in silence for a long time.

"I thought Gabby was nice," said Kylie after a while. "I thought she had it all together and she knew what she was doing."

"People hide their struggles."

"She had it worse than me. A lot worse." She swallowed. "I think she was trying to kill herself when she jumped. It was only luck that saved her."

"Her father tried to control her," Ajay said. "He was a user just like your grandmother." He let out a long sigh. "I don't know. Maybe that's who I am, too."

"Papa," Kylie said.

"No, I know. I'm better than them, but I haven't always been. I guess I've never really thought about it before, and now that I do, I'm seeing all my flaws."

"But you *try* to do the right thing."

"Yeah," Ajay said. The weight of guilt pressed hard on his chest. "But I haven't always succeeded." He looked at her. "I try to be a good parent, too, you know, and I don't always succeed at that, either."

It was a long time before Kylie answered, and when she did it was barely a whisper. "You don't always fail, either."

As their ride rumbled along remote Minnesota roads, Ajay brought Jocelyn's data up one more time to peer at what they had stolen. "Do you remember that diamond optical quantum computer I had a while back?"

"The one that's broken half the time?"

"Yeah," Ajay said. "Do you think that thing still works?"

Kylie looked at him and blinked slowly. She suspected he was up to something. He could see the wheels turning in her head. "Well, it does and it doesn't."

"Kind of like a—"

"Stop!"

"Schrödinger's—"

"No!"

"Cat. Machine. Quantum. Thing." The joke had been much better in his head.

Kylie shrunk into herself a little. "I might have observed it the other day."

"Oh?"

"It rolled off the workbench and, um, its quantum state might have collapsed into, um, the broken state."

"Oh."

"Yeah," she said. "Sorry."

"Do you really want to go to that school?"

"They have a summer camp."

He scanned through the school's data again. It was everything he was trying to provide Kylie. Discipline through martial arts. Social skills. Networking and relationships. The school could provide everything he failed to give her.

"I'll think about it," he said, but he knew in his heart that ultimately, the choice would be hers.

BECOME A PATRON

It can all be yours. Become a Patron now and gain access to raw chapters of future books, short stories, and even early copies of every Anthony W. Eichenlaub book before it's released. Every tier gets access to the private Oak Leaf Collective Discord—the perfect hangout for readers and writers alike.

Patronage isn't for everybody. Not everyone can wants to chip in a few dollars to ensure the future will be written. Joining the newsletter will get you updates when new books come out. It'll get you progress updates and pictures of my dog.

But becoming a Patron is an incredible opportunity to not only support the work you love, but to also gain access to exclusives not available anywhere else. Some people are content to wait and see what the future brings. Others prefer to nudge it in the right direction.

If that's you, come join me and help write the future.

https://www.patreon.com/AWEichenlaub

AUTHOR'S NOTE

Thank you for reading this third installment in the Old Code series. This series has been so much fun for me to write, and your support means that I can keep going. It's been nearly two years since I started writing full time, and it has been the absolute best way for me to spend the pandemic years. Now that some kind of normal is being reestablished, thoughts of employment are creeping into the edges of my thoughts.

But you, my readers, are making the writer life work for me, and as long as it still makes sense, I'll keep writing. I love it, and it lets me get the absolute most out of my Minnesota summers.

So, thank you.

Also, big thanks to my family. I, of course, couldn't possibly do this without them. Thanks also to my editor, Dave Pasquantonio. As always, he not only gave my grammar the support it needed, but also gave some suggestions that really helped the story come together.

As of the writing of this note, the next book, Grandfather Zero, is nearly finished. It might not be up for preorder by the time Grandfather Guardian is released, but don't worry. It's on its way.

And hopefully many to come.

Anthony W. Eichenlaub

Old Code

Grandfather Anonymous

Grandfather Ghost

Grandfather Guardian

Colony of Edge

Of a Strange World Made

Upon Another Edge Broken

On a Forsaken Land Found

From a Barren Seed Grown

Above a Distant Sky Seen

Metal and Men

Justice in an Age of Metal and Men

Peace in an Age of Metal and Men

Honor in an Age of Metal and Men